I KNOW A PLACE

First published in Great Britain 2025

dougiemarlow@gmail.com

ISBN: 978 -1-80541 -714-9 eBook
ISBN: 978 -1-80541-715-6 Paperback

I KNOW A PLACE

A New Way - For The Youth Of Today

Dougie Cooper

An Author with our new generation at Heart.

Having lost his young wife, in a tragedy hard to imaging worse; heartbroken he leaves the very next day his once happy UK home/ architectural design studio never to return. • Off to faraway places on a hopeful mission to save other lives. • In a small mud hut on Kenya's, Massai Marra, alone under an oil lamp he designs a modest school and eco-toilets. • Back to London for a sponsor and a new school for 150 children without such things is built. • He discovers within: dreamy imaginings to help the youth of today, and this very book: ***'I Know A Place'*** was born, with a 'Sequel' and a completed Autobiographical/ Fantasy - ***'Heaven Knew My Name'*** [shortly to follow] • If this wasn't enough; having now moved away from a life in architecture, he studies Breast Cancer for two years under a top UK Senior Consultant Surgeon; wrote a BC education/awareness book, and a sixty page portfolio for: *'Mother Teresa University for women'* for [possible Nat. diplomas] • He had lost one precious life so, launched himself off on a mission to save many. Lecturing to countless female students from deep South India, to the far North (Assam) on BC awareness at: Universities, Colleges, then to Rotary Clubs, Lyons Clubs and Hospitals. • Next, Bhopal mid-India to help the children effected by the worst industrial chemical disaster in history. • Then far south India again to help the orphans of the 2004 Tsunami disaster. • Has run two London marathons for blind, and partially sighted children [stills runs daily]. • From his own tragedy a broken heart doubled in size, and *hope* for many was re-kindled!

TABLE OF CONTENTS

INTRODUCTION	1
ESCAPING FROM IT ALL	3
A WORLD ON MY TERMS	19
FANTASY DREAMING	31
FIRST METAMORPHOSIS	39
MAIDEN FLIGHT	45
A REQUIEM THEN OFF WE GO	51
IN AND OUT THE DUSTY BLUEBELLS	65
SETTING THE STAGE	69
MANAGING INHERENT MAGIC	75
A WORLD WITHIN A WORLD	83
THE RELUCTANT JOURNEY BACK	93
MY TURN TO DREAM	107
A RUDE AWAKENING	111
RETURN TO REALITY	119
LIFE AROUND THE MILL	129
WHO SHOULD COME CALLING	147
FEET BACK ON THE GROUND	153
TIME TO CREATE THE SETTING	159
FURRY CREATURES	167
BACK TO REALITY	175
THE CALL OF THE SEA	179
HOMEWARD BOUND	195
TRAVERSING TIME	207
A WELCOME DAWN	213
NEW AMENITIES	219
WELL-DISCIPLINED	229
THE HOLLOW MOUNTAIN	237
HIGHER UP THE CHERRY TREE	253
THE FLOWER FINALLY OPENS	263

INTRODUCTION

The story is based on the dreams of a thirteen-year-old girl, Freya, who, for so long has dreamy imaginings of finding a world that moves away from the pitfalls of growing up years when young. As teenagers it would seem, apart from the process of learning, many crave opportunity to move outside of the accepted habitual, boring routines of young life so often subjected to school bullying, belittling, and generally struggling to impose one's ideas on so many self-opinionated, supposedly more 'cool' contemporaries. Who as it happens, for some strange unfair reason, seem to attract more friends? Then there's the 'pecking order', based on who can boast of countless social media 'likes' and 'followers', feeding their false imaginings of being greater beings. Freya becomes aware, there is so much of this precious lifetime being lost in mental trauma and anxieties in a 'bodiless' world of 'Instagram', 'Tik Tok' etc. along with endless communication 'platforms' and 'apps'; with psychiatrists declaring a 67% increase in teen depression and self-harming probably linked to: *'doomscrolling'* in those early hours; more so intended for sleep and the flight of night owls!

She discovers another way, a way embracing many wonders, and becomes totally committed to sharing all her discoveries with other youth in this modern-day world if only to offer some hope of an escape; to a place free from hurt, restrictions, and embarrassments. A place where Love, and total happiness abounds, where bright new young situations are there for the taking. The story takes us into Freya's discovered world of magic; in which she discovers degrees of romance and adventure the majority of us seek for an entire lifetime -- demonstrated so well on family holidays, with so called 'grown-ups' enjoying childish imaginings; revelling in the joys of seeking out sea creatures, who play 'hide and seek' behind delicate drapes of seaweed in clear rock pools by the sea. The occasional sneaky peak at a Rupert annual, venturing into caves where no receptionist sits in wait, and trying to catch a falling autumn leaf. Escaping into a dream is inherent in us all. Here Freya shares how she achieved this; she sets out to show us a way and shares the many wonders she finds, all the way through to womanhood where romance and love gathers her up; with full understanding of how life, in every area, could really be.

ESCAPING FROM IT ALL

There comes a time in those growing up years with all the group participation, such as: school classrooms, playgrounds, and walking to and from school … supposedly chilling out at weekends, and maybe listening to music recorded by artists, who, in all probability one will never meet. This life's patten is presumed by all, to be normal, simply just what we do … but to me, much of it feels somewhat shallow, lacking in meaningful purpose; and filling in time in one's life, so often disappointingly unreliable in terms of lasting friendships. Plus of course, it can be a difficult task to mould oneself into this seemingly complicated growing-up stage of life; apart from that is, the essentiality of becoming unhindered when able to hide midstream in the classrooms of academic learning, although the bright ones do seem to catch the teachers gaze, so the 'pecking order' begins.

Even outside those classroom boundaries, academia spills over with the need to learn the latest youth slang language, essential in order to elevating myself to appear a *'cool', 'Alpha' girl.* Then, for those reaching that higher echelon of: '*wicked*' [as in smart]; other lesser mortals fall by the wayside becoming fuel for the *'wicked'* ones' ego, as they struggle to raise their own profile. Once, having fallen into the lower ranks, there is no way back; contemporaries no longer laugh at your jokes or compliment you in anything you do or wear. There's no way back in this cruel competitive school playground of learning … your stage is being set!

Once, having recognised most of the stuff, outside of the classroom is outside of my control; I began to realise, as with many of my contemporaries, one can too easily be 'put down' or manipulated by others.

I became shocked while so young at what life for my youthful journey has been made to embrace; much of which, being shared on 'smartphones' and various other devices, in all directions by so called friends. Along with many predatory sites hovering ever near, like a 'praying mantis'... looking for an uninformed, innocent enquiring prey. Also, presumably what a girl must do, in order to be promoted to the premier league; I wanted none of it. You see, I learned what the girls did with the boys, the boys shared with other boys, thus increasing their communication *'likes'* total, taking them up their league-table at the expense of a girl...umm! I wondered: would those boys, when becoming men, lose this dreadful egotistical boasting at the expense of others, not least their girlfriends, and perhaps, even their eventual partners?

Relating back to the subject of 'classrooms' ... having always been a bit of a thinker, often gazing around the class thinking; which of them will make it in life, or who will fall behind. The inevitabilities of life unfolding for a modern girl seemed so gloomy; even in a human biology class, I noted the teacher made a reference that according to statistics, at least one or two of the girls, will, in all probability, fall victim later in life to a serious disease relating to 'Boobs', which had me looking around at faces, wondering who that might be; promoting fear in me ... then relief; as it was declared 95% of such victims are curable, if the problem was found early; after all, a pea-size intruder takes around ten years to form! *Umm,* I thought; best I learn what to look for ... but who, I wondered, would be teaching me such lifesaving things?

You see, even when so young, when considering the above; I had that left-behind feeling in the growing up 'pecking order' as my 'bumps' were, at that stage, far from complete. Then realising; although the more developed girls looked somewhat smug ... they might well qualify earlier than us more lacking souls for such a disastrous disease. The boys appeared smug and completely divorced from such a threatening albeit brief tutorial -- *is this equality?* I thought – My friend whispered: "boys do get things".

I was certainly left with a little wondering to myself about life's future possibilities. Even if studying hard to achieve a degree these days, one would be lucky to find a good job at the end of it all. I wanted something more, with bright new horizons: a happy journey; one that comes easily without worry, devoid of so many crimes my generation seemed to be drifting into; involving drugs, 'tip-toeing' into the 'Dark Web' world. Not forgetting knife possession for tasks other than the intended purpose! Where did they buy these things and without questions being asked? Then I thought, as with other dreadful stuff, it was obviously 'online websites'. Those knives I had seen pictures of were certainly not for cutting bread, chopping salad, or Sunday roast … When I say 'seen pictures of', one boy, in his attempt to impress me, did actually show me one weird, frightening looking knife. I said nothing, and simply walked away, looking back at him in a 'put down' kind of way! Mind you; I did have to stop and think … *God, I'm only thirteen with such images coming my way, probably leaving a mental scar, with recall remaining into my old age!*

Being a girl, my mum and dad constantly watched over me and my ever-expanding media lifestyle, fretting over what I was being introduced to, and, if I am really honest, I think I understood their fears; it's so easy for all youth to stumble into completely unsuitable 'electronic' non-real life strangers. With parents engaging in protective measures … then new algorithms arrive, from mega-rich providers … to suck us youth in.

I was soon with a promising teen shape developing to become a fourteen-year-old girl, with, I like to consider, quite good looks. But in order to gain those *'likes'* which, if I am really honest, I secretly did seek, my *'selfie'* presentation needed to show my pretty face, quite a bit lower than my chin. With some girls sharing videos of themselves doing things that in my own secret little world of enjoyment was, in my opinion, somewhat mentally contaminating, to say the least. I was left wondering …

am I appearing: 'not with it', 'vanilla', someone other than normal? They were, without knowing it, racing toward that second-rate citizen status; with their little secrets now in visual format [with a facial ID attached!] Beauty made sordid, slipping through the net and fired out into cyber space, 'up-up and away' to some distant satellite, only to return like acid rain to thousands of global receivers, by way of mobile and pc 'apps'; there for the thrilling of and gloating over by total strangers. Yuck!

Little things in my day-to-day life began to grate on me ... such as many funny jokes made by my contemporaries which were often at the expense of some other person being derided in their absence, in order that the 'teller' be seen as cool in the eyes of others. My attempts at what I thought to be: 'cool' comments, and 'funky' jokes went nowhere, and, as mentioned, once one has entered those lower ranks it was almost impossible, to rise up again to raise a laugh. Unless that is, one could beat everybody at everything considered normal, such as skateboarding, difficult video games, schools sport, music, singing, dancing, or, in fact, any other event that could promote envy from those unable who so often would attempt to put down the successful at such pastimes, in doing so, making fools of themselves – that was a plus?

I once paid the best-looking boy in our school to have a heads only *'selfie'* with me, which I *posted* on my smart-phone ... then, would you believe, my list of *'likes'*, rather than soar, halved in number. So even that didn't work; envy had crept into the equation and other girls hated me, for supposedly scoring so highly with my secretly contrived *'pulling'* skills with someone they all wanted to get their hands on. The boy, tall, handsome, and sporty, with, I noticed at school swimming sports, what my giggling friends referred to as his *'six pack'* and quite a lot besides. Liking my adventurous spirit, with that *'selfie'* bribe idea of mine, he agreed to walk hand-in-hand through the school grounds for free, but for two days only... then benevolence passed, and he dumped me.

All such silly games to play, and to what end? I was young, and to some degree part of those silly games. I wanted out. I just knew in my heart there was more for me, but where to find it? For someone so young, I could recognise in my own way, I was always 'looking outside of the box'.

Even my school RE [religious education] classes seemed so outdated for my generation with countless old stories, leaving us having to trawl from Genesis to some sad Green Hill faraway event. This was the only bit that brought tears to my heart, seeing a man hanging on a cross suffering terrible abuse, and to think, if in fact it actually happened, he was put there by other men. I did somehow get the idea though, the Jesus thing that is. It had been trying to teach forgiveness, spelling out that everybody has goodness inside somewhere [they are born with it] simply waiting to be teased out. *Be nice,* I thought, to find that 'somewhere' and create a situation where it is possible to tailor likes, and dislikes, to suit one's own dreamed of world, or at least have some influence on such things.

Then, in my own private time and place, I redirected that ever near 'thinker' gaze of mine, and eventually found a target ... a beautiful secret place in my dreamy imaginings, which, believe it or not, with much patience eventually became real ... it became mine alone, and I am desperate to share such wonders.

It had all begun with me wondering if my love of art may help. You see, the inspiration in me dawned when, having once read of a man who had successfully dreamed of painting a very large, most beautiful landscape scene, into which one day he might step and in doing so find such a welcoming and wondrous place where, it being his own consciousness' creation, he could create happy daily situations and events free from sharp edges, pointed corners, and so much being tainted or fouled up by others.

It all sounded amazing to be able to create a place free from those who would seek to better their lives at the expense of others, which, when I was on the receiving end of such, always seemed to hurt me so deeply. I wondered ... could I do that? Create such a place, I mean.

Apparently, it had taken many years of him gazing, dreaming, and moving his creative brush in two dimensional shapes and colours, watching a beautiful English scene unfold ... always hoping a third-dimension *'dream scene'* would one day manifest into *reality*, inviting him in to venture on through this wondrous place and make it home. It would be a new life, one he could make of as he so chose, free from countless troubles, many of which he had in fact endured in his life on Earth.

I read his story over and over, especially when feeling a little down, as it always gave me such hope of there being something better. Apparently, the day did eventually arrive when he actually achieved this unbelievable manifestation and, quite amazingly, he could come and go to his secret place without anybody knowing his movements. Each time he went there and returned, it was as if time had stood still in both venues so, when re-engaging either way, all returned once more to life as he had left it! He had continued to do this; until one day, he never returned to life on Earth! That bit did frighten me a little.

It all seemed a little complicated for a thirteen-year-old girl. Nevertheless, it had gathered me up and fed my yearnings to bursting. Since reading his story, whenever sitting quietly in the school library, I would often sit leaning on my elbows with chin in hands, just gazing out through the windows daydreaming of such an adventure where, thinking of his words: '*he could make of it as he so chose*'. The implication being I did not have to embrace his 'out of date' to my generation association with English Landscape. After all, there had been others before me, the likes of 'Alice in Wonderland'; young folk looking for adventures, for magic, attempting the impossible, and moving outside of the proverbial 'box'.

I did so want to take part in a similar experience apart from those scary bits Alice experienced. I had, as I say, dreamed and planned around the idea, but would, as did this man, want to return on occasions to check it all out at home, to see all was well, not forgetting, of course, my education. Gone would be the amalgam of earlier unhappy memories, like demands for incomplete school homework, such as English, which

I so hated [where incidentally I learned that new word, 'amalgam'], with the associated reprimand from the head for such incompleteness. Gone would be the conflicts of life's way whilst growing up, the bullying and taunting by so called friends over my tiny collection of those social media *'followers'* and *'likes'* along with, at the time, as mentioned, my tiny 'boobs'.... Not forgetting my love of nature, which they thought somewhat basic [boring]. I would at the time, tell all 'I don't really care about your silly things', but I did, and whilst so young had already been delegated to that second-rate citizen status to commence my precious journey through life.

If, along with 'Alice in Wonderland', that adventuring artist could do it, then with much practice, why not me, I wondered. He had made one particular comment in a book he wrote, which implied it could also be mine to grasp and embrace. There he states: 'no matter how young you might be; seek and if such seeking is from your heart, you will find.' Well, guess what ... I was 'seeking', so that must include me. I was inspired to at least try, although it felt strange whilst so young to be adventuring toward another world, alone, without talking to friends or family. I did wonder why, I wasn't feeling nervous... you see, the whole idea felt somehow safe and welcoming. Could that man be picking up on my dreaming, giving it his blessing? And who was he ... a strange, almost fatherly figure I felt love for, and what could 'love' for a stranger mean to someone so young? It was as if I was being prepared for that alternative existence I so sought. With much searching until at the point of almost losing heart… I finally, wandered into my bedroom and sat down to explore 'search engines' and 'Web browsers', entering: 'inspirational picture prints' and, as if being managed by some higher force, the very first picture that popped up was that very full scale copy of his wonderful English landscape in beautiful English tones of colour, with the cost, including delivery, £10, the very sum most probably in my 'piggy-bank'; immediately accessed with a heavy piece of wood, followed by a 'superglue' job!

The postman arrived, with a long cardboard tube, commenting with a smile when I went to the door: 'Um … a telescope for stargazing Freya?' – My print, seen here, had me a little surprised at its size, 3ft x 4ft., so very large, actually, so large it really did seem to invite one in.

I had made an investment in an item that was to change my entire life … both now and forever! I couldn't wait to select pride of place in my room, where it would hang, simply inviting me in … an event seemingly not intended for quite some time, allowing a young, jumbled mind such as mine time to ease up a little!

I would dream away, wondering where exactly in his scene so long ago he had entered. Would it have been the tiny lane moving on from the stone buttressed bridge, or perhaps the wooden foot bridge over the mill tributary where boys played 'pooh sticks'... and who were those boys? I began to wonder if I were successful where exactly there would I choose to suddenly go. I realised I was helping my hoped-for transition by simply dreaming. After all, the man had stated at one point in his story… if when, gazing peacefully, you feel to actually be there, then your consciousness will one day make it so. He had continued to say: "always remember consciousness is what you really are". I didn't really understand that bit. All that seemed to matter was he eventually succeeded!

There were the usual stupid remarks from those supposed friends leaning on their newly acclaimed, not really savvy *'woke'* awareness, who would seek to mock me, asking why I should want such a picture for my room, not one of some young pop artist posing in a shot which had probably taken all day, with makeup, stretching his image to appear slim, going to work on the face, not forgetting to enhance a certain bump in his tightly fitted, almost sprayed on trousers ... then at least ten *'takes'* prior to a completely false 'fit for purpose' shot. Who is this guy? We should wonder. I just knew these boy posters were for doting teenage fans like friends of mine, wild with false imaginings, praying for a 'touch of his … robe' … Ha ha!

I tried unbelievably hard for so long, just dreaming and gazing at my print. Then a little voice within called to me: 'Your seeking is known ... but you are simply trying to *escape*. Why not try dreaming of a *reality?* Lose those ever-surfacing doubts of you're ever finding such a new discovery. It's a place so full of joy and untold happiness and it is there, waiting.' That 'little voice within' was new to me. Maybe I had heard such a thing on the odd occasion when tempted to do something wrong. Something inside always gives me a nudge with a … 'NO' … but one has to be quick, or you miss it. I wonder, most of the time we do all hear it, but ignore it?

The day finally came. Whilst in deep and dreamy quiet time, again lost in that distant gazing -- I think they call it meditation -- when all that surrounded me in this worldly place I was currently living in [my bedroom]; seemed to fade as I drifted away, becoming free from my busy mind, until in just one tiny moment everything stood still, and I sensed somebody quietly calling to me ...'come'.

In this fresh, unfolding consciousness; I felt somehow older than my years, and always somehow knew I was different from the others and did realise this, my entire thinking process, was, to say the least, a little unusual for someone my age. I didn't care. There just had to be a happier way of life, and I had found it, and all on my own!

Time passed, and I would eventually find myself successfully dwelling on a quiet spot in that beautiful scene: a small area of shallow, stony-bedded clear water between the two large boulders. I could see water reed, slowly moving this way and that just below the surface, like a maiden's hair. Sun rays pierced down to dress shiny naked pebbles adorned with constantly moving dappled patterns from refracted sun light. I had strayed beyond simply 'looking' with me *here,* and that *there* ... I *felt* to be a part of it all. Suddenly proof of such a feeling was offered up as I gazed skyward in the picture only to witness further glimpses of that third dimension so desperately sought: the leaves, on just one of the tree tops quite close, I believed an oak under the influence of an easy summer breeze, were teased into a slight swaying motion, with an accompanying sound of those same leaves, rustling in soft tones telling of youth in every leaf ... so it was spring! I watched rays of sunlight dancing between leaf and branch, granting me intermittent glimpses of sky blue. Not solely to please the eye, but nature's way of just harmoniously doing what it does. Seems winter had passed, and I could now say hello to those full branches casting shadows. I pondered on the implication of this dreamy apparition, manifesting before my very eyes. After all, it was mine alone ... how could that be?

Near to the water's edge, I spotted a beautiful tree, I think a rowan, and, having read of Norse mythology, learnt: she was thought to be the tree from which the first woman was made. Just maybe I'll learn some hidden meaning there, if ever that is, I fully make this *'heavenly place'* my own in which to dwell and enjoy. For the time being, it all appeared as one of nature's beautiful gowns, and I was simply touching the hem of *Her*, not some pop star's robe.

My heart had developed an overwhelming desire to perfect this astounding discovery, make it complete, step in there, and create a world for myself. Maybe one day inviting in only those who I chose to participate with me in my very own dreamy world, which, I decided, I would call: '*Reality*'.

My dreamy precious moments passed, presenting myself in front of my mental landscape dream. It became, with practice, more rewarding at each passing day, until one day, there in front of me, the entire scene came to life, and the worldly existence that surrounded me drifted away into a pink mist, a mist which, having turned to gaze back without fear of loss, began to form behind me.

My young mind interrupted for a moment, compelling me to call out: 'I can do it!'... I was immediately refocused back into my room, somehow knowing my dream had been granted to me. I was consumed with such joy knowing other wonders must surely be there for the taking. I sat for a moment cross-legged on the floor, imagining what I could create with my excitement bubbling over. After all, that could include lovely friends, trendy cloths, easy conversations with telling and laughter heard, listening and laughter given!

This entire process had given me, as mentioned, a more grown up feeling than my years ... almost as some kind of approval of my growing worth. I was a young woman, not for the teasing of certain school 'geeks', but complete, with things most of my age could only dream of.

I waited for Saturday, tidied my room, then, on with fresh clean pretty white underwear, with a hurriedly put on pretty dress, moving away from the school uniform dress [bordering on 'pelmet']; with hemlines ever rising from leg to bottom area! – *A line,* I thought, not too short, moving away from a tease to a country 'May Day' gown look patterned in tiny pink flowers, with 'Monsoon' styling, flat plain shoes in a grey that seemed to match ... No, I looked like wallpaper, trendy brown shoes suited my hair colour, so brown it was. I thought to add white ankle socks, a securing of my place in youth but that might add an 'Ivy League' touch! ... Oh yes, and I thought to take my newly purchased, colourful 'cross body shoulder bag' customised with my name: 'Freya' in pink, bringing me back into a thirteen-year-old zone. I felt somehow grateful. I was about to journey on, free from: 'tattoos', 'nose', 'tongue', or 'belly-button' rings as accessories … simply a clean-cut cute me … that's it!

I sat and quietened myself, gazing and gazing until a kind of easy humming and a glow came over me and my dream was there once more. Now, along with those rustling soft leaf sounds, songbirds and streams rippling could be heard ... I had never really noticed such harmony, all coming as music to my ears. I stood, steadied myself, along with an almost consuming excitement, stepped through that coloured mist into the scene. This time no longer dreaming in my growing consciousness ... but actually for *real,* and quite close to that old oak tree at the mill pond edge, where a corn meadow, accompanied by the odd poppy, had strayed toward the coolness of the mill pond to mingle incongruously with riverbank bulrushes. I again, heard that little voice within quietly say: 'now make as you will, this beautiful dream you now know to be your *'Reality'*.' I knew immediately there was some 'inner force' watching over me; *It* had just mentioned a place name, one that only I could be aware of ... *'Reality'* ... and it was mine?

I wanted to shout out loud: *'I know a place'* -- because I do! – I had found that place. It was my consciousness, a quiet place within to be found by everybody if they sit quietly dreaming. Mine I had called *Reality* because; when I compare it to that place back there [on Earth], it all seems so real and distant from all manner of falsities.

Looking around, I could see no other, yet felt somehow safe and unafraid… I placed my new shoes by the water's edge, close together, which did seem right as they were after all, a new pair. Then, completely lost in the moment, unbuttoning the front of my pretty floral dress; then, as if a film starlet, let my cloths fall to my feet with a mental camera shot of bare feet and underwear lying there, with falling dress to follow. Strange, I felt no shame, almost pride at being able to present myself a million miles beyond such 'taint' of lovely things I had left behind. Naked, I walked deeper into the crystal clear water, allowing myself to fall forward, turning, as I became part of *my stream* to lay on my back there, gazing skyward. It had all the magic of a school art lesson: Ophelia laying in such a way, painted by John Everett Millais, but unlike her lost life this was me creating a new one, and so real: I could see my wet hair moving here and there in crystal clear water … a union of humanhood and nature, so pure.

My first thoughts as to how I could, or should, use this power I'd been granted were a little intimidating. As time moved on, I would make more and more similar visits, no doubt being prepared for the new way of life I had found. I learned for the first time what law existed to maintain perfect harmony in that, if one detracted from it, a sign would manifest by way of guidance. I learned of this law early on in my adventure, obviously intended for me to become aware of such things, in order to instil an obvious awareness of when to act upon it. That *'law'* was actually brought to my attention due to less than good behaviour on my part and, as you will gather, this early demonstration of mine was not the best of me. You see, what I pictured in my dream in terms of living things would simply appear just when and where I pictured them, and I was untutored in the use of such power demonstrated well by a first temptation, resonating from life back there, which needed cleansing?

I had strolled across the little wooden bridge to the mill with absolutely no fear, as I somehow knew nobody yet existed who could harm me, until of course I considered what, or who, I wished to create. Firstly, quite consumed with this newly acquired power, and certainly with a completely wrong motive, my mind wandered back, almost as if to gloat over a bad teacher most at my school despised. I guess we can all visualise at least one. I invited into my consciousness a fat, miserable old bat, no sense of humour, wart on her nose, ugly teacher ... (I'll refer to as: 'Miss Brown') who always had it in for me ... to join me to sit on the handrail, gaze down at our reflections, and contemplate *'pooh sticks'* passing by on the racing millstream beneath us both ... then I pushed her in. The entire scene went a misty grey and I became afraid in the knowing I had done wrong.

She sat in fairly shallow water, with long green roach weed draped over her head, her glasses remaining swinging on one ear. I felt such guilt, in fact pity, for her as my naughty humorous vision made manifest another participant in my silly creation [never to be repeated]. As she sat there, a frog appeared up between her somewhat generous chest, then, forgiveness, and I will admit a degree of shameful love for her crept over me as I hurried down to the water's edge to help her out.

She stood for a while, water draining down from her wet, saggy, by now somewhat revealing togs. Regret and shame rushed into my mind and the mist, as if in forgiveness, began to change into beautiful colour tones, then cleared. That 'forgiveness' continued as pretty, slim, no wart on her nose Miss Brown smiled and just faded away, gone from my dream scene forever.

I was learning about the power of love and forgiveness, along with a little shame, I might add. It would seem there was to be no place in my dream for negative thinking and silly games, even if it was motivated by my odd sense of humour. If ever I were tempted to picture other discordant scenarios, the scene would immediately begin to fade, with that inner voice quietly calling to me ... 'that's wrong!' I was being tutored and tested to see if I was sufficiently qualified to be a participant in my new dream world on offer, and there was for sure, no place for deriding, or humiliating somebody else.

The first experimental lesson on silly things learned. It would seem there was a short period of time in which one can correct or foolishly stay with a situation one was happy to perpetuate. Clearly, I would need to be careful, as I was actually creating a world I wanted to be part of. A new world scene devoid of the likes of not simply atmospheric, but also mental 'pollution'. My new creation would be *mine alone* to build on and enjoy. [It went slightly misty.] I added to my thoughts the words: 'to share'... and clarity returned.

As my adventure progressed, when returning back to the world as I knew it, this always seemed to arouse feelings of disappointment having to face all those freaky geeks at school who were never happy unless they were hurting me in some way. Along with friends who would frequently come and go without saying goodbye.

If only, I thought, all my contemporaries knew what wonders I had found, which of course I must assume they could also find, with more peaceful quiet time given to create their very own safe *'Reality'* to step permanently into. A place to find such happiness where every person and situation was just fine, with caring, sharing, and keeping others' feelings in mind.... You see, everybody knows wrong selfish actions, but they usually continue to act them out.

It was all so wonderful to think the only special secret place I had previously possessed was under my bed clothes with a torch, before, that is, I came out from under to sit crossed-legged on my bed and enter the media world of text and other devices for electronic communication. Then, there was: *'being in the world but not of it'*; my head looking downward almost permanently into a tactile-less 'smart phone' world, talking bland twaddle without the feelings or emotions found in eyes, soft sighs, touching, or body movements ... bumping into trees and strangers, not looking where I was going, looking at things sent to me by nerds hoping for a reaction about things that any decent boy or girl should not be subjected to, much of which spelled out dark worlds of indecency, sowing seeds in the minds of some so young that will sadly remain... sometimes forever.

How lucky for so many earlier generations before me, who had not been tainted with such unsavoury actions, images, or temptations becoming imbedded in one's mental receptors, surely to resurface in old age memory recall. After all, I had learned in school 'human biology', old events are far easier to recall for the elderly than recent happenings in their lives, with no hope of them ever being removed and shredded for a mental cleansing ... not even I fear, with a stroll through a car wash! What happened to the phase in life of wonderings by boy, and girl, on delicate secret unknown matters that always somehow, eventually seemed to 'tip-toe' into everyone's life, not on 'smart phones' shoved into ones' face in just moments of shock time, cancelling out those natural years of yearnings and wonderings that must have existed prior to a 'media-tech' world. I decided to concentrate harder, raising my consciousness to greater things, preparing for more time to be spent in my new wonder world of '*Reality*'.

A WORLD ON MY TERMS

After much practice I was able to visit '*Reality*' anytime my yearning heart gave me a little nudge and could stay there for as long as I so wished. The remarkable thing was that everything would become motionless, like on hold whenever I stepped out of my *Reality*, likewise, when returning back from my Earthly world, it would remain as such, until such time as the moment of my return. When arriving at *Reality*; my powers of creativity would be reenergised for me to re-engage once more in the enjoyment and creation of my new surroundings.

God ... I felt so lucky! Mind you, I did wonder about that dirty look Miss Brown gave me, passing by in a school corridor. I suppose she had drifted back into her real nature in the world I sought to escape from, with something lurking in the back of her mind of her sitting somewhere in a millstream ... maybe thinking she had had a bad dream. The point is, strangely enough, I now liked her.

Anyway, there I was, back at '*Reality*', and the sun was shining.... First thing was to create a friend to share my new life with. I thought, for me anyway, a boy, a little older, quite trendy, well mannered, up to date in his thinking, and of course ... being a newly created person, he would be free of all that mental dross so many of my generation were being subjected to. I would then have the ingredients of male logic and my girly emotional thinking. Plus, in order to find a good give-and-take balance, I'd suggest we sit and write all the issues we would like to see in each other, with some room for variations as we grew. We would become those people, to build on into later life … um …sounded a bit permanent, that. Who cares? I couldn't wait.

On reflection, I had just said, 'on into later life'... how could that come drifting out of the mind of a teen girl? … but it did. I was doing this all alone and strangely enough felt no fear or loneliness, probably as it was all drifting out from my seeking heart, so, I guess my onward journey must surely come without intimidations. In any event, what could such limitations mean? If I needed good friends, nicer surroundings, nice clothes, and happiness; I'd simply create it all!

This time I sat close to the mill-stream edge with tiny flowers in blossom ... I pictured butterflies and bumblebees, not forgetting small birds singing, then, as expected, as if by magic, they appeared! Before getting too taken up with this abundance of pure joy, and in order not to have to repeatedly refer back to untold events that have taken place prior to *'his'* arrival, I needed that boy to begin the journey together with from the very start. To set the stage for us, I'd keep it all rural for the time being, devoid of motor vehicles and electronics. Let it grow quite naturally, in what would prove to be a timeless place to start with, then, see what unfolds.

So important, to initially get my creation visually correct and ready for launch, then let life take its course. *Seventeen for him*, I thought, *his name will be Luke*. – Not far from where I sat, he's riding a pushbike, short sleeve navy-blue summer T-shirt, with a logo in large upper case pink letters: 'PAX', Latin for all that surrounded us: 'peace'. Hope he likes pink. With a smile, he'll wave, hand spread open in a way that felt as if perhaps we may know each other ... I return the smile, with just a small, quick, hand-movement kind of wave, so as not to appear too inviting, and then I thought … why worry. He began in my consciousness, so he'll be just fine for both our friendships. Then, there he was, coming my way, and with that very smile he introduced himself.

'Hi, my name's Luke, but I somehow think you knew that? You see, before you created the young guy standing before you, I came here long ago as Dougie, lived a long and peaceful life alone, writing stories, painting pictures and falling in love with all the beauty that surrounded me, including pretty girls like you. Until that chapter in my existence ended with my passing,' he continued...

'I sat … as if to reflect on the loneliness I had suffered so much of in my earthly journey, there quietly beneath a large oak tree in the middle of a corn field, my eyes came to rest on a single red poppy, until, as with my life; the scene simply faded in a beautiful, coloured haze.... I picked the poppy; as if to capture and hold close to my heart the beauty I had so enjoyed and embraced in my arms along the way.'

Oak trees and poppies ... this was ringing bells. For just one moment I was in total shock at what he had just revealed. Could this lovely guy in my consciousness really be the 'Dougie' who had inspired me so with his artwork in my search of greater things, now being reborn, and to me? ... Having 'Googled' and read of such a person at the school library, this would be akin to meeting, albeit not a star, none the less, an idol in my world. He continued in such a humble way, actually confirming that very identity and, praising me, of all people... just a slip of a girl!

'Seems you have given Dougie a new youthful life. I do, however, feel I have retained all that creative wisdom which I think will help to take us on together into a wonderful expansion, of all that you see around you: it will be new! Welcome to my beautiful world, which, from now on will be of *our* making! You felt my creative heart feelings whilst fantasising over my picture and have been sent to join me. Thank you for making me seventeen in your dream. You have taken away old age and, I can feel all my earlier youthful dynamics that go with that. A chance to enjoy the innocence of youth once more ... by the way, we don't have mobiles, webcam, iPads…' and with a smile, he added '... and, believe it or not, we have, *'steam'*, not *'search'* engine facilities here. We actually talk person-to-person, face-to-face, and learn to read facial expressions and body movements to see if one is sharing truths or telling *'porky pies'* ... I'm sure you know what I mean?'

In shock at the realisation I had found Dougie in another guise and that he was actually talking to me almost on equal terms, I plonked myself down on a sunny grassy bank in total disbelief!

With a degree of shyness, I introduced myself as Freya and said that I was just coming up fourteen.

'A pretty name,' he declared, 'now I know you were sent ... you see, I know that name and its origins: a derivation of two special people Dougie once knew in his previous life: Frannie and a girl Riya from Assamese India -- the meaning of *Freya* in Hindi is: '*beloved Goddess of Love*'.'

With such a description, feeding ones' mental ego with 'Venus De Milo' re-incarnations and, in order to avoid any 'grey misty' stuff, I thought to ask if only to get a true picture in my mind.

'Do you remember in detail that previous life as Dougie?'– I needed to know the answer to this or my entire adventure, albeit wondrous, would be like inheriting somebody else's dream which would, for me, a new coming up fourteen-year-old new kid on the block, be a little dated? I so wanted it all to be fresh by way of discoveries for two new young souls coming together in my *'Reality'*. His answer put everything I dreamed of back into focus. As he smiled and sat down beside me, and I could see, as I gazed into his eyes, they were young and seeking, surely the eyes of any seventeen-year-old guy. He continued ...

'I have learned areas of Dougie's past, which embraced a partner with whom he had a deep love. She was with him during those landscape creation moments. Two souls that bonded the very moment they met! What you have done, Freya, is to bring into existence a completely revitalised soul, almost like a younger created 'satellite' of that person, but rest assured, I'm brand new. I do somehow know I have inherited degrees of his guidance, which will surface on occasions when help is needed.' I think he meant like a 'Guardian Angel' sort of thing. He continued with a point that made me realise why I had become linked so closely to him and that Dougie tie.

'Try to understand; countless people of all ages over time have managed to move through that secret screen to another place of wonder. Your seeking heart led you to Dougie's painting; others will have been led by other expressions such as, say, music, poetry, or for that matter any channel where an uplifted heart comes into play!'

Eager to stay with such an interesting teaching, I asked, 'Do you really mean there are countless numbers of other complete worlds like *'Reality'* in existence somewhere, a bit like those 'parallel universes' I'd heard about back there at school?'

'Yep, Freya, that's exactly what I mean. There are literally millions and millions of untroubled, happy existences going on in the 'cosmic' universe!'

My young mind was being stretched beyond its limited capabilities, so I decided not to enquire further on the point of ... 'cosmic universes' but did just wonder if there were other people like me back there in my world, moving around in a fairly normal kind of way. After all ... it couldn't just be me. So, I asked Luke on the point, also on the fact that others now treated me differently when returning from *'Reality'*, to which he responded ...

'There are many, Freya. Have you never noticed certain people had an extra pleasant manner about them ... demonstrating that 'caring' and 'sharing' you hoped for with your *'Reality* ... in fact very much like you now? Well, many of those, without you knowing their secret, are those to whom you refer! I know you have experienced for some reason on return visits, school students seem to treat you differently, and now want to be your friend; isn't this true? You see, they can notice and feel pleasant differences in your manner.

'Occasionally, with such joy, you will meet some of those 'Cosmic' souls to share secrets with, and they will tell of their *'Reality'* but under their chosen name; maybe something like: *'Harmony'* or similar.'

My mind latched onto this revelation, promoting somewhat elitist wonderings, and I asked … 'Does that really mean there is like a 'Secret Order' of people who have become special, there on Earth to change the world?'

'I suppose you could call it an 'Order', as you put it ... such people, are, at this very moment, moving amongst the population of the world, demonstrating truth, compassion, love, unselfishness, forgiveness, and so much more. That does include, by the way, your dreamed of 'caring' and 'sharing'. Without wishing to get too religiously serious for you: John 4.48 in one version of the Bible back there makes reference to 'signs following' and 'by their fruits ye shall know them'. Well... you, along with so many, are already members of that 'Order', as you put it; peacefully working that magic without any thought of reward! As time passes and they go on to have families of their own, can you see, with parental sharing, over time the world will become a much lovelier, better place?'

I think I knew what he meant and quietly thought about so many I had met in my short journey to date on Earth. I had never thought to associate so many with a 'Secret Order' that sounds like something out of a 'Bond Movie', and they must surely come in all age groups.

I began to mentally wander back through my short life span and noticed Luke gazing at my somewhat vacant look, obviously not wanting to disturb my train of thought or such 'wanderings'. It was as if he somehow knew I was learning something so profound ... and I surely was.

I could see it all in pictures. Firstly, there was a girl, Jane, in my school beginning days, coming from a very poor family, who so young, would share her small, packed lunch with whoever asked. There was my grandfather, who I saw sitting in heavy pouring winter rain, mending a strange schoolgirl's bicycle puncture as she fretted over getting safely home. Then there was a woman of obvious wealth, judging by her clothing, who rushed forward to help a boy knocked off his bicycle outside our school, removing what to me looked like a very expensive fabulous overcoat, only to fold it to form a pillow, and carefully place it under the boys bleeding head as he lay calling for his mother. I never forgot her name, it was 'DIOR', which I saw on the collar label of her coat. Then there were many who simply said encouraging words to various people who were sad, despondent, and the like. I decided to end my private mental video show with the joy of being able to say ... *yes I have known them!*

'Feeling good?' Luke said with a smile. Well, I certain did feel privileged, so young to be taught such wonders that obviously surround us back there, without even knowing who and what they are. It was time to get back to, as my Ma would say with a reprimand, 'act your age'. So, with a little humour I did... act my age that is. You see I was so happy, and quick to add a little light-heartedness to such serious things by jokingly saying ...

'I'll stroll along back there, without ego, laugh to myself when I do something special, and somebody in a cool kind of way remarks: 'Cosmic'... with me knowing I really am... 'Cosmic'!'

All that mattered, after all that serious stuff; is that we were both now in *our* new world together, ready to begin a wondrous journey, one without those sharp edges, lies, or the transference of blame, along with the power to wreck other people's lives. Everything we would do, or say, or share would be in good faith and trust, each to the other. It would be two people finding and enjoying everything together. In good humour, acting quite childishly, we intertwined little fingers as a sign of trust, faithfulness, and sharing, followed by a Luke demonstration of a 'fist bump' which, I must say, although it hurt my delicate knuckles, seemed a little more grown up than 'little finger twirling'. We looked at each other and declared: 'Okay then ... let's go'.

'So, the small distant cottage from the picture, it is ... you first Luke,' I suggested, simply to engender trust and to offer up a little authority for him, in order that I would feel safe as evening fell. After all, he had initially created this wondrous place he was now sharing with me. As if in a way to suggest togetherness, he held out his hand.

Hard to imagine, my family had no idea where I was, and what I was up to, because the other world, their world, had stood still. I was now living in a safe parallel universe, like Mr. Evans, my physics master, had tried to make us understand. Would I, I wondered, fall to temptation by telling him at my next class that I am actually qualified on the subject and am able to visit one?

Luke immediately focused up on the obvious by suggesting the first thing to do was to create a base from where to plan manoeuvres. As mentioned, the first thought, the little cottage with the thatched roof a short distance downstream from the beautiful mill house, seen there in his picture, seemed just fine. We headed off to check it out as a possibility to begin this new life of adventure together.

Somehow, I felt quite safe that there would be no *'hanky-panky'*, whatever that meant, as this was being orchestrated by my consciousness, mind you I must admit, *'hanky-panky'* had started to cross my mind a few times back there, without, as I say, me really knowing what it all meant. Then it suddenly occurred to me: such thinking was a little unfair and one-sided. How could I possibly be allowed to orchestrate both lives? I thought to make a pact with my consciousness, in that I would write a list of qualifications we must try, at all cost, to abide by.

My *'bucket list'* for a good life was under way ... Thoughtful, Unselfish, Trusting, Caring, Loving, Honest, Peaceful, Sharing, and Romantic: that seemed enough to start with ... which should almost guarantee harmony? Even the 'Romantic' you probably noticed I had slipped in at the end could, for the time being, simply imply gazing at a beautiful sunset sky, with birds drifting across the scene as they head home to roost, that kind of thing. It doesn't have to suggest that Adam and Eve, Genesis scenario. We were innocent teens, well me only just, with no actual experiences of all that stuff, which had not been presented in a very nice way to me by my school friends in that other world.

I felt sure we could improve on such a scenario, where Adam asks if he can have a nibble on Eve's budding fruits, only for her to refuse, leaving Adam feeling rejected and off looking for other fruit on offer. We would allow life to unfold with magical moments step-by-step. I liked that, after all, I was untutored and totally without boy/girl experiences. I felt sure it would all come naturally in an easy unhurried dreamy kind of way, that would gather up both our emotions and be acceptable to both of us to participate in.

So, there we were, standing in sunshine, ready to begin a new second life together, one that would be of our own making, with occasional trips for me back to the world of sneaky things and ignorance of what was actually true in all matters, both stated and acted upon. A difficult world back there with much time being spent trying so hard to read the signs; it all seemed shrouded in disguise and innuendos. A world where everything, it would seem, can come crashing down around you in the blinking of an eye. Remember those two days of me having suffered for the pleasure of strolling through school at lunch time, hand in hand with the school dude, feeling pretty cool, I might add. I found out later, he had told everybody of *his* generous and kind offer ... the horrible nerd!

'Would we become a couple one day, Luke?' I asked, in such an immature, looking in the candy shop window kind of way, with such profound implications ... I did add: 'I think I'm a bit young for that?'

'Wow!' Luke responded, 'that really is setting the stage for adulthood, Freya. Best we remain good friends for as long as intended.' This was his suggestion, coming across with such authoritative sense, I was already beginning to respect him and it meant I had no need to fret over my growing up ... I did somehow know I was 'growing up' although my bumps had been a little slow on that *'front'* ... all the associated mind wonderings, that seem to go with such a period in a girl's life, were certainly getting active ... about which, I seem to recall my Ma saying: 'you're just growing up' ... with my human biology teacher Ms French, adopting a more tutorial stance, mentioning the wonders of the female hormone messaging services around the body and adding: "Tres magnifique" as a winding up comment, as if to play games with her surname; we giggled, if only to keep on her right side!

It was time for some clarity, regarding who's who in my wonderful new world; after all, it had all started back there in my bedroom when I had begun seeking *'Something'* and what was that *'Something'*? So, I asked Luke to explain.

'Glad you asked, Freya; means you are now ready to understand, which will make your journey so much easier, so I'll try to explain. Firstly, there is the true *'Inner Self'* that everybody has *'in there'* somewhere' ... pointing to my heart area which had me staring at his finger tip to check which part of my chest he was pointing at with a new feeling of hopeful expectation surfacing in that my small bumps might finally be qualifying for *womanhood* and his finger tip just might be making contact. He continued without the 'hormone' association ... 'that is your consciousness, your guiding light, your 'Jiminy Cricket', the inner voice you can hear quietly advising and guiding you through life. Then of course, due to your association with my pre-Luke consciousness via that landscape; you came to me to be guided through my dream. Next, as you had earned the right to formulate your own beautiful new world, due to your youth, it was decreed that you should have someone of a suitable age as a friend to grow with through that new life together, for as long as that is, as it feels right for you in your heart. – You chose a boy who you named Luke, who, I am so proud to say, was me as a seventeen-year-old.'

I did notice, with my now new life unfolding in *'Reality'*, my lovely friend had the attitude, and mindset, of that seventeen-year-old, so he really was my Luke, with the most wonderful persona I could have ever dreamed of. In fact, a really nice guy, who incidentally I had noticed wasn't as yet actually looking at my bumps, which I was so obsessively self-conscious about. Although a little disappointed, I did like that: after all, this is *my* friend evolving from *my* consciousness in a pleasant way.

His older wisdom, only when required, came out when I pressed the 'enquiry' button of that consciousness ... when I would then hear what I assumed, to be the wisdom of Dougie projecting through him but in Luke's easy way of articulating things, as I pointed out to him.

'Are you saying, Luke: that certain *'Something'* is actually part of me?' I asked, still trying to pin down this unseen figment of my imagination.

'No,' came his quick, rather knowing response, 'you are part of the *'Something'* not the other way round. A bit deep for you to be dwelling on whilst so young, but best get the matter out of the way, at the start of your new adventure, so I'll elucidate on the point as best I can.' I think he meant 'put it across', but I liked 'elucidate': it sounded really grown up, and I had used the word 'articulate' which I did note caused Luke to raise hie eyebrows in surprise.

'There are two ingredients: 1) your mind, 2) feelings [that silent voice within]. *Mind* is at work 16 hours a day ... it can work things out and take good, bad, or indifferent actions; this differs in every living being! – *Feelings* come from the heart [maybe just five seconds a day]. They bring to your notice the need to love, care, and understand others, etc. Some 'beings' act on these, some don't. It takes time and practice to recognise the differing approach required for such a plethora of varying situations.'

Of course he was right; it was all a 'bit deep' for someone so young, although I had I noticed, as mentioned, he had used words like 'elucidate' and 'plethora', obviously assuming I knew the meanings, which I didn't, but it did make me feel really grown up.

FANTASY DREAMING

It would seem I was finally ready for the adventure to commence. Luke again took my hand and came out with something I had never really considered but loved. Something that must have been lurking quietly in my consciousness, where I had often questioned the so-called *rhythm of life* generally adopted by my peers, one which was, to say the least, finely balanced.

'Let's make this different?' he declared, 'and take ourselves away from homework, study, job prospects, courtships, marriage, having a family, etc., which, as I understand it back there, apart from some true 'soul mate' bonding, never seems to last very long anyway. I am aware it is an age-old pattern of life that sometimes flows along beautifully to the end, but more often than not it all seems to go sadly wrong at some stage alone the way.' He continued with, 'we could create a fantastic adventure, a fantasy full of joy, true friendships, maybe just a little sadness, much caring, and of course the love for others.'

Boxes in that bucket list were mentally being ticked, and all did appear to be going to plan. Apart from our little cottage along from the mill, we decided we needed a secret base from which to orchestrate fantasies that would add adventure in so many ways.

'A tree house,' declared Luke – his logic was good, although I seem to recall, everybody back there on Earth was falling in love with tree houses, which did have me wondering if people, especially children, were trying to get off the planet, if only by as little as ten feet or so. He continued to explain how he saw our version coming together ... a loftier vision beyond childish adventures: A tall oak, with much foliage would be favourable, which, if around two hundred years old would be protected here by '*Reality law*', so we could feel untroubled, and could venture out from such a place after we had made it safe, warm, and homely.' I liked the 'homely' bit, which would present an outlet for girly things to manifest.

Clearly, there would be the need to use the cottage as a winter base, to be once more safe and warm, but we could design such things during warm summer evenings.

I took out from that quite trendy cross-over shoulder bag I had been given whilst on a holiday to the Greek island of Skiathos, embroidered with a motif of, along with my name, summer things. A pretty bag which had now journeyed with me through 'cosmic' space, it held a sketch pad and pencil, which I offered to Luke. He began sketching our new lofty abode, which soon started to take shape and -- look -- great, strong with a good number of cross supporting members ready for the flooring, then up went the walls and I dared to include a pretty, very dense ivy over the timber roof to look like thatch. It would then be lost from view due to countless years of growth, of this ever-present evergreen, offering privacy for occasional winter stays. As I gazed at the unfolding design; I interrupted with, 'What did you mean a moment ago ... '*Reality Law*'?' And he answered.

'Not the complex, impossibly expensive legals grown-ups back there might know of? Here anything wrong becomes known to the offender by a slight grey mist appearing, a mist that allows time to correct the bad action considered... if not acted upon, the 'mist' darkens until one will simply disappear from your '*Reality*' ... does that make sense?'

Well, it sure did; it had come my way, you might recall, due me lowing my sights over a certain Miss Brown! But I think he knew this. Having accepted there would be plenty of time allowed, before one 'disappears' in a puff of grey mist, I thought, with a little nervousness to get off that subject quickly, so I suggested …

'We could include some mistletoe, that's evergreen'. Luke glanced up from his sketch and repeated my idea with a smile.

'Mistletoe... that sounds promising.' His smile had me wondering if the implication was for some grown up kissing there-under. I had never actually done that... 'Kissing' I mean! I'd only heard of such things from a friend who told me her boyfriend's breath tasted of toffees.

Design finished and, with a retractable stair added, we sat quietly gazing at this lovely dream surrounding us. I glanced up at Luke, we smiled, looked around, only to see our new home appearing exactly as his design picture, with surrounding tree and general foliage moving in such an easy manner as if a deep friendship was being formed with a passing breeze ⊠ this was surely consciousness unfolding.

We finished the tree house in time for tea. It did all seem a bit grown up for two teenagers, well me only just, but it was nice. Luke went to a cupboard to find a couple of old mugs, but I was having none of it... '*remember, you are individuals in your consciousness*'... came that little voice within, so, I took action and there on the table was a pretty gingham tablecloth (pink) – Luke gave a sideways glance, and I made it blue.

The scene was being set with things we would have forever ... a tea pot, *two cups and saucers*, a little cake stand in the middle with jam tarts and rock cakes for my new friend. I did say I liked the 'girly' side of life, and there it all appeared, similar to my library day-dreaming moments on '*Alice in wonderland*', all far removed from those 'fast food' hang-outs and bottles of fizzy drinks ever to hand back there.

Why do dreamers so frequently drift back in thoughts of yesteryear, I wondered, with me having again just mentioned '*Alice*'? Bearing in mind, we were able to create whatever we fantasised over in our consciousness here in *Reality* ... the time seemed right to ask …

'Now, what about that fantasy you hinted at earlier, Luke?'

'Well ...' he began '... it's so exciting, when you consider the fabulous subject matter in other spheres in earlier times of dreamy worlds so sought after and loved? To think, there had been 'Watership Down', 'Wind in the Willows', 'The Hobbit', and so many more stories of life being changed into wonderful adventures, beyond the supposed normality of *'that world'* back there. Our choices to create for ourselves something totally new was limitless, even to the point of 'morphing' into other living things ... so why don't we?'

That suggestion shocked me a little; after all, it really was 'outside the box', as they say.

'But what shall we become?' I asked, as my mind raced between 'T-Rex' and 'Tigers'.

Luke was quick to introduce the acceptable parameters to be followed by pointing out, 'Our choices are limitless; however, they must fall within the loveliness and scale of that envisaged and in keeping with *'Reality'* Both having a deep love of nature and all things associated, we agreed: small animals, birds and wildlife were an absolute must for consideration, and Luke's parameters happily ruled out the likes of earwigs or elephants with that obvious limited tree home access!

As evening drew in and darkness fell, it seemed like my destiny was unfolding, as I gazed up at a full bright moon just peacefully resting there creating for us shadows of evening slowly lengthening across the floor. We decided to sleep on the idea of what super specimen we might choose to become up in our little tree top home so cosy. Luke had made timber frames around our beds and hung such fine white mosquito nets, I guessed, in case of nighttime creepy crawlies ... not forgetting a little privacy! It had the appearance and feeling of the 'Arabian Nights'.

The end of my first day away had arrived. We changed in a small separate room with a window overlooking the mill pond, with its reflections revealing a moon [times two]. Its wondrous light came flooding through that window and across the wooden floor to my feet.

Strange, as I removed my clothes for the second time in *Reality* … the first, unbeknown, and certainly unseen by Luke with my secret Ophelia fantasy. I was ready to put on something cool to sleep in, but once more it felt like a romantic movie unfolding as I glanced down at dress and white underwear falling to my bare feet on that moonlit floor. I felt so proud to observe my first, albeit quite small, soft fabric bra lying there, completing a small gathering of such delicate femininity. It had all moved away from the usual modest teen girl 'hiding' procedure; here, for some reason, I had no shame in my nakedness or need to cover myself in front of an uncovered window so high up. I somehow knew there would be nobody out there peeking at my newly developing young profile, promoting such pride! In any case, my consciousness did not include naughty voyeurism (another word I had learned in an English lesson). I think it meant the likes of 'peeping-Toms'. So, I was protected, although, just maybe, I was actually creating and enjoying my own naughty little scene of exposing myself momentarily naked, albeit to a 'pastoral only' world outside, with cool evening air passing over my now exposed young breasts. It all had a feeling of first time freshness as in: *'the first flush of youth'*, and I was determined to hold on to such a wonderful moment of 'growing-up', which for sure, as with all things in time would become just another thing to do … like, removing ones' grown up clothes ready for bed without prompting a compliment or even a sideways glance.

I remained in that pose for a while to enjoy the moment of such things alone, exploring my moonlit silhouette shadow, as I turned here and there, noting it was changing to that of a woman. Surely, the very silhouette that drew artists in, attempting to replicate such perfect angle-poise and firm profile line of female form, before that is, such silhouettes later in life, would begin to sag … as seen with my mother and aunties. This was all my learning time, for example, having picked up my tiny bra, I stood with one hand stretched sideways to let it hang there, swinging it slightly and immediately noticed those shadows had changed, from artistically beautiful, to sensual and somewhat provocative, which had me thinking: if I could see such teasing fantasy, what would boys be fanaticizing about? Umm? This clearly needed filing under: 'future secret girly ammunition'. Such first time, laboured thinking brought an end to my secret awareness and naughtiness.

'Let me know when I can change into my things,' came the friendly voice I had, so soon, taken to my heart, obviously getting a little impatient to change his togs. I had quite unknowingly become hypnotised by the marriage of moonlit shadows and form along with, those hovering, ever near naughty thoughts. I put on my night cloths, picked up my remaining things, and hurried through to part the pure white netting and hop into my beautiful bed.

My first night was pure magic, behind that fine white netting, so high up. It all felt, as I say, like something out of the Arabian nights; *there's the 'romantic' ingredient from my bucket list taking shape,* I thought, even the floor was covered with something resembling Aladdin's magic carpet, which could surely at some time send me into further dreaming of wondrous journeys to faraway places.

I lay, face down, in what I have always described as my 'frog sleep' position, with my arms up under my chin, and one leg bent fully upward to one side ... when I heard.

'Good night, Freya, I've pulled up the ladder ... sweet dreams.' I dared to turn to peep over my shoulder, pushing down slightly with my hand on the folded white linen as I did so to glance across to where he lay, to return the comment, now feeling safe and secure so high up with no ladder for 'others'! I could see, due to two layers of netting, a vague outline of Luke lying on his back, hands behind his head, in white boxer shorts and a navy T-shirt, probably contemplating an extension, or if the stairs had been secured properly for our safety. My bed, with a coloured patchwork quilt, was a veritable kaleidoscope of colour, as I gazed at pretty pink flowers in squares, soft and comforting with a large white cotton pillow. Luke's bed, not far away, was a plain looking duvet in navy blue. I could already see the boy/girl differences appearing along with, I noticed peering across at our little table and chairs, he, whilst I had been contemplating me as 'Venus De Milo', had secretly swapped his cup and saucer, for a 'mug'! – Such joy to use the word *'our'* as in *'our table'*... I felt I belonged.

Questioning thoughts rushed through my busy maturing mind, which I somehow knew I needed to control and await answers to at some other special time in my growing up journey.

Strange, my feelings were that of excited wonderings without really knowing why. Probably due to the entire dream experience we were safely sharing. Although this strange stirring inside was new to me, even at my 'other world' home, where such thoughts would usually pass, they were becoming more frequent and always left me with a feeling of something unfinished, which somehow I knew one day, would surely be fulfilled, but when, would be that ... *'one day'* ... after all, the ingredients were surely coming together ... for just a tiny moment, that very thought of 'coming together' seemed a clue ... as it eased my longing.

I lay, feeling reassured that my mind had not been tarnished by quick glimpses of what school friends had tried to make me view on smart phones. My thoughts and those wonderings remained a mystery so fresh ... an exciting journey to be shared with another ... *'one day'*.

Quite an unheard of situation, I pondered as I resumed my 'frog sleep' mode, and lay thinking: *Me, so young, lying here with nobody back there having any idea where I was, and what I was up to?* Plus, there was a very handsome young man lying just feet away, leading me to thinking: *do boys dwell on such things?* As is my way, this was all silly uninformed endless thinking, which in this case, needed to be overridden with time to sleep, so I did, and dreamed those 'sweet dreams' offered up by Luke of magic carpet rides.

FIRST METAMORPHOSIS

Morning arrived and, having washed in a large china bowl, with warmed-up river water, I changed for the day, and thoughts of breakfast began to surface; so easy, one simply had to envisage the breakfast required, open a cupboard, and there it all was, ready to be prepared.

We sat at our little table, complete with gingham cloth [blue] and began to think on the subject of what we would like our main fantasy form to be ... with adventurous thoughts arising of perhaps us changing to other creatures, but, of course, able to change back to Freya and Luke when required, in order to interface with any other human beings we were surely to come in contact with on our journey. Luke made the suggestion that we would always make our transitions in the secrecy of our tree house, where no others could witness such metamorphic magic.

'Sounds great,' I chirped, 'so what will it be?'

'Do you like water?' he replied. Our conversation became excited as we both realised we had spent every opportunity we could find in our growing up years to be in and around water. When I say *'in'* I really mean *'in'*, as it would seem, he and I had similar desires, me in my current youth, to swim underwater whenever I had the chance.... always, when at the seaside worrying our parents by disappearing below the waves for extended periods of time, no matter how rough the sea might have been.

A little of his ego crept into the conversation, probably to assert his need to make me feel safe, as he informed me that, when young in that other life as Dougie, to the envy of all his friends, he could, when at a local swimming pool, swim 40 metres underwater. Our experiences prompted the thinking: why not choose to be water birds? They can obviously fly, but in addition swim under water and walk on the land; such an exciting idea that included all areas of travel mode and so many species to choose from. We finally decided on the 'White-throated Dartmoor Dipper', which Luke described in detail.

'A pretty bird with a chirpy song, a little smaller in size than a thrush, easy to spot one when bobbing up and down, as they do, as, apart from dark brown patterned body feathers and reddish brown head, they have a pure white breast, plus all those attributes: like in water, in the air, and on the ground, with which we could so enjoy life in our new world,' he went on to say.

'I love the feeling of permanency with this bird, Freya: 'Dippers' have been known to use the same nesting site for well over one hundred years. Can you imagine generations living in the same location, probably leaving little notes hidden in the moss, telling of good food destinations, wishing those following on a happy life, prior to flying off to 'pop their clogs' somewhere!'

'Do you really think they do that? And where do they fly off to … to 'pop their clogs', I mean?' I replied, lost in Luke's dreamy idea before realising what a stupid thing I had just said.

Strange how wonderful that feeling of an easy life was manifesting itself, no threats, no feeling of being seen as half rate, no smart phones with the odd '*like*' granted to me for what I thought to be a cool *selfie* shared, with my attempt at humour, sitting on the loo with the lid down, peering over a book with a 'six pack' guy on the cover, followed by a quick text coming through from the school 'fat-boy', who just happened to be a friend on my mail list, to say: 'If that's meant for me, I don't think you're very funny; what about your two little 'bee stings' hardly visible under your tops?'– You see, anything in that world, in just the blinking of an eye can go 'pear-shaped', or in my case at the time... 'bee-sting' shaped! – At least he'd been looking.

I once gave a girlfriend a big, long-lasting hug as she cried, due to a boy she had liked going out with someone else. The school buzzed with rumours of us being a pair of devoted 'doughnut bumpers', whatever such a stupid comment meant. I innocently declared, 'I love doughnuts', only to be laughed at even more for having made such an ignorant mis-understood admission; prompting some to giggle in a pretence of being all grown up and knowledgeable about such things in life, which, in all probability, they weren't, full details of which my friend Jeni whispered in my ear.

'That's seems odd,' I would say, 'surely people have a right to choose,' promoting even more scorn; not that I really understood who should, or who should not, love each other, that is.

A subject covered at school back there; under 'Gender identity' – probably when I had been gazing out of windows thinking of 'The Hobbit'. Although sensing that our teacher was seemingly 'treading on eggshells', wondering which student might, or might not be, or thought *'to be* or *not to be'* or quite fancied the idea of a change for a while? Along with fear of upsetting 'his' parents or 'her' parents or 'their' parents. Then relief for him, the teacher, stepping off the 'eggshells' to escape into a fresh class on 'English Language', when, oh dear, the matter of 'eggshells' and 'Pronouns' arose yet again along with further fears of a School Head calling with possible dismissal in mind, following parental reprisals for calling Leslie, my friend, 'Les'!

The RE teacher, hearing of his colleague's conundrum, welcomed his class with…

'Let's move on from a certain subject matter covered in your last two class studies. Please turn to (Genesis 2 - 3) of the school Bible on your desks to consider the 8,000-year-old teachings of 'Adam and Eve'… Oh, hang on a moment, I've no wish to hurt anyone with such historical content. Excuse me, I need to discuss a 'third party' gender possibility on this with the Head.'

A shallow world! Little wonder I had been seeking some greater place.

We looked out at a glorious warm spring morning. Butterflies were up and about, songbirds sang, as they do, in fact all the harmony that spring brings far more reaching than just birds and butterflies. It was almost as if every living thing knew its rightful place: honeybees on this plant, not that one, bumble bees on this plant, not that, damsel flies with iridescent blue wings, simply pleasing themselves, dancing this way and that, with a preference of Mill Pond's watery areas nearby enabling her to tease all with her reflections. We thought 'wow' as it dawned on us; we could create whatever we desired to surround us as a living backdrop to our new life's way.

Having considered the dipper's modes of travelling facilities, we contemplated, should we fly, descend to ground level and walk along the water's edge, or dive down into the clear mill pond to swim below?

'Decision made,' cried Luke, 'let's try it all.' Seems our consciousness was clearly aligned, and, with joy, I reflected on my dreaming of Aladdin's magic carpet the previous night. He continued with such enthusiasm: 'What say we begin with a flight. We could survey the surrounding area to get our bearings, sweeping down to low level, passing so close over golden corn fields, smile at that lone poppy resting at the Mill Pond edge, then along, sharing reflections of ourselves with the sparkling stream, as we drift over its sunny surface. We can, whilst enjoying our maiden flight, mentally record good spots along the stream for future visits for picnics when reverting back to our human form, also for fishing for delicious trout, which, by the way, would instantly, simply be re-created as if never having been caught. We should take special note of features on the riverbank, and, who knows, we may catch a glimpse of 'Badger' 'Mole' or 'Ratty', we do need to make some friends along the way, after all. 'Wind in the Willows' was born so long ago, in 1908, creating such friends for us all to find.'

We sat chatting at our little table high in the oak tree, eating a Devon cream tea of scones, jam, and fresh cream, as Luke continued to elaborate on the magic we were about to engage in.

'You see,' he explained, 'the author Kenneth Grahame drifted away into a mental dreamland in his consciousness so long ago and left such magic for thousands to enjoy for all these years, although I'm unsure if he ever took it all to this level where he actually stepped into his created riverside world. But remember, Grahame was writing for others to read and enjoy, taking themselves into the story to use their own individual imaginings. With us, we are in the story, we *are* the story, we are making the story … can't you see, those 'others' read and look into the story, we, however, are in the story looking out! Quite good, that, don't you think, Freya?'

I found that statement fascinating; to think we could actually go beyond such 'imaginings' to actually find his animals and friends. If in quietness we pictured them on our travels along the river then this would surely happen... thinking along the same lines, Luke voiced a little uncertainty on this.

'Not sure if we could ever find those dear friends. Remember they were created by somebody else's consciousness, not ours, however who knows, they might find us ... they are a friendly bunch and know the riverbanks well. Mind you, I do recall, 'Badgers' can be a little grumpy, especially with strangers intruding into their little world, but remember our consciousnesses; we must always remain nice happy people … so I'm sure we'll be fine.'

We decided to build another small stairway up from our tree house, winding up through the evergreen ivy and mistletoe to the crown of the tree, and there, build a flat platform from where we could in consciousness, launch ourselves out into clear skies as birds, 'dippers' that is. I handed Luke the pieces of timber he had prepared as he went about the commencement of the build process.

Knowing we had always planned to keep our transformations from teenagers to dippers a secret, we decided to always make that transformation for flight to and from the platform, on which we painted a modest green 'H', a bit like a helicopter landing base, in order to make relocation easily visible when returning from sky-bound adventures.

The first sunny day for our maiden flight arrived, and up to our launch pad we climbed. On the way up, I asked, 'Do you have any fear of the unknown and what lies ahead, Luke? Because with the thought of launching myself into space, I certainly do.'

His response was forthright, but reassuring, as he reminded me … 'From the moment we learned to step into that picture, you more recently than the earlier version of myself, whatever we did was already formed in our hearts as *reality*. Doubting, would only introduce a weakness in that consciousness. We need to have total faith in this wonder, or, for example, in flight. Were we to consider with limited human minds: 'this is not possible, I was born without wings', this would bring us crashing to the ground and out of the dream scene, me landing in my studio of long ago, and you on your bedroom floor at home!'

The word *faith* rang loud and clear in my ears, all we really had to do was enjoy the journey and never allow doubt to creep in, as every time it did, as I understood Luke to mean, the perfection would diminish directly in proportion to the degree of that doubt. Frightening! Especially, when a few hundred feet up in the sky, and there below in the Mill Pond, eat-anything Mr. Pike, would for sure be on the lookout for a lunchtime snack, which would surely include the occasional nose-diving dipper bird.

Clearly, I needed to really develop total trust and confidence in that divine *inner being* called consciousness. Pinocchio with Jiminy Cricket again came to mind. Mine was real, his was an adorable little friend, but for children growing up so long ago, the same message was there to be heard and to learn from. It was our 'consciousness' from 'within' – as in … 'Jiminy Cricket' within 'Pinocchio'.

MAIDEN FLIGHT

We stood on the edge and apart from a few things that aroused fear in me... like space! Newton's apple theory and a winding stream far below, we looked around at blue skies with the odd small wisps of white cloud drifting by, as if inviting us to join them out there in space. With such joy, we glanced at each other, closed our eyes, and suddenly there we were teetering on the edge, two beautiful birds with white breasts ... then, as do all dippers, we 'bobbed' up and down a couple of times, looked up, not down, dived forward ... and took flight!

'Wow ...' we both cried out as the very first rush of cool air passed over our faces, which, I noticed, soon began to speed up!

'I'm falling...' I called out as gravity pulled me toward the Mother Earth and in quite a hurry, I might add.

'You're a bird, stop thinking you're an apple!' Luke cried out, and I desperately tried to believe it as I pictured myself as that beautiful dipper. In a moment, I felt no pull to Earth as I levelled out, calling out to Luke '... I can fly!'

'Well, there's a thing,' was Luke's response, '... that's what birds do.'

We stayed close in flight formation for a while, taking it all in, and then the experiments began. We soon discovered with a slight movement of one wing or the other we could turn and bank, from one side to the other, then move apart, followed by a couple of bumps into each other as we attempted to regroup, and we were flying side-by-side once more.

'Make mental notes,' Luke called out, 'of easily recognisable landmarks, such as large trees and any special feature you might see to recall some other time on future outings, also down by the stream, look for some riverside features on the riverbank ... that might also come in handy.'

I could see Luke reflecting on earlier days in his ... what we had taken to calling: *'the other world'* when he as Dougie was learning to fly. This came as some comfort and in order to gain confidence and build on the simpatico we were beginning to develop, I stayed with him for a while before banking away and dropping down toward the stream where, never having previously tested the law of gravity before, I somehow felt a little safer being closer to the ground.

After practicing a 'loop' and 'roll'; he followed me down ... and I was happy. *This is already feeling good,* I thought as I reflected on the days when all my past friendships, for some unknown reason, seemed to have fizzled out. I needed to remind myself we were really together in the dream. After all, apart from all this flying stuff, and him being a bit of a dipper ace, I needed to remind myself he was the reborn originator of this; just one tiny part of a trillion such scenes and places created by, I assumed, the Creator of all things, and... he was now my friend!

I skimmed along close to the water surface, in almost disbelief at the clarity of the water, sun reflections sparkling like priceless jewels so close to my underbelly. I spotted a green mossy bank bathed in sunshine, tilted both wings upward slightly to slow me down, then fully upward to stop [Luke told me this], and after a little tumble head over heels, settled on that pretty bank by the water's edge. Luke, clearly almost spellbound with our discovery, with cheeky confidence probably dreaming of being a young flying ace, flew at outrageous speed just millimetres above the water surface, then climbed up high into a loop ... reaching the top of the climb, over the top, and diving down to arrive at the that same frightening distance above the water surface. Turning toward me, he flared his wings out like an open fan and, quite intentionally, as he explained afterward, he *stalled,* dropping right in front of me, staying on his feet without any of my circus 'tumbler' demo ... just like that!

I was a bit young to know what girls were supposed to do when boys try to impress. I was tempted to throw myself at him and say, 'You're my hero, my Batman, you have mastered the skies,' but that had smacks of school amateur dramatics! Then I remembered one of my 'smart arse' pretty girl friends at school, who, when a boy passed by doing a *wheelie* on his pushbike, or a skate board *flat bar* along a metal fence handrail to catch her eye, she would just ignore any such demo and remain looking directly ahead, continuing to talk to whoever she was with. I simply said … 'Gosh…' That seemed enough for my immature attempt at praise.

He, in turn, and obviously to ease himself away from ego, said in such a sensible kind of way. 'I just needed to refresh my flying skills to keep us safe. Will you understand?'

'Well of course,' I replied. This was my first chance to flicker my eyes [just one flicker] in a coy *thank you for being so thoughtful* kind of way.

Clearly the interplay between boy and girl had begun, and we needed to take it all in for a while; it was all so beautiful and exciting. We sat and watched the water ... so alive and vibrant, rushing over half-exposed shiny wet rocks, creating long white bubbling water *pigtails*, in fact, the very conditions dippers must surely love.

We dipped, and dived, and swam against the flow of the stream for a while. Eventually taking to the air once more, flying a little above the surface, avoiding overhanging trees and branches of weeping willows by now forming springtime veils of green reaching down to kiss the water surface ... such romance … that very first touch of spring. We flew in one side of the veil of green, and out the other, just passing through, as we headed back to our 'God's Little Acre' seen there in the picture.

Apparently, dippers do actually built nests up under bridges as well as on riverbanks, so, we *zoomed* up under the little stone bridge opposite the mill. The water reflections danced on the bridge underside creating ever-changing designs. It would be impossible to become bored looking at infinitely changing art creations of such beauty, resembling mobile wallpaper for us, should we decide to build a nest home there. There was no end to the wonders of our dream.

We did think, whilst being dippers, that it might be nice to have a really '*twee*' nest as a holiday home for weekends and overnight stays. We could await the return of the mill house 'barn swallows' from Africa, to form new friendships ... but that would have to be for another day. I thought to ask Luke, 'The swallows, 'back there on Earth', return mid-April. How does that timeframe work here, Luke?'

'Anytime you like,' he answered with a smile. 'Look there,' nodding his head toward the mill pond, and there she was: my barn-swallow skimming over the water surface, then up over our heads with a sweet swallow smile. 'You see, Freya, you had that in your consciousness, and it happened! I must say, that was a master of the skies like a fighter ace; such control at high speed, it made me feel like a 'bumbling along bomber'.'

Now I loved him more, in such humility he had suggested he'd just been 'bumbling along', whatever that meant. I think he meant flying at lower speeds than the one that had just zoomed over our heads. A chance to grasp at a contribution to our relationship, so I added ...

'I doubt my swallow could do 'loops' and 'rolls' like you, Luke.' I think that worked, as without looking my way he nodded his head with an '… umm!'

We returned back to our tree top landing platform, morphed back into human form, then down to our cosy little parlour for tea to sit quietly and talk over the events of the day.

I was left wondering how one could feel so happy and free from *'the world'* of teen things I had left behind. It was all a silly game back there, deception and manipulation that I so hated. To think, after just a couple of days in our dream world *'Reality'*, my experiences, if shared, would increase my social media *'followers'* and *'likes'* a thousandfold, and that most sought after handsome senior boy at school would just feel good to be seen in my company, chasing me like *Pooh Bear* for his honey pot! That would be lowering my sights, I fear. Mind you, it would be so nice, but childish of me, to say when he approached me: 'Sorry, can't stop...up yours.' Whoops! The room went a little misty; I was being warned, either for the implied 'ego' or the 'up yours' bit – it didn't really matter which. I was being made aware of the warning sign Luke had mentioned and it was, after all, just a light mist.

A REQUIEM THEN OFF WE GO

Knowing, as I did, that Luke had evolved in a creation made possible by way of him being a younger version of that Dougie, the very one who, so long ago, had created the wonderful picture scene into which he eventually stepped for a new life. People always assume teenagers don't dwell on serious thoughts on life, but we do.

With curiosity arising, and a mind wrestling with wonderings, as to where it all began for Luke, I posed a rather searching question, followed by an immediate wondering if I really should have. I was about to enter a place and situation in my mind which would have me scurrying up-up- and away from my *Reality* … to a nowhere place, a 'never-never-land' of false imaginings, fears, and, much of what I had conquered by leaving life 'back there'! – That quiet little voice within, heard by all of us on occasions, called out to me: 'don't!' But remember, I was just coming up fourteen and those school day jealousies found in the minds of teenage girls surfaced. So, still leaning on my elbows, sitting at our little table with the pretty gingham tablecloth [in blue] drinking tea, I did – ask, that is…

'Dare I ask Luke: how life back there progressed, and ended, for you and Dougie?' After a short thoughtful pause with him smiling for just moments in time, during which I felt strangely separated from him, knowing I had attempted to take his mind back to a place in time where I simply did not exist which, for obvious reasons, had me feeling absent, not simply from a relationship, but an entire worldly existence. … and loneliness rushed in! Picking up on my 'lost and lonely' look he'd spotted, as he always somehow does, he elevated my thoughts, understanding of myself, my prowess, and more, to a status so far up the ladder I needed to stave off 'Miss Ego' which would undoubtably promote that 'grey mist' to begin to form! I found myself adopting a straight face quietness surely to be found, I thought, in the persona of someone very special. He was about to retrieve Freya from 'up-up-and-away' to 'up-up-and-back-again', thank God, as he said to me …

'Time for me to reign you in from such uninformed mental jumble Freya, in order for you to re-focus on just how such a special an elevated 'chosen one' you really are. You see, 'life back there', as you put it, never ended for me! In fact, it never started. There was never such a thing as Luke alive on Earth! Are you forgetting it was you who gave me a new life … remember? By the way, I love my T-shirt!'

He continued to rush into my silence, driving out such silly things as fear, jealousy, not being understood and the like, all things I had left behind. He looked at me with such a reassuring smile, and said: 'Look across the mill pond Freya … there, can you see that beautiful Water-Lily?' And of course I could. He continued: 'close your eyes and be 'still' – picture a pretty Damsel Fly resting there … now wait awhile,' and I did … 'now, open your eyes,' and I did … and there she was: my Damsel, certainly not one 'in distress', but one just moving wings of iridescent beauty '*here and there without a care*'. There was no need for me to say, 'did I do that?' … because I did!

'Getting the idea yet, Freya?' said with a Loving smile. In shock, for the first time I really did understand the wonder of it all! And from high on that 'ladder' Luke had made me climb, it wasn't 'Miss Ego', it was 'Miss Freya' … and that's me, having reflected, saying to Luke …

'You mean a boy on a bike, a T-shirt in blue, a Latin word for 'Peace' – Oh my God Luke, I've been drifting along in a kind of daydream … almost taking such wonders for granted.' He continued to offer more data to get my head round, which had me realising I had almost, unknowingly, been granted an almost divine right of creation … although, to date, with a certain Miss Brown in mind, well mismanaged by me I do admit!

'I think fair to say Freya, it was you and your consciousness; having felt so close to Dougie's back there; as you tried so hard to feel your way into his life via that landscape. I'm absolutely sure he jumped at the chance of a resurrection as a seventeen-year-old me; to make a fresh new adventure possible! Think about it: you could have created, say, a teen girlfriend, or the likes of say, a policeman to keep you safe … you had that power!'

For sure, Luke had seen me drifting away to some non-existent place of loneliness when there had been no need. However, I could see with such a mammoth scenario unfolding, we really did need to cover at least some past issues, prior that is, to heading off into a wonderful adventure. He continued to say briefly …

'Having found 'Something' special, it would seem *Inner Love*, guided him out of heartbreak and '*wandering lonely as a cloud*', put so beautifully by the poet Wordsworth, but for him, it was far from beautiful. In fact, a hard road travelled since childhood, which did not equip him well for later life, and grown-up things like marriage at just twenty-three years of age.'

Well, I did ask, and if I am really honest, with a bit of Luke's historic association surfacing, a little immature selfishness on my part surfaced, so, even though it was hurting a little, I dared, as we young girls sometimes do, out of shear childish curiosity, to allow such hurt to continue, with my mother's words ringing loud in my ears: 'curiosity killed the cat'! I had entered into a thinking process well out of the youth league. He had just stated, relating to Dougie: '*marriage at just twenty-three*', to a fourteen-year-old girl, that was like … getting on a bit. Up until now, I'd been on the outside of a story being told, simply a listener looking in, so, I asked …

'And where do I fit into this story?' Clearly seeking, if only in a trifle childish way, a feeling of belonging.

'You don't,' Luke replied -- a bit 'john blunt' I thought -- he continued, 'you are the story, you created *'Reality'*... you asked for a little history, and you are getting it. It is, what I say, 'history' and you simply weren't there.'

By now standing there with a slightly hurt appearance on my face, he quickly gathered me up, and I could see Luke, was since we met, trying to focus me on the fact that I was just a teen who still had a lot to learn and achieve in '*the world*' back there. A world which, unlike me, he was never really part of. The implication being, I suddenly realised with adolescent shock and hated saying it to myself, stating the obvious: he as Dougie, had actually died! A realisation that somehow impersonalised the entire matter, knowing as I did, this whole experience meant he was on a new fresh journey 'to the lights of home', now in the guise of Luke, my dearest friend.

'How did he die, Luke?' ... a question lacking in sensitivity, one which seemed to just come tumbling out. With someone as young as myself, there was obviously fear associated with the word 'death', along with me trying to bring two totally different people together, like Dougie and Luke, one of which was 'dead'. *That can't be easy for any girl*, I thought. In the short moments before he answered, I was left doubting and wondering if I really wanted to hear the answer, but responding to my question, out it came.

'An unrelenting feeling of loss, and a broken heart!'

Such a shocking response, I suddenly realised, why he was alone here in *Reality*. He did give the impression that, just maybe, he was searching for that special someone, who might have caused that 'broken heart' and, I dared to wonder, could that very someone now be me: re-emerging, re-incarnated, re-born, or whatever they call it, in some new youthful version of that special one. With such a heart-wrenching realisation of possible unknown outcomes, I found myself suddenly dropping to my knees with tears of both joy and sadness running down my cheeks.

Feeling my hurt, he lifted me up into his arms and, for the first time, embraced me so closely, my legs quite turned to jelly as I felt his form and strong arms around me. He added,

'At death, he was granted the right to step into such a new beautiful world on a permanent basis to begin his search, a search which now embraced me, which must surely have meaning.'

I decided to leave that matter to time, with I do admit, the feeling of 'joy' winning over the one of 'sadness'.

After all, we were as close as it's possible to get, it would seem. I, having gazed for hours in quietness at his landscape, had achieved my 'rite of passage', as it were, by feeling his consciousness and feeding off it, really. It was based on the beauty of a dream scene I had learned to love, so much so that it began to embrace me, drawing me in, to share it all. Apart from those soft clean and unpolluted breezes, there were untold revelations of nature's gems, such as the smell of wildflowers, heather blossom somewhere nearby, and damp moss from the mill pond margins … a hint of 'humanness' offered up, with a scent of bread perhaps being baked by someone at the mill.

You see, even though so very young, I could see the darkness beginning to engulf '*the world*' around me back there, with the likes of stabbings, shooting, drugs, rape, child abuse, disgusting websites. Then there was almost out-of-control world pollution and a generally depleting of a once pleasant adult world, which it would seem according to history, had at one time enjoyed sound political underpinning, and order. Why, I pondered, could I, so young, see that runaway situation growing and moving exponentially away from harmonic order and balance, yet grownups couldn't, or could, but refused in small-mindedness, to acknowledge the fact and act upon it? A young girl, growing up, articulating such as: 'exponential' and 'harmonic order'.

All a bit 'old head on young shoulders', I thought, but there clearly had been a restless mind of a thirteen-year-old on those shoulders of mine, creating a desire to be free from my world of falsities and the selfish desires of others, for me to live in a beautiful world... and this had been spotted, so, there was my link! Dougie, feeling my sincere yearnings had, with his applied help, allowed me to picture my own manifestations there, even to the point of seeing him as a new blood, and just seventeen. He liked that but advised me to try to make something of my life back there, and to remember: the love of my family and those who truly [not sneakily] loved me and would be with me forever.

'Tell me, Luke, would you know how Dougie became aware of my seeking?' I pressed on with the point, a bit like a child with a new toy, and I'm glad I did, as his response was pure fantasy magic as he volunteered ...

'I learned, he had been gazing into the clear mill pond, and your face, albeit in shades of coloured mist at first, slowly came into focus. He knew immediately you were not just looking at his picture, but he could feel you looking into his Heart. But you must remember, Freya,' he continued, clearly trying to get my feet back on the ground, 'Apart from truly 'seeking', to some degree you were escaping all that you did not like back there, so please remember, you are young. You can come here whenever you choose, to pick up exactly where you left off, similarly, when you return, nobody will even know of your absences.'

'Does this imply I will be two different people?' I questioned.

This had become a serious tutorial on life itself and I wondered if I was really up for such things. When you consider, I hadn't, at this stage in my life in *the world*, even kissed a boy, let alone all that other stuff my 'smarty pants' so-called friends were always droning on about, simply to prove how advanced and grown up they were having attended a human biology class on body bits and various hormones, without realising they were throwing away, or just maybe, side stepping all my innocent ways, ways which were, quite rightly so, directly related to my years, in what might be considered the correct process of growing up, which I quite liked.

'Yes, you will be two different people,' volunteered Luke. 'However, do remember you are being tested, and if you abuse your newly discovered consciousness dream world, you might lose it, and you don't want that to happen. You see, this dream world is a stepping stone to one day entering the next dreamed-of world, and that's called *paradise,* which is real and forever!'

This was all serious stuff and I was so desperately trying to understand it all, but one thing was for sure: I had somehow earned that right to step into his consciousness dream scene, and *something* within had led me to obtain that large, coloured repro of his landscape picture.

I needed to stop constantly considering my young age and accept such wonders are available to all, if that is, a straight path through life is taken.

'Stop limiting your understandings with age,' Luke suggested, with once again just a hint of reading my thoughts, as he was about to explain his own.

'I can think of a certain boy aged twelve who had obtained that higher consciousness, He left home, similar to yourself, and went on to change the world. *His* name was *Jesus,* remember *Him*? Do you think you'll go on to change the world, Freya?'

Naturally, that was never going to happen. However, I had been gifted with something so amazing, and certainly far above usual expectations of somebody my age. I was at the early stages and had to take it all in, step by infinite step, with wise old/young Luke there to guide me. Seems he was getting that guidance from *Somebody,* or something, maybe divine, completely out of sight.

I had burdened Luke with so many questions relating to background things, to a point I personally had become bored with the tutorials, which, in fairness, were all of my own making. I was keen to get on with my new wonderful world of *Reality*, with all the continued magic of 'Dipper' life and such things. This desire to move on, I could see, also applied to my Luke, after all, I had elevated this lovely fellow, from a handsome young guy on a bike to a 'wise old owl' kind of thing, and that didn't suit him at all!

As if to move away from such complex mind games, I witnessed a demonstration by him of utter humility, as if seeking out simple things beyond intelligence and the need for explanation. I noticed an almost strange demonstration of that humility, as he felt led to carry out the most basic tasks -- undertakings where he could do or say no wrong which might affect others. He stood up, ready to leave the table, smiled and, with one hand, squeezed my shoulder and, with such a sweet smile, declared.

'I'm popping outside for a little air ... won't be long.'

I went to the window to watch him arrive at the base of our tree below, only to see him commence chopping logs and moving large granite rocks about, separating the ones with a good 90 degree corner, as if considering the building of some unknown structure. He then swept an entire woodland area of leaves for much of the day, almost seeking out any task involving relentless hard work! It would seem I had invited myself into an area of understanding, beyond the mind of a slip of a girl. I scurried off to make myself scarce doing odd jobs, occasionally looking his way, strangely feeling a little nervous inside ... finally going out to say 'Hi', perhaps really, strangely enough, me also wanting to feel part of something quite ordinary, distancing myself from such serious rhetoric we had been sharing due to my ever-present inquisitive nature.

He finally stood there, having removed his T-shirt, shining with perspiration, looking like a powerful lumber jack, at least that's how I thought they might look, and me feeling a bit of a miss match, a sort of little girl in tight knickers, gazing from afar at her hero, awaiting more pearls of wisdom to come her way, from, albeit a boy of seventeen, someone who now appeared as a bronze 'Adonis' from a league much higher than her own. It was my Luke, and that 'wisdom' was about to come in a way that would raise me up again. He finally with just one hand took up his long-handled axe, raised it high, and buried it deep into a large log, rendering a loud hollow sound that echoed long through the woodland, making me suddenly jump. He lent on the handle with one hand and looked across at me, obviously about to share something quite profound.

This, to me, all felt so adult like and powerful. I found myself standing, slightly pigeon-toed, hands together in front of me as if hiding my preciousness, with a feeling of such virginal youth. I had lost that exciting blossoming into womanhood feeling the night previous. I was a young girl again, and due to my inquisitive mind, had stepped out of my depth. It was like having been taken by the hand from a Saturday morning children's cinema of old.

Strange how body language can say so much without words to a point where, in this case, after a pause, I noticed I had by now, having said to myself: 'he's my Luke', gained confidence again, now standing with arms crossed, my feet positioned together in a more self-confident pose, as if ready to listen. By now, my thinking of a silly Saturday morning children's cinema analogy, now becoming more along the lines of '*A Streetcar Named Desire*', a story by Tennessee Williams being taught in an English literature class, along with scenes from Steinbeck and D. H. Laurence.

'You are a perfect demonstration,' he began, 'of a teenager girl feeling things are beyond her, a limiting mind, which holds back so many young folks back in your other world. I could see you looking at me a moment ago as if I were someone special. Have you forgotten you created me from your consciousness at the beginning of your new journey? You have been blessed, unlike me in my previous life, who waited a whole lifetime to realise that something wondrous was available to all, but you have been chosen whilst so young. You must have read or heard of stories over the years of children seeing, meeting, and playing with fairies that adults could not see. It was their complete trusting innocence at a stage in their lives where they were un-attracted to, or tainted by, the lower things of that life. Can you not remember in your RE classes at school, learning the meaning of Jesus' words: '*...unless you become as little children you will never enter the Kingdom of Heaven*', not that seeing you, standing there with sun behind you in a see-through dress, puts you in the 'little children' category.'

Now I felt special! But found my confident stance changing as my feet crept slowly closer together, reducing the give-away visual merits of a thin cotton dress.

I was beginning to feel a little like a student being infatuated by her lecturer back there. Emotions do seem to fluctuate here in *Reality* ... one moment I am a growing young lover, albeit, not really knowing what young lover's do. The next moment, I am being tutored by my guy. Guess that will settle down in time, as there is much to learn here. Luke continued his chat in an easy kind of way, somewhat dissolving that constant reference I seem to make to a student/tutor relationship.

'Just accept that all things here are special, and feel good, in that there will come a time, when you will recognise a friend, or two, in *"that world"* who could be trusted to be brought here, as he, or she, demonstrates a readiness for higher things. Even if you make the occasional mistaken choice, that won't be a problem, as any wrong action by them, will, if perpetuated, instigate that mist appearing and have them returning back without ever knowing they were here.'

My thoughts rushed back to the room going misty when having those bad thoughts about Adonis at school, and of course, fat, ugly, wart on her nose, actually, nice figure, pretty, good at Pooh sticks, nice legs, charming Miss Brown ... another lesson learned!

Luke, having by now walked across to where I stood, leant over and whispered in my ear ... 'Exactly.'

'Can you read all my thoughts?' I enquired, with a little wondering, I might add, if I might at some time be in the embarrassing position of having some of those ever increasing, naughty ones to answer for.

'Only on major issues of importance in your growth,' he replied. 'You must feel confident that you are building a private life of your own here, without any intrusions by others.'

My immaturity surfaced again! You see, he had, in order to assist me, just stated: 'you are building a private life of your own'... now I felt lonely again! Oh dear! Guess that's growing up, and what all teenagers have to go through. – I didn't want to be alone, I wanted to be with him, and really close. – No mist appeared, and I felt safe, knowing I could, if I so wished, be a little sneaky in my thinking.

'I cannot go back,' he continued. 'So, when you do, always know that I will be here waiting to help and guide you if I can. Without, that is, sounding too far out of touch with *the world* and being well past my 'sell by date' on modern views. After all, as mentioned, you did make me seventeen for your journey. You have no idea what a wondrous thing has happened for me in your dream consciousness, what with you being led to use my landscape scene from my previous life. You had the power to make me this age, and maybe, just maybe, the plan is you will remain with me as my younger self, and we'll journey on together to wherever I am heading. Let's wait and see.'

Then with a knowing look, I felt sure, in order to give me options to feel happy with, he continued...

'You never know, in your world back there, you may have many partners, one of whom will perhaps, one day become your eternal loving partner.'

God ... I suddenly felt so important and grown up. We were not talking about, a new bra, smart phone, nail-bar appointment, or even belly button, nose and tongue piercing, we were talking about grown-up boys and loads of them! One minute I felt alone and free, the next minute I felt Luke and I were close, and then, with mental flirting, I wondered if there could possibly be another, and another. Had he released me directly into greed?

With that discerning ability he has, plus the faraway dreamy look Luke had spotted on my face, he declared...

'Getting greedy? – Don't go breaking hearts along the way Freya, maybe even mine, and remember my earlier advice of relying on 'Heart, not mind, feelings'.

My mind grasped at one little piece of his guiding words. He had said: "maybe even mine!" Could this, I dared to wonder, have implied he too had some sneaky feelings about me? My mind was doing exactly what I knew from my teenage friends at school, dashing from one issue to another, liking one boy then another, loving/hating, plus those ever surfacing secret thoughts. At least back there, my mum was around to guide me, making such comments as: 'it's just growing up, Freya, your hormones are swishing around all over the place, that will all settle down and you'll be just fine, you'll see.'

Clearly, I needed to slow down and do a bit of growing up at normal speed.

'Live in the moment,' Luke chirped up, as if he was fully aware of my mental jumble, and added: 'As I have pointed out: there is only '*The Now*'... one cannot see into the future. – How do you know, or for that matter want to know, what lays ahead on this, our journey together. The ultimate Highest power may say to me: 'You have struggled in your Heart for so long to find the dearest friend you ever had, and here you are with Freya, without you realising, she is actually that friend, and has been all along. I simply made her different in appearance for this journey.'

He had just implied my earlier thinking may have been close -- that seeking-heart scenario of Dougie seeking someone special he had lost, was now a youthful Luke, and what he was seeking is actually standing right in front of him ... like me! Such advanced thinking for such a young soul like me. The content was so profound I felt the need to simply journey along and stop my inquisitive mind working away so much, as it would surely get it all wrong, and just maybe, the eventual outcome could actually be beyond my wildest dreams.

IN AND OUT THE DUSTY BLUEBELLS

An incredible journey had clearly begun. Luke began to explain that the first stages we had so enjoyed, like the 'dippers', were intended to ease me into all this adventure and made the comment.

'That was just an intro, Freya. Remember me saying: 'you can be anything, assuming that is, it is honourable and correct'.'

'Do you really mean anything?' was my fairly obvious response to such a powerful statement with mind-boggling implications. It was a cornucopia's treasure trove overflowing with adventures, and I had the key.

'Yep, try this.' was his somewhat inviting answer.

We sat down by the mill pond edge, peacefully glancing around, until he pointed to some beautiful white water lilies languishing on the surface of a fairly quiet section of water, just off the main stream, and a beautiful butterfly danced across our view and settled on one particular bloom.

'Your thoughts... or should I say feelings?' he asked, and I was honest in my response, in that I was thinking how wonderful it would be to be sharing such a sunny spot in such surroundings...when it happened I had become a beautiful butterfly sitting on the large flat leaf looking up at my newly found, equally beautiful friend.

'Don't stay there,' this beautiful little *Papillon* called down to me, 'Mr Trout might take you. Come up and join me on the flower petals.' Whilst in a state of pure bliss, I quickly did just that, and commented, 'How lucky you are ... so beautiful, and able to enjoy such surroundings.'

'Be careful Freya!' warned my new little butterfly friend. 'Enjoy each moment, one after the other, that's all you have to do, as they are infinite; one moment arrives, then it's gone, making way for another moment. Watch your desires and, by the way, butterflies only live for a few days. Not many 'moments', eh, Freya?'

Having considered my options rather quickly, as I fancied living for a little longer than a 'few days', suddenly there I was sitting back with Luke on the grassy riverbank.

'That was amazing,' I blurted out, 'and he knew my name.'

'Sorry, what do you mean?' was Luke's vague response, almost implying he had no idea as to what I had been up to ... mind you, I really believed he did.

'I had no idea you'd been anywhere, Freya, remember it's your gift to enjoy, maybe it was intended as a lesson, in being careful what we wish for.' Probably, I suspect, making hidden reference to the somewhat short life span on offer of about five days. 'Can you see?' he continued, 'this is the beginning of something any person in *'that world'* would do anything to be part of. But do remember it was your consciousness, not mine. ... Clearly, as you came back, I must assume you didn't do anything that might have cancelled your dream with you drifting into a fading mist and out of sight ... I would have really missed you!' I was reminded of that slight *mist* event by the mill, with Miss Brown! I paused to reflect on Luke's words, then realised the underlying implications, in that, had I been selfish, I could have lost everything, whereas his existence in *Reality* was forever. In a heart fluttering moment, I knew exactly what I would have lost. You see, he had just said, 'I would have really missed you.'

It was such a great lesson. I was being tested and made to realise my destiny was solely in my own hands. When you consider I could have been greedy and languished in such beautiful surroundings with such a handsome butterfly partner, however, for any more than those 'few days', along with my new friend, we would have died, with Luke and my 'togetherness' ending there and then on that grassy bank, there before him, without goodbyes ... End of our story!

SETTING THE STAGE

For sure we had begun a new venture with countless joys to discover, and it was all so exciting. We finished our tea and sat talking for a while. I recognised, indeed welcomed, what Luke began to discuss. He knew very well that before we continue on this wonderful dream journey, there was a need to set the stage and the general underlying philosophy of it all.

I so enjoyed the following conversation, but could recognise my contribution was erring a little on the somewhat teenage girl emotional mumble-jumble understandings of things.

'Staying on that subject of meeting other creatures and people here,' Luke reflected. 'Even though you are quite young, Freya, this is so important for you to understand, without that is, allowing sadness to creep into your thoughts ... I am sure you can recall some person or pet you lost along the way, maybe a granddad, grandma, pussycat or a dog? Make a list of these, and in doing so, you will be bringing them all to the fore of your consciousness in readiness.'

This immediately touched a nerve in me, as sadly all those instigators of love he had made reference to had come my way in their Earthly journey, and I felt a little hurt inside. In such a reassuring way, he continued.

'This magic world we live in here is, as I have explained, all based on uncontrived heartfelt *'feelings'*, so any of those people or pets you have lost, if based on true inner *Love,* will one day be found again, and when you meet, you will immediately be aware they were waiting for you and, like yourself, they may appear the same as when you last saw them, if unwell then, they will be healthy again or some suitable age which I can't elaborate on now. They'll call your name, or of course, purr or bark as they run to you... how about that?'

He was quick, with sadness in his eyes, to point out: 'I learned from the story of the one from whose origins I came, of a loss from *that world,* of a most beautiful girl, a few years younger than you, and her adorable younger sister, half English, half Italian, with deep trusting love and friendship between them grew. He worshiped them. Then in a moment, that became a devastating lost! Maybe, one day, I also will hear them call my name again.' He continued, 'so much to understand, Freya, so be patient. if we go rushing off here and there, in all directions all too soon on our journey, it will all become a jumble of events. Better to savour each moment, remember, some of those moments you, as well as me, will want to keep as a permanent part of our wonderful world here, so, step-by-step, and in the right time, and only the right time, things will present themselves. You'll see.'

I began to make a list of those resurrections I so wanted to be with me again. Actually, my list was quite small, and I realised suddenly that Luke's list would be of greater interest, based on the mystery of his life here prior to my handywork in bringing him to me. I had now learned my suspicions were well-founded, in that, as I have suggested earlier, he had a mission to find a special lost one, this time to cherish forever ... and that just might have some implications relating to me. Having allowed that emotional dust to settle a little, I dared to ask about those 'implications', probably, with a little impatient teenage jealousy creeping into my mind.

'What about us, Luke?' To which, in his easy comforting kind of way, he put the matter straight, well if not 'straight', at least on hold, for my tiny little undeveloped heart. I think he knew, as the subject had been hinted at of what I was looking for, maybe proof, that I was that very one that Dougie had dreamed of finding again, him now in the guise of my Luke I had now resurrected, and, it might just be me, taking my part in that very reinstatement of true Love.

'This is your dream, and in that dream you wanted a boy of seventeen to share it with you. *Something special* chose me through my landscape setting for you in order that I too, could savour the life force therein. We have a lovely journey to enjoy together based on another deep trusting, sharing friendship ... any fluttering in your young heart will for some time be the same love as you had for that little pussycat 'Milo' that I spotted there on your list. Regarding *"us"* as you put it, there will be new discoveries for us both to embrace.'

'What...back to Adam and Eve Luke?' I questioned, adding a little uninformed young humour.

'No... That related to *temptation,'* was his response.

'Being tempted with what?' Seemed the honest and obvious follow-on, especially as in all the pictures I had seen of Adam and Eve in RE, they were both *starkers*. Seeing where this was going, Luke, in a shy kind of way, with, I was amazed to see, a hint of a blush on his cheeks, added.

'Can we leave that one for the time being, you will know when it happens to you, and me too for that matter.' I went a little quiet for a while, trying to imagine how I would know 'when it happens', as he had put it. On this major point for me, he steered the subject more in the direction of a fourteen-year-old girl and, as always, made the whole matter seem correct with a scenario of sequences so sweet, filling in gaps of life, adding up to years in time before permanent relationships could be in order.

'Every person, be that boy or girl, is different,' [I did know that much!] he volunteered. 'Be patient. One day in your world back there, you might look at a boy and something, just something, will attract you, it may be his manner, his smile, colour of eyes, his height, sporty type, or swat, who can say? Then you will feel a pleasant yearning to be with him and, hopefully, for him to want to be with you. Next comes contact, holding hands will do to start with.'

Sounded a little silly, as if taken from an old romantic movie, however, I was beginning to like the idea, and it all seemed an easy, not too intimidating way of boy and girl coming together, especially that 'pleasant yearning' bit, which as mentioned, I think I had felt a little of on the odd occasion since I was about eleven, around the time my monthly girly things commenced.

So glad, I had not been 'tempted' to take on board all that boy/girl 'stuff' on smart phones my friends seemed to be forever nosing around. Who knows? Maybe this is why some Higher power had given me this wonderful opportunity with my new dream world. I asked Luke his thoughts, only for him to say.

'This is, as I repeatedly point out, your private journey of discovery. However, to clarify the point you have just raised, consider the clear sparkling stream you swam in yesterday, then compare this with what your friends had been tempted with, '*that stuff*' as you put it, which they were always trying to make you look at. Their little stream is running like a polluted drain, leaving memory imprints that will be difficult to clean away over a lifetime ... this seems like a good example of that 'Temptation' we have just discussed, which in fact you seemed to have turned away from.

'There is pure magic in the air waiting for you, Freya, and remember, there are few boys out there who can be trusted with that precious little heart of yours. You really *must* learn to rely on those *feelings* about people. Look into their eyes, look out for too much ego, and listen out for gossipy false things being said about others.'

He finished with, 'That should be good enough to go on with and, remember, as I say, I will always be here to guide you, but no more than that. It's your life, not mine, but you must know I will always be there to offer my support based on somewhat limited knowledge on many things.'

He always seemed to counter a lowering of my heart feelings, and here again he somehow sensed my imagined separation from him, along with related disappointment based on what he had just said, you see he had just implied once more that our togetherness, which I had only just begun to savour, was perhaps to be for only a limited period, based on the fact that he had just been through an entire outlining of me and other boys. Then, I was utterly shocked at his next remark.

'Who knows where our destiny lies ... I surely don't.' From this, his own honest demonstrating of the inability to offer clarity, I felt nervous ... after all, I was beginning to think Luke knew just about anything. He was offering up an honest lack of understanding of the entire dream we were both part of together ... for a moment I felt quite unsafe! Then, as always, he made an observation that made it all 'togetherness' again, possibly on an even greater higher plateau, as he continued.

'Thought to point out ... the guidance just given on 'boys' and 'you' is all based on that other world, which is an entirely separate affair to *Reality*. Remember the day will arrive at some time in the future, when you leave there forever, to live your life out here.

'How do you or I know if, in fact, this could be a wonderful new life unfolding, where you have been chosen to join me, and,' having paused to consider, he added, 'I might be getting another chance of a new life with magic moments that I had day-dreamed of all through the loneliness I endured in the latter years of my previous life. Just maybe, as I have already hinted, you, in another guise, are that very person from my previous life who broke my heart and was destined to be with me once more. – To be really honest with you, I have seen certain little characteristics in you that surely remind me of that lost love ... characteristics being carrying over to a new Love!' I could swear I spotted the tiniest cheeky '*wink*' prior to him continuing with,

'We may be destined to grow together here, when, that is, your ties from that *other world* are ended at a predetermined time, so not long to wait, because you may recall, I have explained, time has no meaning here.' He had given me, although patience would be required, some of that inner joy I so desperately sought, leaving me satisfied thinking 'fiddle-de-de' to those other boys.

Clearly this wonderful journey had to be eased into something like a love story, in fact a new life unfolding with each moment special, just as he had implied earlier. That supply of special moments it would seem, really is infinite. It was time to move on into that story, with I guess a few tutorials along the way when needed, which hopefully would not be too often, if I stop asking so many questions. After all, this was life unfolding like growing up, and too much mental tinkering with my busy, still very young inquisitive little teenage mind would only spoil a natural rhythm of it all.

MANAGING INHERENT MAGIC

Our plan the next morning was to wander out and about a little in our new world, if only to get the feeling and layout of it all ... strange, during these early stages it always seemed to be sunny.

Thinking back to Luke's earlier reference to 'feelings'; we had only walked for about an hour enjoying so much beauty when I found myself attracted to, along with his easy humour, my new friend's confident manner.... I began having, albeit brief, those 'pleasant yearnings' about him. Remember those? ... 'Behave' ... my tiny mind called out, so, with a little uncertainty as to what my mind was up to, and what in fact I had needed to behave from doing, I went to the water's edge, kicked off my new brown shoes, and stood ankle deep, bending down to rinse my face in cool clear water.

'Cooling down?' asked Luke. Well I was, but it was more like a calming down, from the distractions of inquisitive mind games ... of something unknown to me. *How strange and comforting the learning process of growing up can be, and in such a safe place,* I thought.

I was so happy, that I had inquisitiveness on things that were not being spelled out to me in degrading ways as in *that world*. Seems I had been plucked out of a madness developing before I had chance to change from a sweet ripening juicy peach into a rotten apple, attracting nasty fruit flies, in what was becoming a dark, supposedly normal world for my entire generation. So many were, it would seem, being taken like Pinocchio to 'Pleasure Island' on a carriage pulled by eight donkeys, which over time had become a convoy of a thousand trains, each with thirty carriages full to capacity with none of the passengers looking happily out of the train windows. They had all become lost to temptation and were now destined for tails and long ears on that island!

Many I knew of who, when so young, due to a premature overindulgence in bad behaviour in what surely should have been a wonderful period in one's life have as far as I could see, diluted, even 'polluted', countless pure magic fragments of life. Putting the picture together back there in my mind, it would seem that 'magic' in any event all appeared to be too short lived. What of those early growing-up moments; of girls' first sightings of private things, and those new feelings rising up. And what of boys' stories told of spongy girls' breasts, felt from outside of clothing, later to experience, for the first time, the wonders of that soft skin beneath. Feelings of naughtiness as we move through moments of discovering forbidden fruits ... but who forbade them? Usually a girl's mother, warning of the eagerness of boys to touch ... which had left me wondering; why would they, boys I mean, want to do such a thing? Probably 'the unknown' due to such things always being hidden under clothing. I was now beginning to realise the difference between 'intrusive' and the 'sharing' of secret things with someone you cared for. And what of the feeling of 'power' which girls felt, to know they possessed forbidden fruits so desirous of boys. The strong fist of the school bully boy that could break a nose, that same fist so tamed when allowed that first feel 'on the inside', an experience which, when told of such things by my friends, I would act out a false air of shock ... yet I so yearned for it myself.

I somehow knew in my wonderings that prior to moving outside of the joyous adolescent box, my 'things' for so long would bring pride, as secrets to be hidden in pretty delicate blouses. There would, one day, come that confident strut to the sea water's edge in a 'bikini', then, when dressing, the cheek of a '*peasant blo*use', and the control of how far it slipped down over a brown shoulder ... the self-imposed authority to appear a little shocked, as with just two fingers, one pinches the *puffed* sleeve top, to raise it slightly. The knowing of temptation things girls were fully aware of beyond boys' understandings, as they become mesmerised by a soft cotton dress pressed 'cling-film wrapped' so close, when facing a strong sea breeze, revealing for them hints of those 'forbidden fruits'... and yet, the same soft thighs, seen in that bikini bottom, were seen as simply human limbs, no longer tantalisingly sensual to boys! Why?

It all seemed so wondrous, until one realised the short life of those 'Adam and Eve' tempting moments, stepping over a line drawn across by scriptures. In just one of those moments the naughty magic times will be gone, giving way to 'the way of life'. Full of loving *friendship*, but now part of all the 'human biology' stuff taught, to include a reproductive system soon to be kicking in. Then those priceless 'things' denied to boys will no longer be seen as soft and secret, with glimpses granted to tease. They will all become as intended, 'purpose built' for breast feeding duties, with all the related responsibilities and the wonders of marriage, and motherhood taking over. Then: an acceleration of unwelcome knowledge given by mothers and aunties ... presumably to appease a teens' inquisitive mind as they rush into adulthood.

So sad to realise those magic cheeky years will all drift away, especially for some, as those medical intrusive facts on *BC*, mentioned in school 'human biology', kick in, to attack those 'soft' precious wonders. I so wanted to find my *'Reality'*, where such things could not intrude on me. Memories of possible first kissing and more, down on some lower meadow, will all begin to fade, eventually to be lost forever! Fine details will be lost, in the fading clarity of the mind with each passing year, denying us mental re-runs of such unions for us to savour once more. It will all move into 'being grown up' as they say.

I was determined to savour each precious moment – to make them last and last, taking each one to its limits, before moving into the next phase for similar joyful consideration. This way, I somehow knew the excitements, teasing, wonderings, intrigues and the like would extend those joyful younger years. It all made such sense, as I recognised, and reflected on some older female teachers, who remained vivacious and, full of joy with young perfume smelt, who could, with a smiling glance, destroy a male, and yet, there were girls at school who appeared to have short lived each of those 'phases' of youthful expansion, and it showed in smiles and tired expressions on faces that appeared experienced and older than their years. We can all look and know things about them without words … their teaching of boys to grow in manliness and pride at their expense. I began to realise, my *'Reality'* world was slowly bringing me up to higher levels of truth and understanding, as my mind buzzed with such serious thinking. I had, as mentioned, always been a 'thinker' and if I'm really honest, it did all make wonderful sense and would surely delay those 'granny' moments of breasts like oranges in socks at Christmas. Where did that cheeky firmness go?

Luke and I were slowly moving through 'phase one' of all those mental imaginings of mine. Most of our experiences were, more often than not alone, simply *'thinking'*, and we were suffering no feelings of guilt, relying on the adage from Shakespeare's 'Hamlet' *'nothing is good or bad, only thinking makes it so'*. The modern 'Hamlet' command performances, tell not of earlier generations 'Adam and Eve' moments sitting in a cinema back row, struggling with 'temptation' as a boy's arm comes slowly creeping around the shoulder of a girl, as he attempts his very first conquest, with the girl fully aware of every centimetre of encroachment, with the power to end such advancing manoeuvrers. All dependent on how far she had survived 'phase one'. The boy quickly retracting his seeking hand as he reflects on a school nature lesson, where the female spider eats the male following a successful advance. It is now; instant access made available at the press of a 'smart phone key' to youth anywhere, along with the worst possible forms of 'temptation' being presented on web sites, ready for sharing on various electronic 'gizmos'!

I somehow knew, I would be 'boring' back there, but I was happy with my time clock ticking without impatience on such things. My new world of *'Reality'* had a natural rhythm, and I felt good. No time to be feeling sorry for those 'back there' in the world, where a complete generation of parents were being tricked by the mega-rich media moguls knowledge of marketing to the young, with endless new 'AP's' and algorithms becoming available to suck them in. Knowledge my *digital-native* generation had developed awareness of and could sneak around any restrictions imposed by parents in so many ways ... solution found. Then more 'Apps' as the media moguls again go to war in their attempts to uphold their multi-billion profit margins, much of it at the expense of less IT tech-savvy youth. So, with a disappointed heavy heart-feeling for that generation, I selfishly move on along that sunny riverside grassy bank to somewhere.

I called out to Luke, and he immediately stopped and looked back, telling me in a reassuring way he knew his new name, confirming to my silly mind the wonderful change really had taken place.

'What's up, Freya?' came those caring words, with him thinking I was about to ask a question.

'Nothing, just wanted to catch up and be with you.'

'Well now you have,' he remarked as he took my hand.

'Lost you there,' declared Luke. 'Have you been working it all out again?'

He knew from my faraway look and the fact that I had fallen somewhat behind, that I was trying to get some understanding of the wonder of it all, and he really did know what I had been up to, made clear by his following comment,

'Ears and a tail would never have suited you Freya. Unlike little wooden Pinocchio, you have a soft beating heart in there,' once more pointing to my chest, causing me to glance down at his fingertip stopping millimetres from my young breast, with me wishing so hard it would make a brief contact, also leaving me wondering how did he know they were 'soft'. 'Phase one' and I loved it! He continued, clarifying my obsession with that subject, by reminding me that my 'soft heart' was created by loving parents. 'As did the parents of all on those countless train loads of children, now sadly with polluted minds, long tails and ears on a one-way track to 'never-never-land.'

'Stay bright and happy, and don't waste such joy available to you, and, by the way, when the Creator of this *reality* place is happy that you are up to scratch, my understanding of your private thoughts will fade in me completely, as they are already beginning to. I've already noticed I only catch quick glimpses of your jumbled mind, so you must be making the grade.'

He put his arm around my shoulder, stroking my neck as we walked, and I felt a strange tingling sensation that I had never experienced; the longer he did this, the more intense it became. He was only stroking my neck, and yet it all felt so wonderful. There was a struggle going on inside as to whether or not to allow this to continue like the girl in the cinema. I felt so important, in that I alone could decide if it should continue, along with a little wondering about where this might be heading.

I didn't ask him to stop; I simply took his hand in mine as we walked, with my mind racing back to the Adam and Eve scenario: could this be that '*temptation*' I was so enjoying? My heart had brought this all about for me, and I loved it! I did notice he had looked at me with a little wondering as to why I had stopped this minor advancement, and I suddenly realised, thank goodness, my secret feelings were mine alone, and he was unable to cross the secret threshold of access to a girl's private world, made 'out of bounds' by a pretty pink ribbon tied in a bow. His 'little wondering' on this, hardly to be called an indiscretion by him, told of a falling behind by me in 'phase one' as personally, I was loving the hormone signals being sent to my 'nether regions' I quickly altered my thinking, removing the word 'hormone', which seemed to be taking naughtiness into the mechanics of 'Human Biology'. I was a girl, keeping safe my femininity.

I did love having that enquiring mind as I grew; I was able to enjoy every facet of the entire process of moving through from childhood to womanhood, able to reflect, re-live, and re-consider each wonderful moment. Many of my school friends back there kept diaries using secret code words for events that some might consider 'naughty'. Then there were some not very bright ones who drifting through life in a kind of daydream, ending up with all that 'magic' condensed into brief moments had with a stranger, having fallen into a hay-rick somewhere!

This time, it was *my* little conscience within, not Luke's, that called out to me.

'Don't rush through youth too quickly.' Clearly, I had much to learn, but it was slowly coming into focus. Latching onto that 'youth' bit, I stopped and picked daisies by the water's edge to make a daisy chain to hang around my neck, which seemed like fun. Then, on looking up, Luke was busying himself on some other type of 'chain' as he tended to his bicycle, left there against a tree some time earlier, putting its chain back on ... simple, I told myself ... boy's things/girl's things, Freya.

I decided, in a silly kind of way, to test my newly developing girly power, and walked across to Luke with my 'daisy chain' at the ready. He looked up and stood from his high-tech chain repairing task, hands covered in the chain oil, lowering his head for me. Indicating he was surely taking in my romantic daydream *'wreath of laurel'* moment, he had moved away from the status of 'bicycle chain repairer 1st class', to a glorious gladiator at the Colosseum in Rome: tall and bloodied, with sword in hand, as I hung my freshly created love token, so well earned, around his neck. He smiled, and I could swear I caught him having a quick glimpse down the front of my pretty, slightly open white blouse. We were playing grown up games, teetering on the edge of seduction, which I had seen on films. As I say, these were early 'games' with me extending that 'phase one' which must surely be nearing its endgame. *Guess I'll have to wait and see. Reality* rushed in, as I noted my hero, rather than covered in bloodied wounds to be tended to with my delicate, oil-free, white hands, it was Luke standing with a bicycle chain in hand, covered in such oil.

With a smile and just his fingertips, he took off my garland offering, made and presented by a maiden to her champion, and hung them over his bike handlebars. Romantic overtures, turned into a trophy hanging there just swinging 'to and fro', that's all.

I was learning fast the secret private, one to another, joys of life on offer, which we have to control with the likes of patience, timing, and sharing. Clearly, we both had things that the other desired, without really knowing what those '*things*' were, even associated body parts never seen. '*Never seen*'? I seemed to have admitted that certain things remained unseen each to the other, which really added to the mysteries of my mind.

Strange, I was, for the first time beginning to feel importantly special. After all, I had asked Luke to stop stroking my neck as we walked together, and he immediately stopped. Also, I had caught him having that sneaky peep down my blouse as I leant forward to place such a beautiful trophy around his neck. Which, although I knew my modesty was slipping in a naughty kind of way, I loved. I had learned of another 'power tool' a girl is blessed with, like on the correct occasion, with good timing and well-chosen clothing, one can lean down to pick something up, knowing full well just a glimpse of the 'Promised Land' is on offer, although the girl must ensure, she appears not to realise, thus, rendering it a stolen glance, allowing, say, two seconds prior to modestly adjusting her top. Must be '*two*' not '*three*' seconds. '*Two*' a modest girl so desirous, '*three*', a danger of being seen as a possible 'trollop'. Oh dear, such is the game of life.

Time had passed, and I was by this time fifteen, in a friend's relationship, a million light years from those back at school who teased me so. I decided, *I am going to ease into and through every wonderful moment and try to develop a real meaningful togetherness of two people in a world not for spoiling.* That seemed really grown up. After all said and done, what was the hurry?

A WORLD WITHIN A WORLD

We finally arrived back at the mill house and spotted another barn swallow arriving in from South Africa, skimming low over the water surface, picking up a water nymph with a dip of her beak, then back up into the eaves of the Mill House roof... her 'second home', often at the same nest site as the previous year. Some minor repairs here and there, and all would be ready for the first of two 'broods' to bring into our world, to fly high and play around the Mill House.

'Bet she'll be tired,' Luke remarked, 'it takes around twelve hours of aircraft flight time and she will have had no *in-flight* refreshments. Travelling around 6,000 miles, she might have looked down to see elephant families with tusks inviting low life thieves to steal. She'll leave such dire things behind as she moves on, travelling over dangerous Sahara sands, sometimes being swept up in [Harmattan] heavy gale sandy windstorms, distracting her navigational skills. At last, leaving Moroccan shores, she'll fly through clear blue skies, across sparkling Mediterranean seas, up through Spain over high Pyrenees Mountains to join 'high flyers', then down along the French coast, finally crossing the English Channel, gazing down at people in tiny crowded rubber dinghies who, unlike her with a home awaiting, were seeking something better. How they might wish they could fly like our 'barn swallow', up over English meadows to our mill stream sparkling. Aren't we lucky, Freya?' My mind, in total wonder of such a journey being described, prompted me to ask.

'I suppose, the thought of us being able to join her, on her return journey as winter draws near, is ridiculous, Luke.'

'Nothing is impossible in *'Reality',*' was his response, telling of deep understandings beyond my young perceptions. He continued with, 'best we grow in this tiny bubble before we head off out into the *Alness*!'

I stopped my questioning at that point, but quietly dwelt on an unknown word to me, '*Alness*', I'd picked up on. A word with meanings of, well, *Alness* I guess, which would either expand my consciousness to a point well beyond my capabilities of understanding or drive me insane trying to make sense of it.

'That would be like giving a baby a five-course meal when it cried for milk,' Luke whispered in my ear.

My questioning mind, it would seem, had taken the intended course, finally pushing matters to an extreme where it had hit the buffers, making it blindingly obvious the best way forward was to enjoy each moment one step at a time, and all would simply unfold with intended harmony. I now knew the time for me raising questions about the unknown had ended, and the correct lead for me was to follow Luke.

By now, back at our lovely home, I slumped back in my chair feeling somehow that its arms were embracing me, safe and sound, as Luke began to chat away, like some grown-up philosopher.

'Can't you see, Freya? We can make of our dream whatever we so choose, even that childish magic that remains ever close in human hearts. Have you never noticed, when grown-ups take their children on holiday to the seaside, they themselves love to play in rock pools, seeking out little things under submerged rocks and seaweed, not forgetting the sandcastles, rock climbing, exploring caves in which to find smugglers treasure of old, then wandering through secret woodland glades. All a million miles away from their corporate and demanding lifestyle back home. They'll hear a songbird and feel to be crucifying such harmony as their mobile rings in that sacred place. Those seeds were sown so long ago when young, and they happily remain there in that 'consciousness' I repeatedly refer to, for the rekindling, the very moment the first of the family, irrespective of age, in their holiday-bound car, calls out, 'I can see the sea!'

As if as a completely fresh idea, we decided to venture out together once more, for another interlude in our *human* forms and excitedly heading up to the top platform. Strange how in my story of life, I jumped at any sequence where childish imaginings come out to play. It was as if I somehow knew grown-up things with my Luke would come rushing in quite soon enough. That child in us all will struggle in all haste to leave 'skipping ropes', 'marbles' 'hop-scotch' and that 'first flush of youth' behind, reaching out for 'bras', and 'long trousers', then, so soon to return to the simplicities of such youth, leaving complexities of life found behind for others once more! I recall, when reading in the school library about that landscape artist Dougie, he revelled in the mischief of painting into his pictures 'a tiny butterfly' and a 'fox cub' in secret places, only to recognise all who viewed his work, knowing of such things, could think of nothing else other than to find where they lived, hidden safely away! I had already witnessed such boyish DNA in my Luke.

Looking outwards, holding hands, we closed our eyes, counted to three, called out 'Dippers,' and launched out into fresh cool morning air once more. After my first five-second, heart stopping, free-fall moments, we were flying down, swishing through gaps in trees, over wild blackberry bushes soon to give up free ripe bounty for making favourite jam.

Luke was, I noted, always looking over to see if I was okay, often laughing when I overshot and headed off into space. I did enjoy some safe separation on occasions, and would, when quite alone, sometimes spot lovely places and events to share with him, for seeking out later.

One such delight I had spotted, whilst on such a solo break-away flight, was an event that welcomed me with open arms. It was an animal picnic on a mossy bank with a little boat I seemed to recognise pulled up onto it. *There's the childish me,* I thought, rushing into my dream.

My little pink 'gingham' tablecloth was always there in my consciousness. To me, it seemed to represent domestic friendliness. This time, I saw such a pretty tablecloth spread a little up from the stream over the soft moss at the foot of a large tree offering shade. I could see cakes, what appeared to be lemon drinks, and small sandwiches cut into four triangles, as only a delicate soul might do. I could see, and feel, a touch of 'times gone by' there.

The happy band of animal revellers I spotted had looked up and called out.

'Flying alone? Why not join us?'

I smiled and dipped my wings first left, then right as if to acknowledge such friendship on offer and, flying a little lower, called down.

'Thank you, I'd love to! I'll be back with my friend, hope that's okay.' They all stood and waved like true new friends, leaving me thinking *this is such simplistic fun, so far removed from all that growing up stuff in human form.*

I had read once, whilst in the school library, that the likes of 'Wind in The Willows' was deemed by some critics as 'an adult novel that can be read by children' and being as I fell somewhere in-between such parameters, I was happy to know our lives would allow such interludes along the way. *Could this mean*, I wondered, *when as a 'Dipper' or other such happy little creatures, our minds were free from human clutter, be that good or bad? That would be nice.*

I headed back along the water's edge until I spotted Luke doing what dippers do, splashing about, and freshening up in that clear water, so I joined him. I couldn't wait to share my own little discovery.

'Would you like to hear my own wonderful friendship discovery?' I asked, almost as if to establish my worth. He seemed overjoyed at the thought of friends beginning to appear in our unfolding new lovely world as I elaborated on my story. 'Well, here's the magic. Guess who those new friends were?' I asked, as I could see him pondering over that very thought.

'Well do tell,' he replied, having sensed my somewhat overexcitement.

'Are you ready?' I laughed, as if to continue to tease. I was learning fast, you see, it is nice to see a boy's expression when teased; you kind of feel in control of a situation. Maybe that's silly. *The things a teen girl can do,* I thought, *offer up something, then make the boy wait.* After all, Luke in human form was now eighteen and I had been assured by my school friends, who were a little more developed, mentally that is, that boys become quite demoralised by such things as girl teasing.... Even as a Dipper, I felt such power!

'Well?' he asked again. 'Do tell.'

'Luke,' I called out with such joy, 'there were many familiar animal friends having a picnic. I spotted, at a glance, a Badger, Beaver, Fox, Otter, Mole, perhaps a Water Vole, and I think a Toad, or, a Frog, not sure on that one.' I then elaborated on the fine picnic they had prepared, one which we had been invited to share.

'Seems more like a veritable feast than a picnic,' he replied with such happiness on his face, 'sounds rather inviting, the thought of such company and food for sharing. Too good to miss especially when, as you say, they invited you to join them. Shall we introduce ourselves without delay, Freya?' Luke had just said, 'shall we.' Now I felt important. Him asking me seemed like a kind of balancing up of our union!

Having spotted Mrs Barn Swallow, we tried to follow her over the rippling water as she came away from the Mill wheels. Fast flowing floating bubbles on the race from the wheel gave the impression we too were 'racing', but she was like a fighter jet with perfect aerodynamics compared to us much slower Dippers, so we peeled off to the left to cut across an *ox bow* in the meandering stream and headed across to that riverbank picnic area.

'A little further on, Luke,' I thought to warn him.

At his suggestion, we stopped on some half-submerged smooth rocks to smarten ourselves up for our special meeting, both keen to ensure our white fronts were bright. Then he remarked,

'Unlike 'Robin red breast', ours are white; some other creatures are lucky... they have two.' He smiled, and I knew he was, for the first time with a rather silly remark, trying to be cheeky. I ignored the fun, if only to boost my innocence, but I really did appreciate the fact that my bumps were beginning to qualify as 'grownup' status, if only in fun.

'Time to go,' Luke called out, 'let's surprise our new friends. We can skim along over the surface for a while, then, when not far away, we can dive below to swim over the riverbed of green reed and shiny pebbles then simply pop up right in front of them all. What do you think?' Although I thought his boyish idea a bit dramatic and out of keeping with the quiet pastoral picnic going on, with a little concern I replied,

'Okay! I can call out to them as we surface 'Remember me?"

It was so exciting to see the trail of little clear bubbles we were leaving behind as we moved below the surface, racing through the water like torpedoes seen in war films my dad watched back there. Luke's signal came, like a wartime submarine captain.

'Prepare to surface,' and up we popped, with water flying everywhere! The Otter lost his dignity as water dripped off his by now drooping whiskers. The Badger declared, 'What in God's name is happening? My cake's gone all soggy.' The Frog loved it all, but did add, 'My tea's been diluted.' The Fox shook his fur coat violently and gave everybody a second soaking! Beaver and the Water Vole thought the whole thing such fun and requested a re-run of the million drops of water sparkling in sunshine, cascading down from that Fox fur-coat shake-down.

'What a to-do.' I whispered in Luke's ear as he struggled to control his laughter. Smiling in such a reassuring way, he quietly replied.

'Let's do what we are best at and make them laugh.'

'Which is?' I asked, wondering what other embarrassing comedy sequence he was conjuring up.

'Dipping, silly,' came his response, 'that's what dippers do best.' So, we re-entered the stream, dipped up and down in the water in perfect time and added a little synchronised swimming, a bit like a watery stage turn, really! They all laughed, the disaster was forgotten, and the picnic was shared, during which time, Badger having, we noted, quickly and discreetly changed his cake for a dry piece, leaving the soggy piece for someone else, decided to introduce the band of friends, along with names of some absent ones who had not arrived.

'Please remember us. Maybe one of you could remember the first five names and the other the last ones.' Luke decided to take the first tranche and declared.

'Okay, I'm ready.'

'I'll start with myself,' declared the Badger, with an obvious sense of authority.

'I'm Bossy, because they all seem to think I'm a bit bossy, I don't know why.' Those standing behind him placed one hand over their mouths, nodding their heads up and down, as if to hide their agreement. He continued, 'Next going round the gathering is Fluffy Fox, then Busy Beaver, Messy Mole (he digs holes everywhere!), then there is Olly Otter.'

'That's my share,' laughed Luke, looking at me. 'Over to you.' Bossy glanced my way and continued, 'Next in line we have, Whiskers Water-Vole, and you will soon meet, I'm sure, absent friends Dotty Door-Mouse and his friend Speedy Field-Mouse, who are inseparable. Then there's Roma Rat, he's always roaming around somewhere.' Badger paused for a moment with forefinger and thumb scratching a chin covered in cake crumbs. 'Oh yes, there's Tim and Tilly Toad, not forgetting lots of rabbits we know, we just call them, Floppy 1, Floppy 2, etc., due to their floppy ears and being so many of them! Guess you won't remember us all, but you will in time. By the way, I forgot to ask your names so I can pass them on to all our friends.' Having suddenly realised we had been asked our names, which presented the sudden realisation that we had other identities, albeit quite exciting, at that moment we were nameless and stood in shock! Luke gave me a sideways glance, and, without even blinking, volunteered in a flash.

'I'm Dude, and this is Dilly'

'Welcome Dude and Dilly... by the way, where did 'Dilly' get such a pretty name?" Badger made this comment with all our other new friends, nodding their heads up and down, as if agreeing with my 'top title'.

'Oh! She *dilly* daydreams quite a lot, but always about nice things,' Luke replied, pointing at me with a broad smile.

'There's a lot for us all to remember,' declared Bossy, then, having enjoyed the picnic, as if to bring the event to a close, with such authority he declared, 'Soon we must all go home, so let's pack up our picnic things. We will meet again many times in our lives as new friendships have been formed.' I think we all knew that.

Suddenly somebody pointed out that the little boat they had borrowed from the mill owner [seen there in the picture] during all the fuss had drifted unseen out from the bank, and was now well on its way down the stream.

'What a bore, we're stuck here for the night,' mumbled Bossy, pointing out that his and Fluffy's homes were about two miles downstream near to some old farm buildings. This was a great chance to demonstrate our friendship by putting the matter right. Luke, having looked my way, declared with a wink.

'Let's go Dilly.' I smiled at hearing my new name called out, thinking Dilly and Dude sounded a little like a song and dance act, to be seen up in lights as 'Dilly & Dude the Dance Duo'. I knew exactly what he had in mind as we both took to the wing as two far greater performers like 'Batman & Robin' and headed downstream in pursuit. We caught up with what appeared like the *'Mary Celeste'* with no crew on board we dropped down onto the boat and gathered up *'the painter'* [the small rope line at the front].

'This will not be easy, you know, as we will be towing up stream against the flow,' I volunteered with concern, really trying to impress and demonstrate how river-wise I was.

'Time to move beyond limited thinking, Dilly,' Dude called out, 'remember if things are done with Love in our consciousness all problems disappear.' Having had my own name dissected by Luke in front of our new friends, I couldn't help but say,

'You're such a cool dude Dude, and where did you get that cheeky name 'Dilly' from?'

'Just popped out,' he said, 'in haste I nearly called you Dippy, that might have been better: Dippy Dipper.' I felt quite relieved, especially knowing certain girls back there that were not too bright had been tagged, 'a bit dippy'!

Suddenly, we were flying with the little boat following like a dog on a lead. We arrived to such happy faces standing on that mossy bank as sun shadows lengthened and evening fell. A couple of them were actually standing in the cool clear water ready to greet us back.

'You are our friends forever,' they all called out, 'this bond with fellow animals is for always!'

'How true this is,' Luke declared, as he recalled when, being Dougie, right up into his older years long ago, when his beloved wife Frannie would buy him the Rupert album every Christmas, he would lose himself in childish memories and adventures over the holiday period. Maybe that's where his dreaming moments began of perhaps one day stepping into a dream picture he might one day be able to create.

Bossy and Fluffy stood with one toe in the water and declared, in a rather condescending kind of way,

'Actually, you know, we could have swum back!'

'Well of course!' The others called out in unison, standing behind them giggling, as they reflected back on the day some time ago when

Bossy had fallen into the river and they all had to pull him out, all wet and grumpy! On this occasion, being friends, we granted them both the leadership prowess so desperately sought, by saying,

'This time, you will have done us the honour of helping you both get home, after which a couple of you could return the boat to Jack the Miller in the morning, as I suspect, you already intended to do.'

THE RELUCTANT JOURNEY BACK

As we flew back to our faithful oak tree home to re-engage as Luke and Freya people, we looked at each other and declared,

'The adventures are boundless; it will be difficult to choose what wonders to pursue next.'

We were home, feeling full in our tummies with cake, cheese and cucumber sandwiches, and drinks; we laid back on our beds, hands behind heads, looking out of windows so high up, as the sun shone through, creating dancing shadows from young green leaves of spring, until we dosed off into light dreamy sleep. I dreamed I had been on a wonderful adventure like '*Wind in the Willows*', then awoke, and realised I really had!

Luke made, although a sensible, nevertheless a little unsettling suggestion: that I must not forget my family and friends back in *that world*, pointing out, as if to ease any disappointment, that when I returned all would be exactly as I had left it, by stating,

'You must keep those fires of love burning with friends and family. They are precious moments that do not last forever. This dream world will always be waiting and available to you whilst you keep your consciousness bright and true: *Reality*, is forever and ever!' I smiled as I looked into his eyes and saw a hint of caring there.

'You see, Freya, I have no friends or family back there anymore, but I know the meaning of true family Love. Sadly, it can fly away so easily as it did for me. I'll always be here waiting for you, if your heart calls out to me, and we can pick up on things which, remember, as I say, will all be exactly as where we left off at the time of each and every parting. We will naturally have aged a little according to the short periods apart, but all that we will have created will be exactly the same.' Which led me to ask.

'Does this mean whilst I am away, we will suffer lost time in our togetherness? Surely, if I am there for weeks or months, we will begin to appear different. And by the way, how shall I go Luke?' I asked, with, I noticed, a bit of a tug on my heart strings at the thought of saying goodbye to him and a little uncertainty as to the nicest way to go drifting between our two worlds.

'On your question about us ageing, this is quite complicated, but for the moment I'll explain in simple terms: You will always pick up on all things, including ageing, when you return back to Earth. The same applies when returning to *Reality*, so you will become almost like two people. However, here, you and I can take ourselves back in time to pick up where we left off if we so choose, avoiding that 'lost time' you refer to. Remember ... they are 'parallel universes', forever independent of each other, and here, as mentioned, there is no such thing as time as you once knew it to be.'

None the wiser, I smiled nodding my head as if to imply that was all so obvious to me! His suggestion on the second part of my question on leaving almost made light of what, for me, was such a serious matter ... I think somewhat intended, as apart from to dissolve sadness, it was to highlight there would be many more departure days for us both to deal with.

Having raised the idea for consideration, he was doing what he always did -- acting positively, almost as though he was not allowing fear or anxiety to have any credibility or power over something so special – a 'something' called *'Reality'* that would be with us forever.

I think we both knew the time had come for a trip back, so I took both his hands in mine, and gazed at him, in a way that told of seeking help, probably made obvious by my lips being pressed tightly together in a half smile. He was about to press the re-visit 'start' button to make it all seem fine.

'Sit quietly by the window, Freya, and let it unfold ... it'll be fine.' So, I did and thought of childish happy things like 'The railway children' I had read of back there... and there we were, standing on the platform of a pretty little railway station about a mile beyond the end of a certain 'Mill Lane'.

Sitting there on the platform with her mum and dad was a teenage girl I presumed to be on a family holiday from some other distant part of my new world. She was looking at a girly magazine, waiting, I presumed, for a taxi to take them to, I somehow felt sure, a small friendly seaside hotel. I did notice in passing as I glanced down, she was looking at pretty dresses in light pink, maybe dreaming of herself centre stage at a party one day.

This steam train theme just had to be my romantic side unfolding, dreaming of days seen in comic books, or maybe some other life, a dream beyond childish imaginings of 'Thomas the Tank Engine'; mine were romantic themes, like lovers waving goodbye out of train windows, prior to the existing back there of being locked in overcrowded tubes with non-opening windows, listening to others twaddle on mobile phones, people pushing and shoving, aged or cripple folk standing with no seat given! There's no romance there. Easy to see what had driven me away from such an unfolding 'wakey woke world', where a gender other than female might give up a seat for obvious pregnancy, only to receive the rebuke: "why? Bearing my child is not a sickness." He humbly turns, only to find some commute pig has filled that still warm seat!

The small train drew into the station, and with a blast of steam like a tired shire horse, it came to a halt and stood there with such presence, almost as if waiting for me to climb aboard, so I did. My carriage had other people sitting there; a young boy leaning on a lady I assumed to be his mother as she read a book with a title I had caught a glimpse of: 'A Tale of Two Worlds'. Opposite them was a smart gentleman quietly gazing out of the window to the other side.

I placed my travelling bag, which I did notice was quite small, on the seat near a window, perhaps indicating a short trip, which felt nice. I lowered the window and leaned out, as they did in days gone by, and standing there was Luke. I was teetering on heartbreak, as I looked at him, standing so confidently, smiling, almost as if it was all a procedure well-known to him, which of course it wasn't ... leaving me wondering why he did not appear sad. After all, it was our very first parting, and it had been said long ago by Juliet to Romeo: *'parting is such sweet sorrow....'*, so where was his *'sorrow'*, I wondered ... before realising his stance just maybe implied, there was no need for concern as we were obviously to be re-united.

Now I felt good as I brushed aside that intruding heart breaker. I distinctly remember thinking in a somewhat positive way: 'I must remember the name of the station' which did seem to imply a degree of my own belief that I would be returning!

'Reality Halt' – Sounded a bit bedtime story-ish, but it fitted my dreamy world quite nicely.

This was our first of many goodbyes that would follow, but each time it would hurt deeply. How could this be? I was just a teenager, but what with that Dipper fluffy feather preening each other feeling, clearly something incredible was going on.

Apart from my heavy heart feeling at having to say goodbye to Luke, I did wonder if my bumps would develop more whilst I was away. This was another question to be answered, oh dear, guess all will be discovered in time. It was time to put all this wisdom-seeking aside. Still at the window, I glanced across at him, enjoying that he was there for me, only to hear him quietly call out.

'You're growing up, Freya ... Hope to see you soon, and remember I'll never be far away.'

I loved the whole scene that surrounded me; it was a million miles from those boring, bad influencing school scenarios I was being tempted with, almost on a daily basis, in fact where I was once again heading.

This was surely a re-enactment of Shakespeare's words on parting, you see, I'm almost sure I noticed with shock for me as a teenager, a single tear drop running down Luke's cheek before he had time to discreetly and quickly wipe it away with his folded-back white shirt cuff.

How could one tiny clear pearl drop tear, have such power over someone so young? And what caused that soft blush of youth that just happened to appear on my cheeks? I had youth to enjoy and all the things that go with that.

I began to reflect on those very 'things', and realised most of it was shallow and going nowhere except, that is, for education and a fine career perhaps, which would be silly to miss. It was surely a matter so common to all teenage girls when growing up, with mothers saying: 'Don't worry, it's simply young infatuation for boys that will develop into something far more meaningful when you are older!' What the heck, I was having none of that, I thought, it was all so obvious: I was falling head over heels in love with somebody, and that somebody's one tear drop had confirmed the feeling was perhaps mutual.

Now I felt good as the train pulled out of the station, passing a large station name board: '*Reality Halt*'. Luke drifted into the distance until he was just a tiny speck still waving slowly in a manly kind of way, with just one open hand at about shoulder high rocking it left to right from the wrist until, I hoped, he would only temporarily fade from view and out of my life.

I felt sure it would all shortly return in my consciousness, and we would soon be together again, sharing a journey which we would both create. It would be without disappointments, being cheated on, badly influenced, and all the limiting things that go on in the place I was now heading for.

With much resolve, I had taken to following Luke's earlier advice to stay and study in order to make something of my life to please my mum and dad, after all ... *Reality* would be there for me to build on forever.

I felt so advanced for my years, knowing I alone had granted Dougie a revised youth again, along with a new name and life at that! Hopefully to include all the eventual romance that one might expect to be embraced therein. I vowed to myself: I would, in a quiet way, stand close when we next saw each other and put my arms around him. Not sure if I could yet do face-to-face stuff, as my thoughts drifted back to me having almost fallen to my knees that time when he had lifted me up with the difference between boy and girl becoming suddenly evident.

I sat looking out of the train window at my reflection, thinking *I'm so young to be travelling alone, yet strangely enough I felt consumed with a feeling of safety and wellbeing,* especially as the woman in the carriage with the little boy looked my way and with a smile said,

'You have a faraway look. Would I be right in assuming this is your first return trip back to a worldly life you had dreamed of leaving, hoping, perhaps, for a more harmonious one, if so, you are very young to have achieved such fulfilment ... do you mind me asking your name?'

'Freya,' I answered, 'and yes, it is my first return trip to my Earthly home.' I thought to ask, 'how do you know of such things, and where did you board this special train?' Her son moved across to sit nearer to me to look out of the open window, so I helped him onto my lap with a firm grasp around his tiny waist. He whispered in my ear: 'we've come from 'Harmony Town' and the train driver told us about somebody special we would meet at a new station called *'Reality Halt'* ... is that person you?' His mother interjected with,

'Ever curious; I think he had imagined, as did I, that you would be older ... it's a pleasure to meet such a young achiever of dreamy imaginings. We have journeyed from 'Harmony Town', another place of perfection I found many years ago. You will be meeting many such travellers over time. Do I assume *'Reality'* is of your making ... and how did you manage such wonders whilst so young?'

Realising I was in the company of other, more experienced achievers, I happily ran through my story of the picture and its artist creator, and explained that I was very unhappy with the way life on Earth was heading, especially with the youth of my generation, and that I just somehow knew there had to be something better.

The smart gentleman had by now turned to listen to our pleasant exchanges and with a smile said,

'Seems that I'm in good company once more; I make this delightful train journey often. But no longer have an Earthly destination to return to; I just stay on the train enjoying the view, listening to lovely stories, then return to my home in my perfect place! Incidentally, Freya, in recent years I have had the pleasure of meeting many similar-aged youths as you. Are things on Earth really changing that dramatically, causing so many youngsters to recognise a better way maybe there for the taking?'

Apart from, with such joy, learning that others around my age had had similar callings, this was the first opportunity I had found myself involved with similar people, with whom I could engage in conversation about such changes, after all, this lovely man had actually just asked a serious question of me, a fairly brand-new teenager.

It was not my Luke, but a naive adult stranger, innocently ignorant of the ways by which the Earthly world was unfolding. I felt empowered to try sharing a modern point of view with someone who had obviously existed on Earth in some earlier time, if only to hear a few comparisons!

My words came drifting out in this sharing in a way that came easily, in fact almost beyond my own level of understanding, so much so that I too was learning from every word I spoke. At each breath taken between imparted theories, I thought of Luke and how proud he would be of me, the slip of a girl who had made a 'daisy chain' for her guy.

My revelations promoted no different points of view arising around me, almost as if what I was revealing was at least close to being factual... not grey areas of thinking. My audience included just one who still moved in Earthly spheres and she was a mum, simply nodding her head up and down like a 'nodding dog', as if in agreement. The gentleman sat quietly with the odd comment such as: 'all so different from my time,' made even more obvious to him when I introduced the latest ever-increasing *'woke'* obsession.

'I note from my 'modern history' studies; life in what was probably 'your time' embraced similar ingredients, but in such times: *'time would have out'*, allowing a settling of adolescent self-taught knowledge. As I understand it, children would grow through areas of adolescent maturing, with excitement driven by an ignorance of the very process. Parents, it would seem, generally avoided certain delicate subjects. The learning of such mysteries, therefore, meant the entire narrative was confined to *their* own, very young, experimenting in innocent ignorance. It was theirs alone, to fumble and bumble through, finally coming out the other side simply okay! Life for all, seemed more black and white, well-defined in all areas of society, be that good or bad, with lessons being learned along the way ... an age old learning curve!' He responded with,

'You speak like that of a person above her years and, I might add, without appearing old-fashioned, but young and vibrant. Your school teaching does, in general terms, briefly sum up how things were. Tell me of this revised use of the word *'Woke'*,' the man asked, obviously seeking a modern take on how life was changing, so I bravely offered my young understandings of the modern studies I had received to date, with what I thought to be a great idea as to how I could give the man something to reflect on in just a few words. After all, my generation doesn't do a lot of 'word play'; it's all IT communication with vocal chords nearing redundancy. So, I made the point again on the sudden changes my generation is having to accommodate.

'When you were very young, you will have been taught such as: 'A

…. of cows' = Herd and 'A ….. of fish' = Shoal. Now we might be confronted with: 'A …. of confused ideas, actions, statements, opinions, suggestions, points of view, etc' = Woke. Why should we have such a re-invented word, leaving us desperately trying to catch up with variations of conduct or direction? Not forgetting discrimination, oppression, injustice, on so many areas of life. A fear has been introduced into what one says, writes, does, or even implies,' I added. 'Thank God, they can't interfere with 'thinking' … a fear that as I understand it, never surfaced during those, what seemed to be, 'fumbling and bumbling' days I have, in my young way just referred to when earlier generations were growing up, a *fear* which now also prevails so strongly with current adults. I'm sure there will soon be Websites: WWW. @ Wakey.Woke.World The man, looking a little vague, then said,

'I don't really understand.'

The woman suddenly came to my aid, from such deep subject matter, one that I sensed had 'explosive' stamped on the package. With her son, by now sleeping under one of her arms, she quietly spoke out, saying,

'I wanted so much to hear such understanding coming from Freya, so young. It told of such mental progress being formed in this wonderful place we now all live in here. Clearly, anybody who could, through her consciousness, create *'Reality'* must be quite special... well done, Freya. Let me help in this wonderful discourse of yours... you see I am a solicitor in my Earthly life, and I think I can clarify a few points quite succinctly for our new friend,' holding one hand palm upward toward the gentleman. 'One can now be exposed to any number of legal challenges in so many areas of Earthly living. I refer to 'actions' and the 'spoken' or 'written' word! One has the need to be so very careful, for example, how one addresses somebody, even if said in fun.' The man interrupted with,

'Yes I have heard of such things, which left me wondering about my youth at school, and what we called each other in fun... not very nice sometimes, but it all faded in time, rendering it all left and forgotten to innocent unintelligent mischief ... some of it, at the time, even feeding the school 'bully' who eventually got 'bullied' in some later school 'Ruck' ... as in rugby!'

'Now I fear, it is no longer interpreted as 'innocent mischief' as you put it,' the lady interjected, then asked the gentleman, 'give me some examples and I'll tell you if, by today's standards, you would be in some sort of trouble,' said in fun with a broad smile. 'I think this is getting near to Freya's reference to, in her quite well put: 'Wakey-Woke-World'.' He thought on the matter for a few minutes then volunteered,

'Our playground was a testing ground of characters, weaknesses and strengths with names handed out such as:

1. A Jewish boy David – 'Schnoz' for his big nose.
2. Split pin – Anybody skinny.
3. Lanky – Anybody tall.
4. Beanpole – Anybody thin and 'lanky'.
5. Copper Knob or Carrottop – Person with red hair.
6. Cocoa – A boy, Mark, of Jamaican origin.
7. Tubby or Fatty – Anybody fat.
8. Spotty – Anybody with freckles.
9. Four Eyes – Anybody who wore glasses.

In such fun, our Solicitor friend burst into laughter, finally with a wry smile saying,

'No comment! Consider yourself blessed, which of course you are, but I mean 'blessed' for staying on the train.' Glancing my way, he was quick to say,

'Despite all of those dreadful insults levelled at each other back then, I would say to those fretting over today's rules of life, 'generally at school ...we were all friends." The lady continued,

'Sadly, now, we grope our way through pronoun mine fields, trying not to offend.'

The little boy awoke, looking a little bored, so I took a small sketch pad and pencil from my pretty bag, and he immediately slid my way again, as if sensing something was about to unfold.

'Do you like stories?' I asked, and of course he did ... so I prepared to utilise my quite good sketching skills, learnt in my Art lessons. It all moved away from such serious grown-up 'gender' stuff, and I became a youngster once more as my mind and pencil in hand sought to create childish things. It came easy for someone drifting between being an almost grown-up 'lover' in the true sense of the word, and an innocent schoolgirl at play with a little fold by the river.

'Tell me,' I asked, 'if you close your eyes, what do you imagine if you think of magical things?'

The adult conversation had ceased, and it went rather quiet, telling of the point I have always known: there is an inherent childishness ever near, which so easily moves adults away from grown up seriousness ... not least *'woke'* confusion! The boy closed his eyes, we all waited for his childish imaginings to shine through, and it began: him telling of wonders in his private world, with me sketching as he became a 'Director', by now watching every movement of my pencil, directing proceedings with,

'I see a small little wooden house where all my toys are kept, where brothers and sisters can't take and break them.' I glanced at mum, who raised her eyebrows as if in recognition of certain design needs. A pretty little house began to materialise, which seemed to fit the bill okay. This was made clear to me, as he was smiling and fidgeting nearer with eyes locked onto the pencil lead, certainly not me, simply an extension of the pencil as an operator. Then, as if as an Architect in the making, his look became thoughtful, and somewhat pensive, as he mentally visualised his scene … he continued once more to direct operations.

'The wooden cabin needs to be difficult to get to, so I want it taken up higher.'

'Do you mean a tree?' The operator asked.

'Yes, make it a tree-house, quite high ... so not to be visible to my friends, actually, only to those I say so, and they will be given a 'password' to use when they have learned from a secret map hidden in different places where my tree is hidden!' One could see by a faraway occasional look as he stared from the train window, he was on his dreamy way, and nobody else's. Returning his gaze to the design concept, he continued, 'I want a rope ladder, with wooden bars to step on, and a string attached to let it up and down, which has a place to put a piece of paper for the password to be written on before the ladder can be lowered.'

By this time the hairs on the back of his young pretty neck were beginning to stand up. He continued with asking for some details relating to the inside.

'Special friends can come if they bring their own picnic, which must include a few little pieces of cake, and I love sandwiches cut in triangles; some can be left down by a stream for 'Water birds' to also enjoy and, there must be enough for me as well.' It was time for me to get involved, by way of flushing out certain suspicions arising in me, and a happy dialogue began.

'Do you want a little table and chairs?'

'Yes, to put cakes on.'

'What about a pretty tablecloth?'

'That sounds nice.'

'What colour?'

'Blue, with a little square pattern.'

His mother leant over to say, 'he means 'Gingham'.'

He continues, 'and I want a name over the front door.' He had become the 'Director' once more, so I followed his direction and personally added a small sign with a name on it, prompting him, having gone quiet for a few seconds, to turn quickly to his mother, calling out,

'Hey! How did she know my name? Before she could respond, I interrupted,

'Well, that's what true friends can do; they hear a name quietly spoken in a whisper, which means they will be friends forever,' said holding out a little finger, waiting for my new friend 'Luke' to entwine it with his, by way of confirmation! His mother looked at me, surprised, and remarked,

'Now he knows what the driver meant when he said, 'you might meet someone special on this train'.' I sat back in shock, knowing full well the meaning of this wonderful encounter, reflecting back on my Luke's words: 'I'll never be really far away from you, Freya'!

After adding a few details, endorsing the fact that it was possible for youth to have such an abode: a pair of boxing gloves hanging, a pair of crossed rowing blades on the wall, and books that dreams can unfold from, I handed the sketches to this young Luke and suggested,

'Keep these safe, always look at them, dreaming one day your little house will come true and be real, and that you will, one day, live in that beautiful place happily ever after.' I felt to be communicating, unbeknown to my little friend, with an unseen, somewhat larger version of a loving male friend who I was soon to be meeting again -- I hoped.

MY TURN TO DREAM

This whole train station idea was, of course what my heart liked, so it had just happened and obviously for well-intended reasons, perhaps to sow seeds of magic places becoming a reality! Maybe for my next visit returning back from *Reality* to Earth life, I could walk hand-in-hand with Luke, turn right at the end of 'Mill Lane', and carry on for about a mile ... simply talking over the day and the new wondrous events that had unfolded for us both together. I loved the word *'together'* ... I felt part of something and somebody that had a completeness about it, with no fear of disintegration!

We would arrive at the sea on a quiet sunny beach. There a ferry would be awaiting my arrival, and I would step board. Then, like an old movie, I'd wave a small off-white, slightly pink handkerchief trimmed with lace, at Luke as I sailed home once more, and drifted over the horizon so far away without feelings of separation! Sailing away into the distance, waving a lace hanky. That really was for 'old farts' ... sorry old films. Changed my mind! I'll put on my soon to be size 32A floral bikini top, with matching floral shorts, hop on to a windsurf sail board. (That'll be a little cooler!) Set my sail [pink], then *'plane'* and *'jibe'* my way across the bay. Finally disappearing into the distance until I drop over the horizon's edge, falling through space glancing around at what one might consider an 'Alness'... I did say 'might'. I'll *'hand glide'* to whatever destination intended, until I quietly land on my bedroom floor!

I did need to watch this consciousness thing of creating whatever one desired, I think I had just fringed on a bit of that 'Alness' with me 'dropping over the horizon's edge'. You see, I suddenly noticed, looking out of the train window, there was a tempting beach with wind surfers on. I could almost hear Dougie's wisdom through Luke's inner voice calling out: 'control your dreaming, or as a result of too much desire, you will dart from one situation to another without enjoying each moment, and by the way the Earth is round without an edge to drop over.' Clearly it was dangerous for someone so young with a sweet tooth to be let loose in the sweet shop that I had found myself in. I reflected back to when I had my first mobile from my mum and dad, who didn't have a lot of money to spend on such things; it was one step removed from an early model by Alexander Graham Bell, who invented the phone! But I loved it.

I was learning fast. Greed can spoil anything ... you know: *'the green on the other side of the fence'* kind of thing.

For some special reason, I had qualified to get to *Reality,* and the more each day offered up, the more I realised I was being trusted not to overindulge myself. After all, quite shockingly, I was beginning to understand, I could have anything I desired, which implied I could so easily with desire overindulge, burn my boats, and lose my place here -- or was it *'there'* I thought … after all I am now in transit. Umm? My mind was at it again … 'does a certain 'grey mist' apply here? Who cares. I had nothing out of order coming to mind.

I smiled at young Luke, who, by now, was again sitting with his mum, gazing intently at his picture, dreaming of that new world, and I noted he had sketched a little boy and girl sitting at the table eating cake and sandwiches, then, having added the table-cloth, he asked his mother for a blue pencil from her bag. I picked a book from my little bag, which I noted was homework on algebra, and began to study quadratics ... Yuck! Whilst having another peek out of the window, I did happen to notice a young guy cycling along a riverbank near a mill house; could that be my

Luke once more keeping an eye on me? I journeyed on, having given algebra a miss apart from the easy bit of basic 'binomial theorem', and was still gazing out of the window at the beautiful landscape bathed in sunshine, until the train finally stopped, with a guard calling out: 'End of the line, please disembark,' which I took to mean: 'time to get off.'

A little unsure as to where we were, I said goodbye to my new friends, telling them we would surely meet again. I hopped out and headed for the 'exit' sign ... walked through a pair of doors out of a waiting room, into what appeared as white mist under a rainbow arch ... and there I was, back in my bedroom with my mother calling to me.

'Your tea is ready; I've prepared your favourites: small sandwiches cut into four triangles, cake, and a lemon drink.' Little events were occurring in an almost 'bringing two worlds together' sort of thing. Her description of my pending tea-time sounded almost exactly like that romantic fine fayre by the stream, not my usual burger or the like. Was Luke again dropping a hint that he wasn't far away?

A RUDE AWAKENING

On that return, as expected ... time had stood still.

I arrived at school the next morning and was greeted by three friends wanting to share new *'apps'* on their mobiles, one playing silly games, one trying to convince me she knew all the trendy *'in'* tunes, and one looking at a boy from our class doing a 'moony'... Nice!

I tried so hard not to appear above it all, but I was, in fact, already realising the dreadful contrast between life here and, what it should, and could be ... as with back at my *Reality*.

There was the girl Jeni, who I really did like; she always had such a sad look on her face whenever I saw her, which I knew resulted from her mum and dad separating after years of squabbling. It was her dad, who she so desperately loved, who had died of what she always thought to be a broken heart. Having apparently never stopped asking how her mum was getting on whenever she met him, knowing full well, she had been going with several men over time.

She had no nice clothes for weekends, and, at school, was not too bright, always being ribbed and laughed at; in fact, I frequently helped her with her homework. She was always ready to share any sweets or treats she might have and must have been the only girl in school who didn't have a mobile phone. Which actually meant she could make conversation and was not lost to the world of shorthand text communication words, which even my father, a business consultant did not understand. No emoji and LOLs ... with Jeni, she laughed in silence, but we all had the pleasure of her really pretty face when she occasionally smiled!

I think you will have guessed where this is going and, in fact, what action I was being guided to take. So young, and yet I was seeing an opportunity to help someone who seemed to ask nothing of life.

We sat one lunch break on a quiet seat to the side of the school playing field, and *something* in my heart was calling out: 'help her with Love' ... so I asked,

'Do you ever sit alone and wonder if things might have been better, Jeni?' With a cheeky smile she replied,

'Do you mean not having to look at Brian's bottom on Jane's mobile?'

'Well, no, not that rubbish,' I replied, and in any event I knew he had, in absolute trust, made her show a lot more than that I can tell you ... video shots, that unbeknownst to her, probably went viral and were being shared around the entire globe!

'I'm talking about a way of life ... one free from sadness, abuse and disappointments.' Raising her eyebrows and twitching one corner of her mouth downwards, she thought for a while about what I might mean and replied with a slight giggle.

'I read about such a place once, I think they call it Shangri-La, but takes a lifetime to find, if you are lucky that is, as it lacks reality.'

'You heard her use that word *'reality'* now say it!' came a loud call from within, and I knew my heart was guiding me! Clearly this wonderful new life and experience was never going to falter, or slow down. I had to keep moving ... so I did -- 'say it' that is.

'I have found a place, Jeni, where one treads a true and honest path, not too demanding, just a happy way, embracing things such as love, unselfishness, compassion, caring, sharing, giving, and a general love of all things in nature ... I think you get my drift.'

As I say, although she had a pure heart, she was not too bright, and I could see she was trying to make sense of what I had just outlined. I think she might have been thinking along the lines of children's adventure stories.

'Where do we get tickets for such a place?'

'Jeni,' I said, as I took hold of both her shoulders and looked her straight in the eyes. 'I really have found a place so wonderful, and I visit there; it's called *'Reality'*. You must keep this a secret, in the knowledge that if you ever talk of it, it will simply disappear from your consciousness as if I had never spoken to you about it, and life will go on for you as before.'

In her usual way as she would, with that same old sad look, she declared, with such loveable humility,

'I doubt I'd be allowed in, what with all my background and failings.' There was just a hint, I noticed, of some regrets, but I also sensed a longing in her tone and was quick to say.

'It's available to all, but most will never dream of giving up what they consider a good life ... simply accepting that every life has ebb's and flow's, you know, 'ups and downs'.'

She was clearly longing to leave behind so many sad negatives she had endured for most of her life. My heart sang with such joy at the thought that maybe, just maybe, I could help... so I volunteered the following advice.

'This is how it works: one has to sit in complete peacefulness, it helps to have a beautiful picture in front of you, and I'll lend you mine and sit with you to help with your nervousness of the unknown.' By now, she was beginning to look excited, as I continued, 'You will have to remove all busy mind games; this will take time. Eventually you will start to feel the scene surrounding you and begin to develop a deep longing to be there as part of that very scene you see before you. Think of butterflies, bees, flowers, birds, etc., all as if they are your dearest friends and pets.

Do you have any pets?' I asked in order to give her feelings of retaining precious things on this proposed journey she knew nothing about.

'Gosh!' She replied, with an obvious longing and ever-increasing belief in such wonders. 'Do you mean my little lost cat 'Pixie', who I loved so much, and could my dad be found there?' That sudden response of actually wondering if she could find lost treasures at such a place told of dormant Love resting there in her heart, and dreams of finding somewhere. In that very yearning, she had the key to the door.

With me by now beginning to feel a little like Santa Claus, I continued, but did begin to wonder, if I was old enough to be managing such things without my Luke on board.

There was clearly the need for focus on such a life-changing experience; in fact, one which I was only an apprentice to myself. I would need to explain a few home truths in order to move away from that 'sweets in the shop window' scenario... so I hastened to add.

'Try to understand, Jeni, you must never adopt the stance of running away from life or picturing too much at once of what you would like to see in this wondrous place. You must just *'be'* there in your heart and let the dream story unfold! Your Heart will make all that is correct for you come to life. On the point of your dad, if you had true Love for him, he will not be far from you, and you will get signs of this along the way, until you eventually meet up again. Understand, you will, as have I, be returning back between here and *Reality* to everything exactly as you left it, so, your pussy cat will be just fine, but your dad? That's special, and I am sure in time he is to be found there in *Reality*. I sense your love for him remains strong, and if that is so, then that reunion is almost guaranteed, and it will be a togetherness which, when all is ready, will last forever!'

I began to realise, due to my deep-rooted feelings of Love I felt within for *others*, I really had been chosen, and was without a doubt, being watched over, so, assistance and guidance for me in this role must therefore surely follow. I finally set the stage for Jeni by suggesting,

'Come to my home some evenings and weekends, my mum would love that, she has always liked you, we can come up with the story that I want to help you study to get through exams. I can begin the task of preparing you with things you must learn about in preparation of that trip to *Reality.* You won't find it difficult, because you have a soft kind heart and that's the secret.'

I studied hard for a year at school, often being reminded that I had a 'faraway' look on my face. I wonder why? Jeni grew in confidence, keeping all the magic to herself as she dreamed of becoming ready!

The first signs that my choice of finding the right person was correct -- she was keeping her new secret all to herself, as I had asked a few mutual friends 'why Jeni seemed to look happier these days' no related responses ever came, unlike most, who would surely not have resisted boasting to 'up' their ego. Feeling good about my choice of a lovely candidate for *Reality*, I thought to give a little encouragement as we walked together after school.

'Be patient, Jeni, I will shortly be heading back to *Reality* and my priority will be to make all arrangements for you to be made welcome and feel at home; you are going to love it. It will help you to make that transition one day, knowing I am there waiting for you to arrive. For a while, you will find things all a little strange, in that I will still be at school and around generally, however you may begin to recognise a... slightly different persona about me, with things like confidence, etc. You see, when I go to *Reality*, time has no place, in other words, even if I have been gone for months, that will be a period of time that simply does not exist here in the world!'

There was such reward for me, as I noted for the first time an easy gentle look on the face of such a lovely girl. Someone who all and sundry had taken great pleasure in deriding. She now had an air of confidence about her, which I noted began to attract others to be her friend... strange that! I guess it is life's way, in that nobody likes a 'loser' ... they like 'winners', but given the chance, they will seek to take away everything that winner has achieved, thus turning them back into a 'loser' once more ... little wonder I had developed that desire to leave.

Why, whilst so young, was I recognising such poor distasteful human behaviour? I think with some discernment I had been a bit of a misfit for years, and it was plain to see why I dreamed of *Reality*. The more time spent in my room with Jeni, sharing some of the early wonders of *Reality*, the more I became aware of how lucky I was. It would seem, when you share anything quite special, the person spouting off can hear and relate to the words coming forth, as if standing bye as an observer! Jeni made a comment one day that told me she was not far behind intellectually than those who teased her, when she said to me,

'Sometimes, I'll look at you, knowing you may have may have been away in no time.'

I worked hard at school, and did notice the change in my consciousness learned at *Reality* had given me an air of confidence, and I seemed to breeze through each day without anybody trying to put me down. It was as if that certain *'Something'* was being sensed by others, as *'Its'* power radiated out unseen from within me.

I had read of such things, where 'Light' drives out 'darkness'. In the knowledge that I felt nothing of this was of my making, my ego remained hidden, and I felt happy about that. Luke had taught me such uplifting things regarding this subject, and I knew I personally, was certainly not a 'Chosen One'! I had, in fact, actually made myself a tiny part of that *"One"*. With such a partnership, if only with a one *'jot'* share, one becomes protected! Made obvious for me when noticing the complete lack of unsavoury things now coming my way, such as bad websites, swear words, running others down, making fun of me. In fact, all the interactions we would all prefer to be absent from our lives. Actually, people now seemed to be drawn to me for friendship.

I couldn't wait to see Luke again to share such tidings, especially to explain the joy I felt at just observing the wonderful changes taking place without any thought of being responsible ... a humble observer.

I sat quietly on my room gazing at my picture, closed my eyes and drifted into a dream scene of a walk along the railway platform. As before, I was passing through a mist, but now as a steam cloud in pink being fired out from my little steam-engine friend… I was on my way.

RETURN TO REALITY

My newly found friend, the old gentleman I had met on the train when leaving *Reality* last time, was sitting in the carriage I selected, with me wondering if we selected such a carriage or if a certain 'Something' did the influencing as to which one I would step into. This was the lovely man who no longer travels back to Earthly life, he simply enjoys the ride, the window views, and the new people he meets, not forgetting his main purpose of something akin to reading newspapers, by catching up with on life on Earth.

He waited for a short while, allowing another older girl to be seated and me to settle, then lowering a book he was reading, with a smile leant forward slightly and spoke.

'Lovely to see you again, Freya; now tell me, are things improving back there?' nodding his head just once in a slight upward motion. He continued, 'be nice to hear of any developments that you, with a young fresh mind have noticed that you would like to change or give an opinion on. It's so nice to hear young views, as older folk are a little biased and almost resentful of change.'

What could I comment on, I wondered … then I thought to mention the general confusion arising day by day at schools between boys and girls, and he so nicely asked if I could explain, which I tried to, although feeling a little strange at having again been asked by an older generation man as to what a teenage girl thought. Adopting an open-minded stance for safety, I opened with,

'I can see from reading modern history, there is a levelling out of equality between the sexes, which most would agree seems a right and fair thing to happen. I personally think the transition should have started long ago, in an 'easier' evolution of events. It seems to me and my friends at school there has been a sudden emphasis in so many areas of life from the workplace, sport, genders, and the like. We talk much about this between ourselves, and all seem to agree, it is so easy now to offend, with what you say, what you do, even where you go; it's a bit like 'treading on eggshells'.' The gentleman, smiled, as if acknowledging the attempts of a far from 'worldly' girl to put the world to rights, and commented.

'I so admire your sharing, isn't that of itself, a recognition of a changing world from the one I must sadly relate to, one which is obviously so far out of date. I am learning from a 'bright eyed and bushy tailed 'teenager'. I was left thinking, *he is showing me, and my generation, such respect,* and that felt odd to someone like me, who was only used to being taught by teachers much older, who were not always up to speed with young minds as they try so hard to knock us all into shape, knowing, it will be a 'world' where one will frequently be 'treading on eggshells'. I liked his description of me being 'bright eyed and bushy tailed', one that I had never heard of. I stopped chattering away. Recognising my pause, my travelling companion smiled and took away my 'old head on young shoulders' ... he thanked me, and gave me back my youth with,

'Not easy for your generation, and from my heart I can only thank you for the update you have tried so hard to give me ... I think I am glad I have finished with that life, which brings me to say: being as I'm no longer a part of that world, and considering my old age, I think I can say: your dress and shoes are so pretty, a dress fabric in colours and design unknown to my time. There, lingering under such prettiness, is surely a great intelligence,' looking across at the other girl in the carriage, saying, 'wouldn't you agree?' She gazed my way with a thumbs-up gesture and addressed my dear friend with a smile.

'There's an example of Freya's reference to 'treading on eggshells' … you see, I know you said something lovely from your heart to Freya, I also know that Freya will have, if she's honest, felt really special.'

'And?' said the man in a questioning sought of way.

'Well, it's a little 'Wokey'.' said the girl, leaving our dear friend to look back down at his novel with a slightly guilty smile, utterly convinced he had heard the sound of 'eggshells.'

The train pulled into '*Reality Halt*'. I said goodbye to the girl travelling companion, then stood, turned toward my so respectable friend, and adopted a fashion model type pose with my feet, threw my shoulder bag over my shoulder, brushed any creases down on my dress, and shot the 'Woke' matter down in flames by saying,

'Thank you for your company, and how do I look?'

'Take care of yourself, Freya … you have just demonstrated something beyond those new rules of life, more so a Heart being allowed out to play'.

I leant forward and kissed this dear man on the cheek, a bit like I would my grandad; I stepped down onto the platform and the entire scene re-engaged. The teenage girl I had left sitting on the platform reading a girly magazine stood, glanced my way and smiled. Prior to her popping it into her travelling bag, I got a quick glimpse of a pretty pink dress she had pencilled around. The family climbed into a rather special looking taxi and were off in a completely silent vehicle. I needed to ask Luke about that.

For me, the joy of seeing my Luke again was just too much to bear. *I must try so hard*, I thought, *to conceal such an obvious giveaway smile of first love … a smile which would surely reveal my heart feelings almost to a point of nakedness.* Back to those feelings again! And they were, I might add, growing and becoming more intense and frequent!

I could see no sign of him as my searching eyes darted up and down the station platform, looking for someone who had become the biggest part of my young life. No sign! It was as though my world had come crashing down around me.

I felt devastated, desperately thinking what to do; *I'm stranded in limbo between two worlds.*

The 'grown up' Freya who had been advancing her knowledge and worldliness in a new expanding world that had opened up for her was suddenly a fifteen-year-old youngster, away from home, lost and alone with nowhere to go! With tears welling up, I glanced quickly in almost desperation to see if the train was still there, at least offering the safety of a trusting fatherly figure to help me through, but it had left, and all that remain of this commute sanctuary that could take me home again was a tiny puff of steam in the distance.

I rushed into the waiting room to sit and gather my thoughts, and 'wait' ... forever, and ever if need be, until I die, having lost everything; after all it was a 'waiting room' with no time limits indicated on the board on the wall stating such.

Seems I was to be fed a window of wonderings, in a place where time did not really exist, wonderings that included: would that train return to take me back and would I ever get over my Luke?

It seemed like forever, as I gazed up at the waiting room clock on the wall ... noticing the hands had not moved, only to feel more 'loss' creeping over me. Then I realised: time, as I knew it does not exist in *Reality,* so I must be there. Evidence of this came rushing back into my lost, overdramatic young mind as it cleared fear away like a sweeping hand across a glass table removing unwanted poison pen letters from its surface! I had caught a glimpse of that young innocent girl with dreams of pretty pink dresses stand, smile at me, and walk along the platform of *'Reality Halt'*. Feelings of *'Loss'* began to dissolve into their inevitable nothingness, only made something by false imaginings of anything being lost forever. I was back to being the bright-thinking girl who had surely not been forsaken!

Then suddenly, there he was, strolling through the waiting room door in such an easy kind of way.

'And how's my Freya?' he called out.

'I'm fine,' I replied, with a little fidgeting, slowly rising, feet together holding my little bag from Greece in front with both hands, not quite knowing how to react without giving the game away as to what my beating heart was now getting up to ... he followed with such reassuring words.

'Our lives are complete again.' This put me at ease once more, as still stationary, my right foot moved in front of the left, pointing slightly outward, losing the somewhat pathetic schoolgirl pose, now reassured that there really could only be happiness at *Reality.* I thought for a moment, then, with refreshed confidence in a rather open book kind of way, stated,

'How wonderful that we both should simply pick up where we left off with our togetherness. It's great to see someone who I feel to be the other half of me again. The joy of *Reality*... True love and friendship is real, and never to be doubted.'

I sensed there was, just maybe, a slight hint of his awareness of my fear of loss resonating in my rather overstated pitch, which in its very nature made me understand once more what *Reality* meant. What we had really was real and needed to be understood as being beyond the limitations, and fears, of 'the other world' back there. I had to raise my game, lift myself to higher thinking... so I did.

I remained stood still for a while and allowed that higher consciousness to drift back in, just as it had at my initiation when stepping into Dougie's picture, and in no time, '*It*' flooded into my being like a welcoming home, with silent, most beautiful words rushing into my head, which I clearly remember, and though sacred I am happy to share them here:

"Refocus and remember; your new surroundings are without sharp edges, snares, traps, and disappointments ... just light, and soft things in colours

beyond that 'other world's' limited concepts and boundaries. No 'clock ticking' time here, or limits as to where things, or others, should be, or not be. You might find many loved ones in streams and passing breezes dancing. Imaginings, made up of particles of light appearing as people, stream ripples, pretty leaves and flower petals, to be shared and enjoyed with friendly animals and birds of every kind. Winds will become breezes, which in turn will explode into a thousand tiny sighs, seen as simple breaths in light pastel shades of colour. For you, this is a destiny of souls unfolding. Relax in it without fear, you, having searched for higher things, have found them."

Some of those uplifting words from some other dimension told of wonders beyond my learning to date at *Reality*, but it all generally told of a place where nothing can hinder. And was that clock in the waiting room standing still a sign? I stood, starry-eyed, revitalised, and walked toward that which I felt to be mine, to have and to hold, in the form of Luke. It came easy for us both: nothing said, just eyes at work each to the other. I felt at home!

Luke took my hand, and off we walked out of the waiting room ... and there was that delicate mist once more, quite refreshingly cool, I noticed, this time in that pale pink hue. We walked through and into those familiar surroundings we had together created.

Down a lane toward the stream, sparkling in morning sunlight as if calling us to witness flashes of radiance, my mind's eye eagerly gathered it in. It all appeared seemingly beyond the norm in degrees of brilliance. The miller's little boat sitting at the stream edge, those sun reflections dancing here and there on its timber side; once more, my scene was set.

Glancing around, I noticed there were other people now, some picnicking, and some laughing happily as they strolled by the stream. It all seemed so harmonious and pastoral, but I did need to ask Luke about those 'other' folk and us. After all we did have a wonderful secret world named *Reality* which, I had dared quite naively to imagine to be ours alone, to live and grow old in. Then I realised the obvious: how could there be a world with just two people? That would be back to the 'Adam and Eve' scenario, and I fancied keeping my clothes on ... or did I? It all went a little misty as my mind fumbled over buttoning up one of my blouse buttons which, when nobody was looking, I had quite naughtily undone on the train in readiness of meeting my guy. *Well*, I thought *that was only a faint mistiness, just a nudge to indicate I was perhaps stepping a little over the line. Not a major error... 'Just growing up'*. That still, small voice within reassured me.

Luke had picked up on my wonderings, as my eyes quickly searched out other people. Maybe, he even saw a tiny question mark, and the word '*Thinks*' in a balloon, hovering above my head, as seen in comic books. Who knows? He was quick to reassure me with,

'Nothing of our *Reality* life has changed whilst you were spending time back there, Freya. It's all now beginning to develop into a fairly normal country life, without that entire aspect of modern tech stuff and gizmos to distract.' I was reassured -- after all, we did need normal surroundings, or we would end up like 'Tarzan and Jane'. My concern was related to 'us'; you see we did have a wonderful dream life we were able to create from our consciousness, so, I responded,

'This is sounding wonderful, Luke, all adding to the *Reality* dream world where there are people we can say 'hi' to and relate to in friendship, but I am unsure how we sneak off to our tree top home and live our wonderful, dreamy world without being spotted? After all, can you imagine someone strolling along a riverbank and glancing across only to see lovely animals and birds laughing and enjoying a picnic? Or in, fact, all such variations and scenarios we will no doubt be creating along the way.'

'I understand what you are referring to,' came his response. 'But do try to understand, all that surrounds you by way of people, animals, nature, etc. is a backdrop to our lives. However, when we morph into a consciousness creature creation, that is ours alone, unknown to other people; they will simply not be there. So, whenever we quietly drift into our consciousness adventures, we can never be discovered in what is our dream alone … all that surrounds us forms part of that hidden world … in fact a world within a world.'

'A bit like that parallel universe you mentioned earlier, Luke?' I added, trying to sound intelligent by demonstrating my recall abilities, also trying to find a place in the universe where I actually belonged. Also, raising a point in fun that did, in fact, have deeper implications: 'so what if , say, whilst 'dippers' we 'morph' into mice, whilst mice we morph into 'deer', then 'dolphins' in warm seas in the sun. We could be moving 'up-up-and-away', journeying on into oblivion.' Luke's focusing response came:

'So, there we are us dolphins, rushing through warm seas, leaping high to entertain 'on deck' photographers in warm Caribbean waters ... where would we be Freya?'

'Well, you just said 'Caribbean'.' It seemed the obvious answer.'

'Nope! You lost your way again!'

'Hang on, Luke … did you, or did you not, say 'Caribbean'?' said with a smile, hoping to catch him out, but as always, he was bound to have an answer…

'Well, I did … however, we'd still be in your '*Reality*', Freya … why not try morphing back through that 'oblivion' of yours to just you and I, simply strolling along in quietness for a while, taking in the beauty, with an overwhelming feeling of belonging which now seems to embrace both of us. Best we complete our immediate surroundings first before heading off to the moon!'

He did seem to say things so easily, always tinged with a little humour and a smile. Mind you, it did leave me with more to think about, in that '*Reality*' was a new world, and this must surely include all that that implies Tea with a Badger, along with: 'one small step for mankind' sorry: womankind, sorry: personkind … like, on the moon! I thought to make a note of that for my next train journey meeting my dear old gentleman friend, should '*Woke*' issues arise.

We passed a pretty village corner shop with many delights in the window such as locally produced honey, homemade jams, and baskets of products made at the local bakery.

'Guess where the baker gets his flour from for baking, Freya,' Luke asked. *That's easy*, I thought, could it be from the mill, which sits centre stage in our newly unfolding dream world? A mill, albeit somewhat obvious and, larger than life., I had to admit, the purpose of such a homely, industrious-looking building had never really crossed my mind.

There was need for me to take in what had been so blindingly obvious: the Mill must have an entire associated purpose for being there, and I had simply let it just drift by without a second glance.

My journey was moving so fast, even to the point of working it all out, as in fact, I have just been doing, after all, this in-depth thinking usually comes from 'old heads on young shoulders' ... with me it's a 'young head on young shoulders!' I reminded myself: *I must try to just drift along, without too many questions* … My questioning mind does seem to spoil the spontaneity of so much unfolding, … I think I'd sooner be a 'bimbo'. Umm …changed my mind on that one!

LIFE AROUND THE MILL

There it stood: the beautiful old Mill House, crying out to share stories, memories, visions and dreamy imaginings; after all it had appeared from Dougie's earlier consciousness as he dreamed around such things so long ago. It was originally simply a picture, but what lay behind those walls, windows, and surroundings was to be an entire story in itself. An extension of the story that was eventually to unfold in our lives, which would surely be as garnish to his vision of our *Reality,* making it all even more wonderful.

It would seem a new adventure was waiting around every corner as we strolled together. After all we were really here, and whoever heard of anyone ever turning a corner, only to find a complete scene frozen, stationary like a camera still shot, or a video stopped in mid-record?

It was obviously time to bring it all to life, but our thinking asked where to start?. Well, maybe not for 'our thinking' but 'my thinking' it would seem, as a knowing nudge came my way from Luke, who, as always when the need arose, sensed my lack of understanding.

'Let it unfold Freya ... that's what stories do. Remember it is us, creating each facet in *Reality,* and once that has occurred, it will always remain that way, to revisit or to spend time with.'

Of course, as always, he had me on track straight away. After all, he had been in the unfolding dream since I first arrived when I was destined to meet this lovely friend. It's just that sometimes it is all a little hard to come to terms with, especially me just a young teenage girl... Luke continued.

'We look at the mill across the stream, Freya, and, as mentioned, no scene in our lovely dream world will ever be a still shot and motionless. We can see over there, where I am pointing, the bulrushes at the water's edge move slightly in the summer breeze, a kingfisher suddenly darts across the stream from one side to the other, clouds unhurriedly drift by and, a thousand other facets of life are there to complete the living scene. However...'

'Do tell ... however what, Luke?' I asked, as I wondered what was coming next by way of something wonderful to learn.

'Look at the Mill House windows. At the moment nothing lies behind that hint of curtain drapes we see, or for that matter behind the front door, which at present, being around the corner, does not exist yet either!'

I always, even before he had finished explaining various things, somehow knew what he was coming to. However, in this case I felt sure I was about to learn something so profound and exciting beyond such knowing. He continued in a way that was far from simple small talk, more so something so deep and I guess quite spiritual. A little of the 'God' stuff I knew he clung so closely to. He began to explain.

'It's really just the same as when Dougie first began to dream of a perfect place to find, somewhere beyond *'The Veil'*; a veil which people have believed in since the beginning of time. One simply has to walk through that imaginary, non-existent '*Veil*' to find what lays in wait for each of us.'

I was quick to show my understanding to Luke; after all, it was our dream now, and for me not to understand would surely leave me trailing behind.

'There's nothing behind those curtains, is there, Luke?'

'Correct,' came his reassurance, but still looking at me, I sensed an expectation of a little more to come from Freya, so, I continued.

'We turn the corner and there is a door concealing nothing. We open the door and much appear inside, we look around the room and across at the windows to see those pretty curtain drapes moving slightly from an incoming breeze, the implication being, we have now created what lies behind both those drapes and the door and have given the entire scene life!'

'As always, you got it, Freya; we are creating the dream. Just standing there, before we open that door, there will be absolutely nothing behind it, not even air, simply 'nothing'. It will become one of untold numbers of those '*Veils*' we must pass through.'

I really did like these profound moments of learning about this wondrous state of being I now found myself in, but I was also very keen to get back to being young and enjoying the very act of growing up with Luke.

I could see we had been creating various events, which would now always be part of our life here, and they would all begin to come together to form a complete almost wonderland in which we could relax and chill.

We already had the tree house scenario, the dipper life, our new waterside friends, a railway station, and lanes down to a beach, along with future trips for me back home. It was growing until, for sure one day, it would all be that complete wonderland *Reality*. Luke, in an attempt at expanding my horizons, added a little infinity to my understandings with,

'Every new scene we observe is made permanent for our lovely world. As we travel, we will be expanding that world. Remember, we have a train with a station and country lanes leading over the hills and far away to nowhere... until we make it so.'

We crossed the little wooden bridge heading for the Mill and stood mesmerized at the water cascading over the '*overshot*' mill wheel, with every tiny droplet of water falling from the wheel paddles catching particles of sun light. The sun that day seemed so powerful, and yet it was only mid-morning. Luke turned to look my way and, out of nowhere, suddenly made a comment far removed from pastoral observations.

'Lovely to see you standing there in sunshine, Freya, looking quite the young fashion model; in just one thousand of a second, you turned your head and your long dark hair 'swished'. It declared so clearly a statement of femininity, especially with the sun behind you; I can see your beautiful shape again through the pretty cotton dress you have on today.'

A little shocked, I looked up at him and quickly adjusting my stance from what he had seen as a budding young nubile fashion model to a stiff embarrassed teenager quickly bringing her legs together and raising one arm up across my front!

Suddenly, it was just the two of us. It seemed he had pulled us both away from the unfolding scene and noticed something so personal, which, I might add, I felt, although a little embarrassed, quite special about. After all, it meant I had accessories, which to me simply came with the slow growing up process that all girls go through, like say, one millimetre a week, so changes come unnoticed ... but for just one moment in time, he had stopped that 'process' and taken note.

It was as though he had pressed my growing up video to 'pause' and seen something he obviously liked, things some of my school friends back there had been giggling about for some time now. What with my solo model posing at the tree house window in moonlight shortly before, and now this observation by Luke, I felt I had received confirmation that I was making the grade as a woman! I was learning to just love this growing up idea, with matters I somehow felt safe with in Luke's company, and knew, somehow, we would *'come out the other side'* just fine.

Moving on with a smile, he made little of the moment, leaving me standing there blushing. He had spotted my secret hidden female form in silhouette, and although he looked as though just maybe he shouldn't have said such a thing, he had approved, making me excitingly aware I was obviously developing more than I had realised. And as fresh thoughts rushed through my secret girly mind, I became once more aware I had things he appreciated and perhaps wanted to share, which to me didn't seem very much ... in any event, I had no idea what 'sharing' meant ... or for that matter how to. I just knew, somehow, I wanted to!

We walked on, and he paused to take my hand, almost in a reassuring way. Strange, I so wanted to continue the moment and posed a rather childish question: 'What did you see?" knowing full well he had probably spotted my developing 'boob/bottom' profile. He answered by reversing that female 'tease' power I have mentioned, which girls can apply by simply raising his eyebrows, with nothing said.

This was that 'romantic' requirement on the first bucket-list I had prepared, blossoming again, and so beautifully. I reflected on what made it romantic; after all I had many times seen pictures of women in magazines breastfeeding babies, and tribeswomen in Africa without tops... all quite normal and not worthy of disrespectful heads to turn. Some, sadly, as with my mum's friend, were savaged by what she had explained as 'breast cancer', the very thing which had promoted that early 'awareness' chat at school I mentioned earlier. That early awareness had, for me, sadly made it all very, kind of biological ... but at this moment in my young world, mine were delicately secret, new, young, unmolested sweet fruits developing outside of any grown-up agenda ... as yet unseen or touched by strangers, and my Luke had had just a glimpse in profile of my braless precious young development. Interesting that I use the word 'precious', because unlike so many girls at school, who even referred to them as a four letter word beginning with a 'T', for me it did feel all so precious still and would remain as such, for as long as possible, like a spring flower bud preamble to that ageing process change I'd spotted with my granny with those saggy boobs!

These lovely interludes of Luke and I on that bridge, I knew, would resurface once in a while, probably with more frequency and, no doubt, with more longing and associated things. In such a grown-up way, I left the subject alone, but did note I was experiencing an inner glow, which felt so good!

Would this magic yearning rise up? Then, as time passed, also sadly fade with age? I wondered. The delicate, oh so pleasant subject matter kept re-surfacing, and I suddenly realised, this newly unfolding world *Reality* was never intended to become solely a fairytale story, as with 'Alice in Wonderland' and the like. It was all so real, and included developing growing-up people, and must, surely, include what developing growing up people think and do.

I had to assume we would be entrusted to make the, as yet unknown to me, progression through delicate issues in a sensitive, learning, and considerate togetherness kind of way.

There I was, working it all out again, as if trying to find correct formulae in a maths lesson, though in this case I actually had little data available to feed into my mental search-engine. I think I was trying to say it was an area to be enjoyed, I guess...?. An area which should flow smoothly along like a quiet stream, then enter the slowly increasing flow to approaching rapids, finally, falling out of control, over the likes of Niagara Falls. That was the only real clue I had gleaned and, if I am really honest, I had cribbed that example from my human biology sex lesson teacher, who seemed to be getting redder in the face at each passing tutorial moment, along with taking drinks of water from her desktop, as her explanation unfolded! The teacher, one would never have guessed, was none other than: Yep... Miss Brown.

Fancy that, I thought, *how did she know all that stuff, and she was not actually married... not that that seems to matter these days.* Pieces of the puzzle were slowly coming together.

We eventually reached the other side of the mill, and there was the large oak door. We knocked with a metal knocker in the shape of a smiling badger's head. I did wonder if Bossy had modelled for its making.

'Come in, the door is open,' came a strong, mellow, somehow friendly voice. 'My name is Mr. Miller, I suppose an obvious name for a man who owns the Mill. I have heard stories of two lovely young people coming to this corner of the world to live. Strange how the years go by in the same old peaceful way, with the same happy folk living, and sometimes passing by in and around our neck of the woods. Then, very rarely, we hear from neighbouring villages of somebody young and special arriving, guess it's our turn with the pair of you coming ... so, welcome.'

We looked at each other, realising just maybe, other Artists, Authors and Poets, in fact anyone with creative abilities who had achieved that wonder of divine realisation, had qualified due to their consciousness to be able to step through that veil between 'that world' and this. He continued along the lines of this wonderful revelation, with certain proof that had us smiling from ear to ear, knowing full well, his words must be truly honest as he declared, something which not only revealed yet another village to our growing community, but also exciting proof of some other unfoldment that was clearly under way.

'We've heard of a man in the nearby village of 'Copsewood' who often sits in the sun by his pretty cottage, stroking his cat on his lap, telling passersby: 'I am expecting a visit from my daughter Jeni'... yet most, having lived there for so long, knew nothing of a daughter named 'Jeni'. People talk of her being another of those young 'special' folk I mentioned who come from a place where many youngsters dream of better things, but are unable to pass the requirements found in 'quiet innocent minds' where dreams which can come true are made! We all feel so blessed to be here in a place where no bad issues or such feelings exist.'

I knew immediately from this remarkable comment that Jeni's consciousness was elevating and closing in on her papa's. She was making great progress in her attempts to get to *Reality*, and I thought, if only she knew there is a beautiful happy sunny place awaiting her, where a new life and friendships are to be found and bullying, intimidation, and unsavoury things are no longer present.

By now, we were standing inside the Mill house, a lovely country scene which appeared to be almost from times gone by, I just loved the feel of it all. Strange, how for me growing up back there in a modern world, with all the multimedia apps and gizmos, this feeling of simplicity was as welcome as with olden days of seeking out those seaside rock pools, which to this day, most modern souls still pursue and enjoy.

It became immediately clear; Luke and I were still, as with our tree house and Dipper world, of the same mind, after all, what I saw unfolding before me each time seemed to be totally in line with what he was picturing and vice-versa. It was clearly an endorsement of our consciousness being in simpatico, as with the first coming-together moments when I stepped into his beautiful world.

The miller looked up from his labour and what was for a young modern-minded girl, a strange, almost medieval task of tending to mill wheels spinning, a large stone corn grinding wheel slowly rotating, large leather straps turning other wheels with differing functions and corn *hoppers* feeding the corn down to be crushed and ground into flour for making bread, all driven, quite free, by that mill wheel turning so methodically outside, by way of a marriage of wooden paddles and clear mill stream waters. So much input ... one might expect a motor car to be an end result!

Many large sacks of flour could be seen at a lower level, filled, awaiting collection by the village baker and other clients. It all seemed so industrious, with so much going on in such a managed and harmonious way and by a man alone.

Then ... a bringing together of our adventure became obvious as I looked across to the other side of the mill house, and there sat some wonderful friends, some of them known to us in our Dipper lives. There was: Bossy Badger, Roma Ratty, and Messy Mole making a mess with some corn, all sitting so happily eating a piece of crusty bread supplied by Mrs. Miller ... I say 'crusty' because I could hear each bite Bossy took as he glanced sideways at his friends' pieces in a greedy coveting kind of way, checking out the size of their pieces, an action they seemed to recognise as they turned heads away to eat. She had obviously baked it in her own oven in the mill cottage. When I said: 'a bringing together', I meant the two worlds of humans and animals.

'This is a world where people who love animals, birds, and all forms of life, not forgetting flowers and trees, etc., can live in harmony together,' volunteered Luke, which did make sense, considering our Dipper experiences, and here we were standing as two people!

'If you are wondering about our animal friends over there,' Mr. Miller lent across to say, 'they come every weekend to enjoy themselves around the mill; you would be amazed at what they get up to, after the wife has spoiled them that is.'

'Might I ask what?' I dared to ask our new friend, causing him to stop his work for a while to explain.

'I guess this has become a centre point which my wife and I welcome so happily, a meeting place they all refer to as 'happy place' where they just enjoy life getting on together and having fun in and around the Mill.'

'Can there be such a place?' I asked myself, knowing that, if so, every living thing would love to be part of it. It would seem, being as such things as mobile phones etc. do not exist in this newly discovered wonderland, every living thing senses when there is some happy activity unfolding, in this particular case, it would appear to be a regular meeting-up and we couldn't wait to see what they got up to.

Mr. Miller got on with his work of making flour; looking over his shoulder with a smile, he suggested.

'Why not stroll around outside of the mill? You will see such fun, which, I can see from the window, is just beginning.' We thanked him and said our goodbyes for the time being, then strolled out into the sunshine, with me thinking that he just said: 'I can see from the window', that was actually one of the windows that earlier had appeared lifeless and without 'proof of purpose!'

My eyes glanced up, gazing at that very window, now open, and a curtain could be seen moving a little in the breeze. It was an area of beautiful pastoral life we had brought into existence. A real life, involving animal and human friends, living and enjoying each other's company.

It was all taking place, at every living moment, but unseen by so many back there until they seek and find their *'Reality'*.

The first demonstration of animal friendship underway was to be seen as we passed the large mill wheel turning. You see, Mr. Miller had explained when showing us around ... his mill wheel is called an 'overshot' as opposed to an 'undersho't wheel at some other mills. His particular millwheel being where the water turning the wheel runs along a man-made tributary (flume) arriving at the top of the wheel and strikes 'paddles' or fills 'buckets' to turn the mill wheel and subsequently all that mechanism inside the mill that I have mentioned, such as various pulleys and corn-grinding stone wheels. The 'undershot' wheel is where the water arrives at a lower level to strike those 'paddles' to turn it.

Quite good of me to remember all that detail, I thought as I ran through it with Luke, noticing him appearing, if not impressed, somewhat surprised.

We heard laughter coming from the little copse of trees where the feeding mill stream seemed to be coming from, then these little friends began to arrive. First to appear were a couple of toads drifting down the 'flume' sitting on water lily leaves, then came several pairs of ducks followed by several water voles standing on small sticks playing Canadian log rollers. Clearly, they were all heading for the wheel going about its work of slowly turning so industriously, producing flour for a love affair between hot crusty loaves and butter. But there was also fun in the air!

First to arrive at the top of the wheel were the two new faces Mr. and Mrs. Toad. Into a 'bucket' they *'plopped'*... and over they went, laughing all the way down as they fell out into the clear stream below, made deep at this spot by years of cascading water. Off they swam to the bank and scurried around for a re-run and to make room for those following.

The ducks appeared quite professional, even to the point of not opening their wings as they fell through the air, remaining in a diving attitude, allowing a deep plunge into the clear water, leaving a stream of white bubbles following them down into the depths. The happy band of log rollers, well actually, twig roller water voles came next, turning the water surface into a lively explosion of white foam and bubbles rising into the air as they hit the water. The entire scene felt to be an eruption of shear happiness as friends played together on a hot summer day in the mill pond.

Then, quite suddenly, they were all gone and appeared to be heading down stream toward the little thatched river side cottage we had designated as our other human base. Luke thought to suggest.

'Why not make our little river friends a continuing reality and extending it by strolling down to the cottage in order to be in readiness for them passing by?' We bid farewell to Mr. and Mrs. Miller and were quite shocked as they smiled saying.

'I see you are heading in the direction of your little cottage downstream. We all knew for some time you had moved in there. Now we have met you, please come often to see us.' We were amazed that he knew of us and our little cottage, and, looking back, thought to ask,

'How did you know this, Mr. Miller?'

And he replied, 'We could see, on occasional cold nights, white smoke rising up from the chimney, and knowing the man Dougie who built the cottage long ago had long gone, with nobody living there after him, we put two and two together. By the way, have you found anything interesting or adventurous in the cottage?'

'Like what?' I asked.

'Well, stories are told that he made maps and drawings of secret places he had discovered where people can live secret lives, unseen or heard by others. It left everybody here wondering where these places might be. One of which has fascinated people's imagination from the day he left, the place he called 'The Hollow Mountain', where people could travel forever upwards, until finally opening a large oak door to reveal a new world of wonderful things! People here have never stopped talking about this mysterious place.'

There was obviously so much to learn in our unfolding world of *'Reality'*, things beyond what Luke and I were orchestrating for ourselves. It was as though we had an inheritance to claim, one that told of wonders to be found, almost as if as garnish to our lives. Seems Dougie wanted to leave certain things to be enjoyed, knowing, as he must have that, when dying, such wonders should not cease to be there to be discovered.

Keen to get along to revisit the cottage and check out our friends' arrival, not least a visit to the cottage loft area to search out 'maps', 'drawings', and possible secret codes that might reveal the whereabouts of 'The Hollow Mountain', I suggested,

'Think we'd better hurry, don't you, or our friends will have passed the cottage by the time we get there,' said with a degree of urgency in my words, and a degree of impatience to get into that loft. Luke's reply immediately had me back on track with a little guidance.

'Wrong,' came his response, 'you are imagining they are still travelling along the stream, unseen by us, but that is exactly what I meant when I said 'imagining' earlier, that's what you are doing, imagining that they are there. If that were the case, then other people could see them, which is not possible as they form part of our dream alone! Bearing in mind there is no such thing as time here, we simply have to be there at the cottage, and what we are dreaming will just happen ... such as being there to await their happy arrival.'

Clearly, Mr. Miller's hint of such an adventure, and us then following up on such a thing, was setting the stage, as it were, for a whole new phase of life to open up for us.

We arrived at the pretty cottage only to see our new friends a little distance up stream separating and also heading for their homes. Maybe our thoughts had made that happen. Further meetings and fun would have to be for another day, and we both had much to do in our new home.

We busied away for some time, with me making it all look so bright and happy and Luke, I noticed, setting up a rather large art easel.

'That looks promising Luke,' I volunteered, 'am I to witness new scenes manifesting on that?' He looked so pleased with himself as new ideas were clearly buzzing around in his new unfolding world.

'Can't you see Freya? Our opportunities are endless, if that is, we choose to venture on. You see I can create dreams within dreams, with other places to maybe go to.' I quickly picked up on: *'Dreams within dreams'* and *'other places to go to'* and asked him to explain. Could he possibly mean other places like *'Reality* to 'the power of ten' (I learned about that on my last visit back to school)?

'To give you an example, Freya ... assuming say I paint a picture worthy of the type of entrance you and Dougie made possible for yourselves. With much quiet time, we may be able to step into that new scene.' My mind went crazy with ideas based on what he had just said ... and 'the plot thickened', causing me to sit down with my elbows on the cottage table, chin resting in both cupped hands, staring at him with a rather blank, lost looking expression. You see, based on one of those: 'crazy with ideas' notions my mind had offered up, I was one step ahead, and somehow knew what he was about to say next ... with the word *'infinity'* screaming at me! As if right on cue, he began.

'So having created another beautiful scene, Freya, assume it reaches that certain standard. Try to imagine, having stepped into that new scene ... we find an Artist sitting there painting a beautiful picture ... stopping to gaze in wonder at such an *inviting* scene, we notice in that picture, sitting there by a pretty stream, under willows bending, there's another Artist at his easel painting a beautiful scene of a sloping green meadow. At the top of the meadow stands a magnificent 'windmill' leaving the viewer [us!] thinking of such a powerful potential rotating thing, 'wishing' and 'willing' for a breeze to bring those 'sails' to slowly, very slowly begin to turn, bringing the scene to life! At the lower meadow of that last scene, next to an old section of wooden fence by a 'five bar gate' sits an...' Before Luke could continue, I called out to him.

'Please stop ... I know... there's an Artist, isn't there?'

'You got it in one, Freya.'

'I'm losing my way, dear Luke ... am I old enough and wise enough to even try to understand where this is going?' I paused, reflecting for a moment that I had just said 'dear' Luke, which almost demonstrated a slight maturing, as that's what older people say, and I had never heard such a comment from a teen. I continued to highlight my concerns with, 'I am only just getting the idea of the boundless wonders to be found in my *Reality*, and now you are revealing the possibility of diving deeper and deeper down into other dreamy wonder worlds, and to where, eventually?'

'Stay happy, Freya,' Luke said with a smile, 'this is all meant to show you there is no limit to the joys that await. It is not meant to intimidate you. You asked, 'to where eventually', the answer to that is ... 'nowhere'! It would go on forever as does space above you, back there on Earth. By the way, you also mentioned: *'deeper and deeper down'*... try always to think *'up'* which can only lead you to the stars, Freya!'

He always seems to find a way to bring me into line with my thinking. He had dissolved my concerns of it all becoming too much by taking me to total extremes in my thinking by implying a bit of 'star gazing' at some time along the way... which had the effect of making a stroll by a *'pretty stream under a willow'* followed by a walk up a *'sloping green meadow'* to stand beneath the 'swish'-pause-'swish' of a windmill's sails all seem like extensions of what I already had. I was back with feet on the ground again.

'Don't forget, you were granted your right of entry by that Higher source, and that must have included the probability of you having to embrace more ... *He* does not make mistakes! We have a long and happy journey ahead in your *Reality*, but somewhere, maybe far off ... I just know there are going to be other doors opening for us, exactly as I have just demonstrated a moment ago. I'll soon start work on this new large canvas, so we can hang it on our cottage wall... I think over there,' pointing to a large expanse of white wall. 'Maybe a lovely composition of a large 'windmill' at the top of a green sloping meadow leading down to a pretty stream under a willow near an old section of wooden fence by a five-bar gate. What do you think, Freya?' said glancing my way with a wink.

He shouldn't have asked: 'what do you think, Freya?' which was inadvertently [a word that crept into my half term English test] inviting me in to comment on all that: 'up, up, and away' stuff. So, I did.

'Does that mean if you were to step into one of those scenes without me, you might find another girl to be with?' said with a hint of silly teenage envy creeping in.

'Think about that, Freya ... and who created me for your dream of living in *Reality* with someone close? Why, you did. It all started back in time with a guy called Dougie, followed by a young girl Freya falling in love with his pastoral heart along with what that heart had created in the form of a beautiful landscape setting. Can you not see; there is a permanent link there. You gave Dougie youth back, and that youth needed a name, which you decided should be 'Luke' ... that's me! It means you and I are linked to *Reality,* which we can expand on in infinite directions... so no need for other venues.'

'But what if we did manage to enter those fresh places, Luke?'

Suddenly, for the first time in so long, the entire surrounding scene went a misty grey, and for just five seconds [which seemed like a lifetime] I became afraid of losing my new wonderful *Reality!* As if receiving guidance from his earlier 'self', he went very quiet ... simply staring ahead, then suddenly, as if he too had his feet put back on the ground, he smiled and spoke,

'No need. We can, as you know, create whatever scene we so desire, and right here where we are!'

His next comment was, I'm quite sure, based on that inner guidance intended to bring an end to such 'wanderlust' and, to be really honest, it had that alright! With a very straight face, he explained in a way that made it apparently obvious that we had both been pandering to temptation and fear ... him talking of 'Dreams within dreams', and me thinking of him finding another girl there, or, as referred to in the following guidance he had obviously received regarding one of us possibly becoming 'lost', possibly me, to the seeking heart of my friend Jeni. He shared so peacefully the following, which can only have come from somebody au-fait with matters even my local church vicar would struggle with.

'That entire procedure of 'Dreams within dreams' is intended for very spiritually illumined people, with the picture scenes moving away from beautiful landscapes to something more simplistic. Eventually, to give you an idea, there can be a blank canvas with just one rose. It can take many years of Earth time in meditation to be in the presence of such a flower and much longer before its fragrance is enjoyed.

'Eventually you are asked by a 'still small voice' to pick the rose and put it into a vase of pure water and cherish it, as it will last forever! The many pictures to be conquered along the way can amount to hundreds; each stage becomes more difficult! Some inquisitive people do try, but such 'curiosity' is discouraged, with many getting lost and unable to find their way back to their intended place!'

'Do you mean people like Buddhist monks, Dougie, sorry, Luke?' said to give the impression of being intelligently interested, with a slip of the tongue in recognition of 'old knowledge' coming through, which, in point of fact, did not sound as if from my young Luke... but in all honesty, I got the point, but the thought of an ochre robe wardrobe and a bald head stopped me in my tracks. Silence followed. Luke and I smiled and sat enjoying the unimaginable beauty of *Reality*. As if in forgiveness, there before us high on a hill at the top of a rising meadow green, with blue mountain backdrop, stood a slowly turning 'windmill' as if spelling out the correct 'metronomic' rhythm of such pastoral life.

We strolled across to the lower reaches of that '*green sloping meadow leading down to a pretty stream under a willow, near an old section of wooden fence by a five-bar gate*'. Luke stood in front of me, took my waist, and lifted me up to sit on the gate. We both sat gazing at what had, after all, originated in his consciousness.

WHO SHOULD COME CALLING

Suddenly, there was a quiet knock on the door, which had us both wondering who could possibly be our first caller; after all, nobody as yet really knew much about us.

We both walked toward the door, full of exited wonderings. Luke slowly opened it, with me peering over his shoulder from behind, only to find a brief appearance of an almost ghostly image of a girl standing there in a misty pink atmosphere with a lovely smile on her face.

'Hi,' came her greeting, said so softly we could hardly hear her. Then she faded back into the mist. I exclaimed with such joy.

'Luke… I swear that was Jeni, my lovely friend from school, the girl who I had shared our secret with, she is so lovely, peaceful and true, looks like she is making progress with her quiet time dreaming of reaching *Reality*.'

'Act quickly Freya,' was Luke's immediate response. 'Open the door wide and place a vase of pretty flowers from the garden right in the middle of the doorway to let her know we are waiting, almost like having friends beyond the '*Veil*' to help her through; she will feel our *Love*.' I ran for those pretty flowers and a vase. Within moments, coming into focus again, there stood Jeni, this time stepping out from the mist to join us, with tears of joy running down her face as she realised my promise was really possible.

‘Now we are three,’ Luke volunteered, ‘come and sit down, Jeni; I have heard so much about you, you’re so welcome to our dream, a place where everything is always just fine!’

‘Since you shared your secret with me, Freya,’ Jeni volunteered, ‘I have thought of nothing else but *Reality.* But with so much doubt, and my total lack of self-esteem, which you know I have always suffered with, I felt I could never make it here, and cried in sadness once more as I accepted my place as a humble girl with so little to offer, just a someone who all would continue to laugh at and ridicule.’

‘So how did you make it?’ I asked, smiling with my head a little to one side.

‘I sat for so long, as you suggested, Freya, just gazing at the pretty cottage in Dougie’s picture, somehow imagining you may be at home, but really knowing you could actually be anywhere out there. With my head buried in my hands, I cried for such a long time, knowing I would have to wait forever, if ever, until I might qualify to make such a journey, after all, I never seem to pass anything!’

‘And…’ Almost as one voice, Luke and I said in an almost questioning kind of way as we eagerly awaiting her next words.

‘Well,’ she continued, ‘I moved both hands away from my face and gazed, for what I thought to be the last time, at the pretty little cottage, with that same feeling of rejection I had experienced throughout my entire life ... I had such a longing, but accepted such lovely things were not meant for me and concluded that at least I had a secret given to me by you, Freya, one I somehow knew in my heart to be true, a secret I could faithfully hold close to that heart forever.

‘Maybe it was reaching that lowest point of, as I say, once more feeling unworthy. I gazed at what I thought was to become just a passing dream for the joy of others... the little lane leading to your door. When suddenly a strong feeling came over me, a feeling that ‘*something*’ was helping me on a strange misty coloured journey, and there I was, standing at that very door of the cottage.

'Then, my limited mind began once more to draw me back, telling me '*this can't be happening to me I'm not that important!*' A mind that had only known rejection was struggling to set me free to embrace such things. I again thought to forsake my little chair, with the misty apparition beginning to fade, when a powerful feeling of 'Love' and being 'Loved' came over me, as I felt your Love calling me on. I saw a pretty rainbow arch diminishing in size as the two ends came closer and closer together, until finally forming, not 'the rainbow's end' but both ends meeting to form a complete circle around your door where stood flowers in a vase... and here I am, for the first time in my entire life feeling important, *Loved* and wanted.'

Such a special reward for a lovely girl, someone who had surrendered once more to failure, as she stood wiping her eyes, ready to walk away from the picture she had dreamed of entering, all based on my sharing such things. Were that to have happened -- walk away that is -- she would have once more risen early the following morning to a new day … a school day, and, the relentless teasing, still sharing her 'tiffin' with others who hinted at liking home-made, cinnamon flavoured 'rock cakes'. For me, it was a demonstration of when such matters as sadness, loss, tragedy and loneliness reach their lowest ebb ... some Higher thing will sometimes reach out to answer a prayer! I learned of such things in an English class, where my teacher made reference to 'The Nadir of Discontent', the opposite of which is 'The Zenith', the highest point ... the very point where Jeni had, through faith, now risen to. There she stood, in a fabulous pretty dress and new trendy shoes, with me, picturing her 'piggy bank' broken, choosing them in some shop, in expectation of *Reality*, and seeing her sitting crying, in such pretty things, about to give up on her dream, before the power of Love gathered her up! And it was a '*power of Love*' because, I knew those reading of such a story, would feel that *hurt* being dissolved by *Love*!

'Like your outfit, Jeni,' I found myself saying, as I gazed at such beauty, not just her attire, but her entire presence, somehow exuded a beauty she never somehow associated herself with. The dulled hair and dower look had gone, and the sun shone on shiny black hair, in a 'natural curly bob', that very sun flowing down over flawless brown shoulders from some Jamaican town. Leaving Jeni, so sweetly covering herself, feeling a little embarrassed at maybe being seen as having been presumptions.

'Not the togs I had on in my bedroom, Freya... must have all happened in the privacy of that coloured mist I came through.' This led me to say,

'Well, 'Somebody' saw the real you ... and here she stands!'

I was so happy she had not waited for those trips to my home with me making the excuse of helping her with homework, but really guiding her in readiness for the trip to *Reality*. After all, I am just a young *'rooky'* myself, also on a learning curve. It was a great lesson for me to realize she had accomplished it with, apart from a few tears, an easy humbleness, also surely assisted by a heartfelt yearning with *Love,* to find and, make happy, her Papa and pussycat Pixie once more!

As she said, *'something'* had been watching over her, just as *It* watches over everybody ... she must have been actually tapping into that special source.

Time passed with Jeni coming and going, forming a new life for the expansion of her own newly unfolding consciousness, a life available to all, if they could only begin to dream of higher things. We would meet once in a while on my returns, and I could see clearly a fresh confidence manifesting in her with new friends and situations. The last time we met, she declared with such an air of confidence,

'Freya, I truly believe I have found my real *Inner-Self*; whenever I return from *Reality* to life as we know it, for some reason I seem to attract people who want to be my friend, people who once teased me over my lack, and their numbers of friends on their latest mobile, not forgetting my out-of-date school bag!'

I guess there is a true perfect *Inner-Self* in everybody but, as with me, some unfortunately leave *It* so far from the surface they may never find such truth. She continued with such a newly found wisdom, leaving me thinking I personally, had been slow out of the starting blocks. 'So many seem attracted to the light, but the wrong light ... a destroying flame, like for the moth, only to get burned and die. Mine, when I sit peacefully waiting to return to *Reality,* glows so bright, it seems to exceed the *lumens* I learned of in science lessons. Just maybe, I exude a single photon particle of that light which attracts many. Who knows ... one particle is enough.'

Listening to Jeni, I found a weak spot of my own make up surfacing in that I dared to allow my ego to pop up with the thought arising, it was me who introduced her to this wondrous discovery. Then I realised the origin was based on a Love for someone so denied and humiliated by the world, and I felt fine once more. After all, Luke had warned me 'choose well, or you will be wasting your time' and my choice had been based on compassion for someone who had, for sure, been dealt a poor hand since birth.

The last time she came to visit us for tea, she was pleased as punch to declare 'forgot to say, my *Inner-voice* told me in quietness that my papa is happy and so content, and I will soon be finding him living in a village not too far away called 'Copsewood'.' Wow ... She heard her 'Inner-voice' ... *I don't hear that too often,* I thought. Also, she had just told of the very village Mr. Miller had mentioned where her Papa was often seen, sitting outside in the sunshine with a pussycat on his lap ... leaving me to wonder the pussycat's name.

On the point of her hearing that 'Inner-voice' I dwelled on the point for too long in my mind, and, I might add, with just a tinge of envy promoting a little 'mist', which then returned to brightness! I was being reminded of uncalled for comparisons being made.

FEET BACK ON THE GROUND

No doubt there had to be a slowing down of our journeying which, thus far, had been such a vast learning curve. After all, in a very short time, it seems, I had been rediscovered as a person, I'd become a butterfly, a Dipper bird and what next? I wondered. For sure it would be of my choosing and I felt the need to slow it all down a little.

We tidied around the cottage, sat at the table and sketched a cosy array of furniture, curtains, fixtures, fittings and the like. We did seem to have similar taste, so it all went smoothly. Mind you, Luke leant across, as I went to gaze from the window, and changed a table cloth to blue. We sat together on a window seat and closed our eyes, waiting quietly for a while, then opened them to see all in place without hearing a sound of this wonderful 'fit out'.

It was going to take time to feel at home, with seats being sat on, tables being ate at, and all the usual things done to ordain a home being lived in. We did seem to have been flitting around a bit, from here to there and back; again, along the lines of that beautiful butterfly.

So, having welcomed Jeni our very first guest, we felt assured we had been intended to be there at the cottage, after all, for her to have arrived at the top of a large oak tree ... being so high up, might well have scared the pants off her! Having enjoyed the cottage for that entire day, I suggested,

'What say we return to our little tree top home for a while?' I think he knew, and sympathised with, my yearning to ease back a little from such a merry-go-round of pure joy we could sell tickets for back there.

We wandered hand-in-hand along the lane leading to our lovely oak tree overlooking the mill pond, with me thinking, what would those back at school think of me doing just this with such a handsome older guy? Once more, a very slight grey mist appeared, and Luke, as always quick to pick up on any disconnected thoughts of mine, pointed out.

'Don't be alarmed, it's just a reminder that you mustn't bring the two worlds together in your thoughts; putting yourself above others. You must, by now, have noticed those little reminders are only a very light shade of grey mist that simply pass by delicate guidance toward the correct path.'

We arrived back at our lovely oak, offering the privacy and solitude we so sought. Luke pulled on a secret vine and down dropped the rope ladder, which would take us up the initial main trunk section before being pulled up and fastened. After which, on small, well-concealed sections of timber steps he had made, up we climbed.

'You first, Dilly,' insisted Luke with a wink, clearly related to calling me Dilly in fun. I sensed his concern that I might slip, and he would be there to save me he added a little rider 'don't worry, I'll respect your modesty as you climb in that pretty dress.'

He really did have such an understanding way of easing me from childhood into womanhood; this was the first time since climbing trees with unabashed school friends, always wearing something akin to school knickers. Now it would seem those indiscretions had dropped away, with me now realising there was such a thing as 'modesty' in my life, and there were things so special and private to hide, and the very act of 'hiding' had the title 'modesty'. I liked that; it brought to mind that older friendly man on the train, telling of times gone by, leaving me somehow knowing we would, in time, as did most be, 'coming out the other side okay'.

I responded to Luke's thoughtful remark in a somewhat contrived manner of silence, as if to indicate I was fully aware of the need for no peeking at my now more feminine attire, and even more feminine things they hid, but in fact, up until that point, it had never crossed my innocent mind. Sadly, many my age miss the transition as in school knickers/body development.

It was all beginning to make sense, that difference between boy and girl and the required related communication between them. I climbed on the ladder, still wondering to myself why such areas are 'secret'. I think I knew ... but didn't really understand why, only feeling once again, that Luke was maybe aware of such things and was extending his understandings to me.

We were obviously building on certain things quite automatically ... I really loved that. I was becoming aware of those girl/boy differences in such a nice way, after all, there were signs to be learned and acted upon, such as, if only in passing by, back there I have noticed girls look at a boy's eyes when saying 'Hi' to someone they know, whereas boys have no embarrassment whatsoever staring directly at a girl's chest area to check on progress!

Everything in *Reality* seemed to be happening in perfect order, even growing up, it would seem, had a correct route, so far removed from the school playground tutorials, from those so keen to boast on ill-informed intimate subject matter simply to impress ... I wasn't, impressed that is.

Even that school human biology lesson included, in a mechanical kind of way, an act which to me came across as unbelievable bodily trespass with 'this goes in that' ... totally devoid of any preceding feelings or emotions, let alone any slow introductory overture. It all appeared more related to a car mechanics course, and 'leg-overs' in the park, my friends talked of, rather than a sacred intercourse, a fusion of two lovers, body, and soul kind of thing. I was learning what seemed to me a correct route without tainted tutorials. My body was teaching me with wonderings, and inner glows, with secret things not for discussion, and a growing awareness of precious femininity that clearly attracted the male species. *How advanced we are,* I thought, *Lions and Tigers, move through jungles spraying trees!*

Luke, also young and untutored in such things, was, possibly without realising it, raising me up nearer to the point where our separate wonderings would surely be thrown together one day, a day when our inexperience would fumble toward the romantic. Sometimes, maybe even shocking experiences, so secretly beautiful, each to the other, in a union we would one day drift into for the first time. A union beyond guesswork an shallow tales told, but in a moment in time where for the very first time, I felt sure, I would lie in perfect surroundings and silently declare 'now I've found it!'

All sounding rather 'romantic', but what else would people expect from a 'dilly-daydreamer' like me, if not something bordering boringly along the likes of 'Romeo & Juliet' ... no need to think about such things as 'this goes in that', which at present, to be really honest, I found the thought of a little frightening. You see, people at school had degraded such things down to an act I somehow knew should surely include some respect and mutual caring, whenever and wherever the location might be, even if outside of a permanent relationships.

The world I dream of will always have 'Dreamers' who dream in an acceptable kind of way. It doesn't have to imply the ancient, out-of-date, romantic epic story line, involving lotharios from times gone by, where their chivalry and all that rubbish play the main part.

Such romantic epics were dreamed up for old films my mum and dad loved, leaving the audience females holding one hand to their heart at the thought of such a catch for an adoring pretty maiden, who, in their dreams, could perhaps have been them ... a 'commoner', who has landed a Royal prince. The film theme being along the lines of:

'The 'knight' hero rides across the open plains to be by her side, his silver breast plate shining in the evening sun, lance held high, no longer in the 'couched' position ready for the attack. His coloured helmet 'plumes' flow in

the wind, as he rides at a thundering pace to be by her side. She hears that thunder of hoofs announcing his courtyard arrival and stands to lean against her fourposter bed in her secret place, one bare foot raised behind, resting there. She's dressed in delicate 'see through chiffon'. Female profile made obvious by the backdrop of window light stealing through to naked form, she waits to greet her hero's arrival, when he will surely stand tall in the now left half-open doorway, remove his helmet to tuck under his arm, and, looking across, smile and declare his un-dying love for this maid.'

Had we been living in such times, most of my older male counterparts at school would probably be greeting her with '*been there – done that – bought the t-shirt*'... so nice!

Luke and I were both so young yet clearly being steered in the right direction for this dream world we had discovered. Too late for the world back there to change its inhibitions. Thankfully, however, there was a good percentage of still modern-minded youth growing up really well, even though a lot of naughty stuff was going on, so not too bad I guess, assuming of course well clear of any network predators!

I realise that nobody is perfect, and many of my generation were just being honest fragments of society, be that good, or bad. I was becoming aware, day-by-day, of the wonders of *Reality,* in that it was not simply a tale of adventure that most dream of along the way back there; it was actually a new wonder world, which could go on forever ... to include fun and happy *dilly daydream* moments, but more importantly, it embraced real human facets of growing up with the pattern of life generally. This time it all seemed somewhat 'proper', to use a rather old-fashioned description relating to the same old thing. Whatever... the way it appears to be unfolding for me has 'magic in the air', which I'm sure my consciousness will provide ... even a four-poster bed with silk pillows and chiffon drapes ... a door left ajar.

TIME TO CREATE THE SETTING

We decided to walk the course of *Reality* to set the stage ... a setting that, once created, would be forever for us to enjoy and relate to. Up until now, we have all the beauty that lay directly around our oak tree home and the mill, plus the '*Reality Halt*' station, and a steam train, with, of course, the stream down to the cottage, the new windmill scene and meadows, but that was about all.

There would always be, wherever we travelled, a natural landscape around us, made up of the perfect harmony of nature, but wherever a man-made item or structure seemed necessary for our unfolding life, we would need to sit quietly, consult, and then create it in our consciousness' imaginings, and it would become so!

We strolled, taking in all that surrounded us into our consciousness to make it permanent for our world but happily had to accept, that it all belonged to a divine order, including the seasons; not for being interfered with.

Realising we hardly had a village, let alone a town to enjoy along with the usual things like shopping, after all, if we continued to visualise all our requirements like food and clothes etc., it would be like living in a world of imaginings, not a completely new world. We sat under a tree for a while to make a list of *setting* requirements which would then begin to tick boxes and suitable locations for our very own creation.

Having completed a reasonable size list, off we went! One cannot imagine the sheer joy of such creativity. First we looked at a small cross-road of two lanes, and on one corner we tailored a lovely corner shop, when I say tailored, I mean to include, you know, all the usual issues, like its name, outside signs, produce, etc., along with a post office counter and a post box outside, fresh daily bakery, confectionary, local milk from a nearby farm [which we hadn't created yet] with a milk maid, Milly, doing daily deliveries to the door in a small open-sided milk van which also served for delivering to the door any products the corner shop sold, a bit like courier companies back there in the world, but not 'online'. It would all be run by quite old, so pleasant Mrs. Pope and her son William (known to all as Billy).

We looked at each other, smiled as if in agreement, with Luke demonstrating such humour with the following quip,

'So now we have: 'Billy' and 'Milly' and 'Dude' and 'Dilly' dipper ... we do need to up our game with choosing cast?' Eyes closed to reflect on all of those imaginings, then open ... and there was our village shop, with Mrs. Pope looking out of the open door waving a greeting. In we walked, bought some food and soft drinks for a picnic lunch, and we were on our way. We walked on for a while and found a nice place to sit and have lunch with him saying,

'By the way, we must practice simpatico in those eyes-closed moments of imaginings.'

'Why?' I asked.

'Well ... I pictured a cheese and tomato sandwich, and I've got cheese and cucumber.' We swapped, and all was well, with him smiling once more ... probably due to him having already taken a bite out of mine.

Clearly Dougie's picture was gaining depth beyond that which we could see in it. The village was to be situated at the end of the lane leading away from the little bridge quite near to the base of our oak tree. Interesting, I noted that is where Jeni's papa was eventually to be found along with 'Pixie', her pussycat. I guessed we'd see them in the corner shop on occasions when she visited *Reality*.

'Okay,' said Luke, in such a sensible balanced way, 'we have commenced work on our super environment ... let's take a break. After all, as quoted somewhere 'In the beginning, God created heaven and Earth...' we are simply creating a little niche, as a stepping stone to heaven, if we are lucky that is, but it will take time; we have already had part of the stage setting with the village discovery of 'Copsewood' not too far away thanks to Mr. Miller.'

I had to remind myself on so many occasions that all matters in my other life back there would always be on hold when I came to *Reality*; simply on 'pause' waiting for me to re-attend. I realised the importance of always leaving my home there on a happy note, and never to treat this as an escape, when I felt unhappy with any given situation, as that very situation would simply be there to greet me on my return. This realisation made me think for a moment... you see, if as stated, all was 'on hold' and unchanged, my length of stay at *Reality* would have no bearing on the way things were back home, so I wouldn't be hurting anybody in any way. This made me think more on the subject, of what was an acceptable length of stay in my newly creating world with Luke. It was all developing into a state of a perfect existence, not forgetting, although still so young, I did want to leave a world which was, in my opinion, developing in a very unsatisfactory way!

'Working it all out, Freya? That's running away!' Luke, clearly having noticed my far away 'check it all out' looks, intervened with, 'having tuned into a little of your thoughts, you are, I sense, actually bordering on the *Truth*, so before we go off on another super adventure, let me enlighten you. You see, we have been chosen, and I cannot say why us two, not forgetting now Jeni, of course. Maybe there are millions of others about whom we know nothing. Who can say?

'There have always been seekers of that 'Truth', something far greater than the world as we know it. For sure, you were very young and blessed when you began to hope, dream, and fantasise over somewhere where all the bad things in the world did not exist and harmony was the order of the day ... this is your reward.'

Wondering if Luke had picked up on all my thoughts, I pressed that particular point which I had been pondering regarding my length of stay, and asked,

'If I am not hurting anybody back there, what decides how long I choose to stay in *Reality*?' His response came quick and in a very knowing way,

'It will only be your love for your family that calls you back, but remember, as it is the case here. At the expense of repeating myself on a point you are already aware of, as I say, everything back there stands still each time you leave, so nobody is aware or hurt by such absence; it's as though nothing had ever happened. Remember your understanding of that 'parallel universe' idea? There will come a time when one of the 'parallels' will drop away, and you will know exactly what that means at a predetermined time.'

I think he meant *death,* so I quickly got off a subject that I was surely not ready to even contemplate at this stage!

I suddenly became aware that my new life here in *Reality* was, from the moment I had arrived, a blank clean canvas on which to build and create what I once dreamed life could really be like. You see, being so young and in school years, a period which is obviously when the mould of life for everybody is cast, I did not like what I saw; well, apart from people the likes of my mother and Jeni that is.

With questions to be answered, there was the need for degrees of investigative thinking, especially for someone so young, with, I like to think, a little intelligence. However, Luke was quick to remind me of happy, positive things with,

'Hard to imagine, Freya, for someone so young, you have been entrusted with such grown-up things and responsibilities. Clearly you are able and have even begun to demonstrate womanhood developing in a way beyond my boyish understandings ... which somehow seems to override what I had, probably incorrectly, considered to be my older authoritative male status. We are learning from each other, and I admit there does appear to be a certain power that a woman seems to develop, which is beyond the understanding of men. He just knows something is going on that he quite likes between boy and girl, and that something, I sense, is what we are both beginning to experience.' He finished explaining with: 'Now I've made you aware of a secret you didn't even know you possessed,' he smiled and added: 'don't take advantage, will you?'

Apart from homing in on his discourse reference to me being at one point 'so young' ... and the next a 'developing woman', I think I vaguely understood what Luke was referring to, but not very well; certainly, that is, not well enough to 'take advantage' as he put it, and how would I do that? t. My thinking took me no further than perhaps one day undoing one more button on my white blouse in readiness for another leaning-forward episode of that newly discovered ploy!

It was time to move on with our newly unfolding world, made clear by Luke's next comment.

'All serious stuff eh, Freya? Let's begin that next adventure and give our brains a little rest for a while, what say you?'

We strolled quietly again, in such a 'young love' kind of way, clearly enjoying the feeling of togetherness and the belonging to someone. Strange that I felt a need to 'belong to someone', especially in such a safe and happy place. I suppose it would take time to adapt to it being just us two, until that is, our new world grows, which will obviously include many others along the way.

'So, what's it to be?' asked Luke, looking for ideas, I suppose, which had me feeling so important as I had always assumed major decisions like that would come from him! I thought for a while and finally suggested.

'What say we have another spell of that childish magic we enjoyed earlier, either with our friends around the stream and mill, after all they will always be there now we have created them, or perhaps, something new we can create to add to our wonderful *Reality.*'

Whilst Luke was quietly thinking as we continued our stroll, I glanced down at our hands, once again entwined, noticing my soft white smooth skin lying safe in a strong slightly hairy back hand. He eventually made a comment which once more made me realise the magic we had been entrusted with.

'I've suddenly realised,' he said, 'we must keep an eye on a good balance between our human form existence and the almost fairy tale life we have at our fingertips, as with our waterside friends, not forgetting us as Dipper birds, Dilly and Dude,' he went on to say: 'hard to imagine, Freya, we have such power, not forgetting, of course, it is controlled by a higher source than us, in that if we abused what we have, it would, you may recall, become misty even to the point of us being denied *Reality* in its entirety! The point being, as you have clearly experienced slightly, we are so blessed to have warnings of any wrong thinking we might harbour, or of course wrong doings we might be tempted to pursue, which means we can always enjoy harmony here, unlike back there when all bad deeds and actions can be carried out with the perpetrators simply creating a list of black marks eventually having to be paid for.'

I quietly pondered over Luke's statement and again realised what a wondrous thing had taken place. It all suddenly came into focus, even concerning romance and all that stuff that goes hand-in-hand with such an affair that was clearly growing between us, even to the point of me being so young, which would not have been possible back there! Luke, as always on factual issues, not private thinking, picked up on my mind wanderings and declared.

'In past times in India, girls often married at twelve or fourteen.' I quickly followed up with a cheeky smile,

'Are you proposing something?' He laughed, and I felt fine, after all, he didn't add to that laugh. 'You gotta be kidding'.

We strolled on, mulling over the events which I so loved. It made me think we two were part of the harmony that surrounded us, as I took note of soft green moss on the north sides of trees not sunny south sides, primroses at the foot of foxgloves, and two butterflies dancing above flowers in bloom. Finally, I had a great idea and broke the silence to run it past Luke, with a little wondering, I might add, if I would be seen as attempting to upstage my wonderful guide. I suggested,

'What say we change the existing plan of always making our secret metamorphous on our landing stage at the top of the oak tree, to perhaps, maybe making that change anywhere where we felt to be totally alone in a secluded place. That way, if we felt a sudden inspiration, we would not have to trek home to our tree top.'

'I like that,' was his reply, as he looked at me and winked, adding, 'I was just going to suggest that,' obviously joking, but implying it was a really good idea … I think. As we strolled, there was again an obvious silence as we played wonderful mind games with what we could next become, with him perhaps flying somewhere as some other kind of beautiful bird species, and me as a tiny field mouse with little twitching whiskers, tiny bright eyes, and a shiny pink nose seeking out my friend 'Speedy' with Luke above as a hawk seeking out such things for supper.

'Would you do that?' I blurted out, assuming he was able to read my thinking.

'Do what?' was his response, making me aware he had not read that horrible possibility! Things went a little misty, and Luke quickly turned to me, wondering what naughty thoughts I had been dwelling on, so I explained, outlining my vivid mental picture of a tiny little thing like me as a field mouse with large wings hovering above, casting dark shadows, ready to take me away!

'The arriving mist was a good indication,' said Luke. 'Anything inharmonious or troubling here, unless it is seen as necessary for improvements in us, is unwelcome.' Seeing the fear in my young eyes, he added,

'This is *Reality,* where no such thing could carry you away.' He then turned the idea of being carried away into something easier for me to relate to, as in fun he swept his arms over me like that hawk and lifted me bodily up into his arms, all far removed from sharp hawk talons, more so, the strong arms of a friend. I have to admit, these close bodily contacts were having an increasing sensation of yearning for that 'something' I knew so little of, as he, by now face-to-face, closely, and slowly, lowered me and my blushing cheeks down. The saying 'keeping one's feet on the ground' came to mind, with, I might add, quite a liking for the slowly being lowered down part to get me there.

'Your choice, Freya, you decide what we should become,' was Luke's decision.

FURRY CREATURES

The decision was made, as I exclaimed, with such a feeling of importance and awareness that I was actually helping with such a major decision, in the creation of our new world.

'Red Squirrels,' I happily declared, 'you see, Luke, we can have such fun moving around at ground level... then, as and when we choose, we can move safely through the trees back to our tree top home to revert back to our humanness ... what do you think?' As always, Luke made me feel good by agreeing with such enthusiasm.

We moved into a quite secret-looking place, held hands, faced each other quite close, in fact, so close I could swear he was about to give me my very first grown-up kiss! I closed my eyes in quiet excited anticipation ... you know, as they do on old classic films, where the girl raises one heel up behind ... not so, suddenly there we were, two beautiful Red Squirrels holding hands and touching noses with Luke commenting,

'Our change always seems to work as soon as we both close our eyes.' He then glanced down and asked, 'by the way, why have you still got one of your little feet off the ground up behind you?' Ignoring him spotting my film star pose, I continued the conversation with,

'Were you about to kiss me then?' His response left a somewhat 'cheeky' mystery for me to dwell on.

'I did notice our noses were almost touching as we emerged.' I was about to follow up with.

'No before that,' then I decided that would surely indicate 'I wanted to', 'was keen to' or 'sorry we didn't', all statements indicating disappointment, and me in the initiative role. Oh dear, more mind games on this boy/girl thing, which did seem to keep presenting themselves as it did with poor old 'Adam and Eve'. I began to think that I pondered more on the subject than did Luke, which worried me ... and then I considered, perhaps he does, but it's a male way of playing 'hard to get'? Then I wondered, if he actually likes me that much. It finally occurred to me... Luke is obviously still able, even as a Squirrel, to pick up on, not my private thoughts, but my complete mental jumble about him and me. He smiled and put his little Squirrel arm around my shoulder and added,

'Are you *jumbling* again my precious partner?' Well, I'd never heard of 'jumbling' but I guess I knew that he had a good idea of what my mind was up to, and, as always, he knew just how to steady the ship, you see, he had just called me his 'precious partner'. He leant forward until we were touching noses... I suppose that's what Squirrels call 'kissing'. I had a tingling feeling and my tail *twitched* up and down ... not quite the soft human lip togetherness prelude to the 'going over Niagara' Miss Brown had scared the pants off the girls in my human biology school class with her, surely, step-by-step re-living the whole thing, taking intermittent sips of cold water, but it was a step nearer.

Amazingly, in our new guise as squirrels, we seemed to automatically hurry up the nearest tree for a feeling of safety, then, branch to branch, higher and higher, until we stopped to consider an enormous gap between trees we were suddenly confronted with.

'Can we do that?' Was my first, as always, nervous reaction. Luke's immediate response, as with every such occasion arising, took away the inherent fear in me, with,

'Remember our first flight as Dippers when we launched into space? This is 'easy-peasy' in comparison.' So, we jumped, and such a distance it seemed as we fell through the air, heading for our own chosen branch.

As I moved through space at such speed, I was thinking, *this is amazing, but unlike Dippers I don't have wings*, then it was over, and we were safe again on another tree's outstretched arms to welcome us, me having landed on her rather flimsy arms which seemed to bend so far down like a fishing rod, with my bottom almost touching the ground it seemed, before springing back up at enormous speed, causing me to lose my grip and zoom up past Luke, finally coming down on his branch, where he stood leaning on a strong branch looking down at me, smiling, with,

'Well, that was impressive, where did you learn to do that?' I scrambled inward toward him in order to locate myself a little safer on that firm branch where he was waiting with, it would seem, ideas and suggestions, as he declared.

'This is just like home,' obviously referring to our tree top residence back by the Mill house, 'let's build another small summer retreat somewhere near.'

We moved through the trees with Luke looking for a suitable location for his suggested new 'pad', advising me with such knowledge well outside of this teenage girl's radar.

'It's called a 'settle',' he explained.

'Do you mean where we settle?' was my somewhat ignorant response.

'No, it's what a squirrel's home is called.' He went on to explain: 'it is constructed of small twigs with an inner chamber of soft dry leaves and sometimes moss to make it cosy and warm for cold nights.'

The thought of lying so close to Luke in such a place quite had my mind racing again. *Oh dear*, I thought, *my mind seems to constantly grasp at any opportunity to reach out for that 'something' between boy and girl that seems denied to all girls until the right time, and how am I going to know that right time?* Back there in earth time, the subject was always close to the surface, but not too close. For example, a group of us going to school one morning passed a 'Pear tree' in someone's garden, with one of the boys pointing up, saying, 'what a lovely pear,' and one of the girls replying, 'do you mean my pair?' … followed by much 'giggling' all round.

I'm unsure if Squirrels blush, but for sure it felt that way for me, as Luke picked up on just a hint of what was puzzling my adolescent mind was doing, as he did. With a sideways smiling glance, he commented,

'Remember, we are Squirrels, and I personally have no idea of what goes on in their world of things you might have been pondering over.' Now I was, again, wondering as to how much he really did pick up on. Luckily my 'Red Squirrel' fur probably hid my blushes.

We travelled around looking for suitable twigs, dry leaves, etc., with me sneakily watching what Luke was gathering. In no time, we had constructed a beautiful large round cluster close to the main tree stem for stability in winds. Our 'settle' was complete, with a tiny access way leading into the heart. As evening fell, in we went and 'settled'!

These were new experiences for us both, and we lay together so close, reflecting on this wonderful world of *Reality* we were creating, with something new unfolding almost daily. I was learning the wonders of a strong trusting relationship with a partner … in this case a male squirrel, as I noticed, he insisted upon lying nearest to the small entrance tunnel to keep a watch out for strangers!

Strange, how this fell so safe and warm; with our tails reaching over our heads, it seemed as though we were surrounded by warm furry duvets. *I am a Squirrel* I thought, *and yet I think as a human teenage girl.*

I snuggled down, surrounded by soft dry leaves, moss, and my Luke. We said good night, and wrapped in each other's tiny arms we slept, with my last thought as my tiny nose and whiskers twitched, was 'I'm sleeping with a boy for the very first time, and I feel a glowing completeness. After all we had touched noses and that's quite personal!'

Morning arrived and, whilst stirring, I heard a quiet 'psssst' from somewhere outside, causing me to whisper in Luke's ear,

'You were supposed to be looking out; somebody is at our front door.'

He jumped up and hurried along the entrance tunnel to peer out, only to see a friendly face of another Red Squirrel speaking in the friendliest voice.

'Haven't seen you in the area before, thought to share some nuts I had stored nearby.' Luke hurried out through the opening, and in no time, they were chatting away like old friends. Felt strange for me to only have to fluff up my coat and do a little preening before creeping out to say 'Hi'.

'This is my mate,' said Luke, pointing to me by way of an intro, well, I suppose I really was his 'mate', as in friend. I hope our new friend didn't assume we had been doing any 'mating', as we didn't yet know how. And Luke would certainly not want to admit to it, I'm quite sure, because that would be private … umm, that felt good, thinking of us having private stuff.

We sat together for a while, chatting and eating Hazelnuts, and we explained we were just visiting from other woodlands, some distance away, near to the old Mill House which he seemed to know quite well, exclaiming,

'I have been that way, but some time ago to visit dear friends who, one might say, are a little different.' Naturally wondering what he meant by 'different', Luke asked him to elaborate, and our friend was keen to explain that he had, over time, befriended a little band of animal folk who had been friends for many years; they often met up for picnics by the mill stream a short distance downstream from the Mill.

With a sideways glance, Luke looked across at me and declared,

'Well now, I wonder who they might be.' Our new friend was quick to add,

'They seem to represent happiness at its best; they play around the Mill House on certain days, with full consent from the miller and his lovely wife. You would love them as friends and they always seem to welcome strangers who might just happen along, as they did with me.'

His story, for obvious reasons, had Luke and me listening to his every word, with a little wondering, I might add, as to how to introduce ourselves into the conversation by admitting our own little secret of actually knowing most of them, so we stayed quiet. He stayed a while, and then decided to leave, calling out with a wave.

'Maybe I'll see you either on the riverbank or at the Mill House sometime, along with those lovely friends I mentioned... and by the way, I'll keep an eye on your 'settle' whilst you're away.'

The difficulty beginning to unfold was obvious; and for sure, Luke would have to be the one to solve a certain riddle regarding two Dipper Birds and a pair of Red Squirrels. Oh, dear, I felt quite muddled, as Luke looked at me and offered the answer,

'Apart from our guise at each and every meeting, we'd best keep all other identities relating to other situations a secret!'

'Sounds sensible Luke,' I offered up with a little relief, I must admit, at finding once more a return to the essential harmony required at all times.

'What about now, Luke? Am I to be something like Squidgy the squirrel and you as Squire?' He paused for a moment, leaving me absolutely convinced I was about to end up as a Squidgy, so I hastily offered up.

'I quite fancy Squat, as I'm smaller than you and you could be Squire, as that sounds important, which you are, to me anyway!' These were moments I really cherished, as they revealed differing aspects of our character, which demonstrated many similarities, in this case humour, so important in the lives of two people together ... when I say humour, Luke remarked,

'I couldn't possibly take an ego-boosting, vanity-promoting important name such as Squire; it implies a somewhat elevated person. How could I possibly be so vain?' Then quickly added,

'Well okay, if it makes you happy, I accept.'

We laughed together, took note of our location with a few landmarks for revisits, and left to head back to base, leaving Squirrel adventures to pick up on later on.

'Come on Squidgy ... sorry, Squat,' Luke called out in fun, 'let's do some climbing, then move through the trees doing branch-to-branch long jumps, umm,' he reflected, 'come to think of it, if we'd been in America, we could have been Flying Squirrels.' I thought to immediately nip that one in the bud with,

'Too late, Squire, best you leave the flying to Dude the Dipper!'

He was obviously not too disappointed at that remark, as, having done a handstand on a branch, he twisted down and over, then headed off to another branch doing a summersault on the way! Then in a girly, demure kind of way, I simply stepped from branch to branch to end up where he waited.

Seeds were sown for other future animal adventures, this time as Red Squirrels, so we headed home.

BACK TO REALITY

Having finally arrived back, still as Red Squirrels, into the outstretched arms of our powerful oak tree, we scurried up to our platform, looked around to check on any activity, and held our tiny little hands, closed our eyes, and reengaged with our human form. That felt nice, as I looked down to see the same pretty dress with a tiny pink flower pattern I had on earlier.

We stayed for a while, which gave me time to tidy round our little pad, thinking to myself, *this feels strangely like a marriage*, as I was doing things my mother would normally do, like tiding beds, sweeping the floor and generally making all 'ship shape'. Luke sat reading a book taken from a shelf on, I noticed, something about building your own boat, prompting me to say,

'That looks interesting, Luke, I wonder what you're up to now?' I continued with a rather ignorant comment bordering on greedy. 'Aren't we supposed to be able to close our eyes and create a boat in our consciousness and there it will be?' His response was straight to the point.

'We cannot go along picturing things, hoping for them to just appear, Freya! Even if such a demanding possibility was possible. In any event, your boat design might be a little wanting, as you have no experience in such things; better I read up on a correct way forward, if only to avoid a vessel to sail away in looking, and acting, like an eventual coffin.'

I felt a little stupid, having received my first 'put down' from my Luke, so I quickly scurried into a humble shell to hide and added in a patronising kind of way,

'Could this be a way of extending our little world to new horizons Luke? It sounds like you have a wonderful idea in mind.'

'That's exactly what I am thinking, Freya, what do you think?' I just smiled so sweetly!

'Well,' he continued, obviously ready to share his little secret,

'Shortly prior to you arriving, I had heard of an island sitting in the middle of a large lake being fed by our stream, before that is, it continues on its way out to sea.'

As always, I somehow knew Luke to be fully capable of the expansion of our world together, but felt so grown up that he should even ask me, so I replied,

'My mind is racing, Luke, with possible trips to a secret island, and, of course, trips to the seaside, why don't we ask Mr. Miller if we could borrow his little boat until you have a chance to build our own? He's such a nice man and is sure to say yes.'

'Need to think about that,' was his response as he pointed out, with a little wondering I suspect, if we would need to visit Bossy Badger, to ask him if he and his friends would be wanting to borrow the boat again for a couple of days. For sure, we did not want to upset our new friends' routine when we morphed into Dippers next time, denying them transport for their little boat trips!

'Best I build our own!' he said, with such conviction and confidence and, which was probably what he had in mind anyway. I dared not ask how, and with what timber?

Luke laboured away for some time in nearby woodland where plenty of fallen trees provided timber, with me providing picnics and tea breaks for times when we would sit and chat away, sitting on a convenient large branch. Using that spark of intelligence I seemed to possess, I asked,

'How do we get the finished boat to the river to begin our new adventure?'

'No problem,' said Luke with his usual confidence and positive outlook on everything; even if he was unsure, I somehow thought, he would never admit it, if only to give me the confidence of being in good hands and, I began to realise, this was not necessarily 'ego', but to make me feel all was just fine. With rapid thinking, he came up with,

'I worked it out before starting. The river is only thirty feet that way,' pointing toward the Mill, 'and I can cut many pieces of large round branches to lay on the ground to roll the boat over, with you picking the pieces up we have passed over, then running around to the front to lay them down for us to continue on until we reach the river's edge.'

'You are amazing, Luke,' I said, with a little wondering if he had just made all that survival stuff up for my benefit and why, in fact, he was not building by the river, which did make sense, even to a mere teenage girl with no such outdoor skills. My guess was that he wanted to work out of sight of the Mill.

The boat was eventually finished, and with a pot of bright blue paint we had ordered when on our very first shopping trip to Mrs. Pope's corner shop, there she was: a fabulous-looking rowing boat, ready to be pushed over the round pieces of wood and down to the stream. I think I could be forgiven by our guiding *Source* for even considering such a thing as failure might exist in Reality as I prayed for Luke's hard endeavours not to be rewarded with any water leaks.

'It's a long way to the eventual sea estuary, Freya,' Luke commented, sitting there scratching his head. 'Do you think we would be moving too fast into a modern way if we just popped a quiet 'outboard motor' on the back? After all, we will have to eventually get a little up to date with some things.' I added my 'two pennies worth', if only to ease any guilt he might be feeling, with,

'We have a train nearby and I saw a taxi at the station, so, why not an outboard motor? In any event, it would take days to make such a long journey if you were rowing, Luke, especially with those oars you have fashioned, you could develop arms like Popeye.' That was my contribution, with a little added fun, but bordering on the truth. 'Why don't we wait until we have reached the river before making the 'out board' happen? It will be less weight to move over all those round logs.'

I loved the levelling up of boy/girl smart thinking; it added to my mental tally of things I could do, not forgetting all that girly power stuff I was being made aware of, which hovers around in boys' minds, keeping them guessing.

'That sounds sensible,' was all I had earned from Luke with my brilliant thinking based on my science lessons relating to 'moving objects', 'velocity ratio' and the like. Actually, glancing discreetly up at that 30-foot distance to the river, any reduction in what needed to be moved would have been welcome to this slip of a girl.

THE CALL OF THE SEA

Early morning arrived in our little tree house, where we had stayed after the short Squirrel adventure. A little tidying around, picnic made ready, and in beautiful sunshine, we were off once more to board our new mode of transport: a bright blue boat, sitting there moored in the mill pond near to the base of our oak tree.

'There she is,' Luke had paused with hands on hips admiring his handy-work. 'Can you see what is mounted on the stern?'

'Sounds very nautical. Luke, do you mean her rear end?'

'Well, of course,' was his swift reply, 'that's boating people's language, and that's just what we now are, and, I might add, with a super little outboard motor. Whilst you were sleeping, I sat quietly by her this morning, with eyes closed, and dreamed of such a thing, knowing if I asked too much, I would surely be given a sign, but there it appeared ... Hop in!'

Keen not to disturb the peace and quiet of the entire setting that we had created, Luke pointed to the engine controls to a switch which stated *'Quiet running for all river work'*.

We were now ready to commence an entirely new adventure, and I couldn't wait.

We steered out and around passed the mill with the engine propeller hardly turning, just sufficient for cruising along the stream, with a quiet *'putt-putt'* sound, hardly audible above the sound of the rippling stream and a breeze drifting through bull rush stem and leaf. Certainly not disturbing the tranquillity, which would surely have included our little animal friends along the riverbank, and with one particular friend in mind, Luke added,

'Can you imagine passing Bossy Badger's home were we making a racket with our boat engine? He'd be looking over his reading glasses whilst reading this month's 'Badger's World', thinking, 'what the hell is that dreadful noise', little would he know, it was two dear friends Dude and Dilly Dipper cunningly disguised as Luke and Freya!'

After a very pleasant journey taking in all the surrounding beauty of the riverbank with grass slopes daring to trespass down into the clear stream, and willow drapes of bright green kissing the water, some much longer trailing with the flow. The perfect setting for an otter resting place to lie, one leg bent up and the other crossed over onto it, front paws behind head, gazing skyward and at ease with the world.

We entered the lake area Luke had mentioned earlier, him pointing to a distant island he had made reference to.

'Let's leave the island adventure for another day,' he commented, so we journeyed on, eventually arriving at the estuary, at which point, our quite wide stream met the sea. It all appeared as a new, magnificent, exciting scene that went on forever as we gazed seaward to the horizon.

'What lies beyond that line?' Luke fired this quite profound question at me as I gazed in awe at such a permanent friendship in my *Reality* of sky meeting sea. Keen to let him know I had been paying attention earlier, I quickly changed my dreamy outlook to Reality, and with the Mill owners' front door in mind, I answered,

'Absolutely nothing … until we make it so!' He glanced my way with a smile as if to acknowledge I had been paying attention and replied,

'Great to see you have understood the magic of you and me creating this wonder world. I think, as mentioned, we should forget the

'Alness' beyond that line of the horizon, until we are up to higher levels of dreaming; I'm sure we will be led to know when we are ready.'

'Suits me,' I volunteered, not yet having fully taken in all the wonders to date and remembering I had already begun to dream of my next return journey to see my mum which would hopefully be across that sea on a 'wind surf' board, with a pink sail you may remember.

In the meantime, there were rock pools, caves, and shoreline adventures to be explored.

'We'll pull our boat up onto that sandy beach just beyond the 'high tide' line, seen at the top of the beach so as not to lose our little blue friend. Hopefully there will be no 'high tide' today.'

As always, Luke was there with sensible suggestions which my inexperienced mind would not have considered; after all, we did need the boat to return to our lovely home territory!

We spent time exploring rock pools and peering under seaweed for exciting marine discoveries, with each discovery, for some strange reason, not darting off to hide, almost implying this creation was devoid of predators waiting to catch and eat you. So unlike the Earth somewhere over there beyond that horizon, where devious *scammers* and *hackers* increase by the day, one of them catching Jeni's dad for his last few pounds he had saved and spent on a new school bag for her ... it never arrived!

'That looks interesting,' Luke called to me, pointing to a cave opening some way off just crying out to be explored. We hopped into our new little blue boat, headed for a piece of shore quite near to the entrance, and pulled our little friend, safely up onto dry sand beyond that 'tide line' ... well, actually, Luke 'pulled' and I pretended to push!

We wandered in and, having gazed up at what appeared a high vaulted cathedral interior, we found ourselves climbing higher and higher, simply lost in the moment of adventure. The driving force that pushed us onward and upward revealed to us as what appeared as a small opening high up with a shaft of sunshine visible, coming from somewhere way above. However, there was another 'driving force' I seemed to have overlooked as we climbed: I noticed, having glanced down to where we had wandered up from, the sea had moved quite near to the cave entrance further along from where our little blue friend was resting safely, well, so I hoped. In my attempts to raise those hopes of us not being trapped forever in a dark cave when the sun went down, I asked.

'Do you think,' I said pointing up toward that ray of sun light, 'that opens up onto a beautiful meadow above the bay?' Nervously said, as I followed Luke up, not daring to mention the fact that we were being pursued by waves that drown 'rooky' cave adventurers!

'Only one way to find out, Freya,' he replied, 'let's keep going.' Clearly lost in a new adventure, his levels of fear had dropped away, and mine had increased tenfold, so I nervously responded,

'This looks awfully high, Luke,'... having again dared to glance downward to check on sea levels, and added what I thought to be a tempter with 'what say we head down urgently, to enjoy our picnic before the cave entrance is closed by the incoming tide?'

At that very moment, what to me seemed like a life saver appeared by way of a small passageway going off to our left, a bit dark, but we could see bright sunlight at the end shining in from the outside.

Strange how one feeling of total fear can be eased with an alternative dangerous situation on offer, you see, I felt relieved at being presented with an alternative... like being able to crawl horizontally along a tunnel toward the sunlight, at least, no longer heading upward to that first higher light source we had spotted on entering the cave. We simply had to be heading for an opening out onto a sunny meadow above the bay. Attracted by not having to make that first climb in the opposite direction ... like downward ... with friendly sunlight on offer, we crawled along this dark tunnel, which eventually opened up into a large cavern, lighted from above by a large opening, which sadly appeared out of reach. In the middle of this cavernous discovery was a small lagoon area full of crystal-clear water. Luke, so sensibly, put one finger into the water, licked it, his finger that is, and declared,

'Rainwater, that's good, it must be fed through that opening above along with surface water percolation.' This presented me with a great opportunity to also show intelligence as I added,

'Well! If we become stranded, at least we will have fresh water! Had it been seawater, wouldn't that imply, based on how high we are, there'd been a 'tsunami' recently?' Luke, having thought about that for a moment, went a little quiet with just an 'umm'. My growing love for him increased ... because he's not perfect!

We had stumbled on such a beautiful cavern with walls covered in green moss and rare small wild flowers around its entire periphery, each facing the centre to benefit from the light source shining through that above opening, friendly sun rays, with the power to make each blossom face its opposite friend across the way over crystal-clear water, reflecting each to the other... beauty times two.

There were crags around, leading almost up to that beckoning opening above, which Luke had already begun to explore in the hope of finding a way out, finally declaring with some confidence,

'There are some large what appear tree roots near the entrance, which, with a run and jump ... I might just be able to reach to pull myself out with.' That sounded encouraging, to a boy that is, but to a delicate, blossoming young girl in a pretty summer dress, blending nicely with the flowers that surrounded her, it was as 'chalk and cheese'.

In such a short period in my life, where back at school I would still be struggling through algebra, I had experienced being a budding teen, a Dipper bird, Red Squirrel, a home-maker [well trying], a teenage girl about to befriend little fish, and now an intrepid rock climber heading for the stars with, I might add, an overpowering desire to get my feet back on the sand!

'Why can't we morph into a couple of 'bats' Luke? We could head out, then change back to us lovely people, one of them who is scared stiff right now.' A slight grey mist began to form, which Luke spotted and called back.

'Don't worry ... just a gentle warning notice to point out that we cannot journey through Reality using that gift 'willy-nilly' to solve problems we ourselves have created, or, in this case ... what I have created, not you. In any event, it might have a little something to do with you calling your Miss Brown 'an old bat' and nearly drowning her!' A guilty look came over my face, but I dared to smile as I reflected on Miss Brown sitting there in the pond, struggling with her modesty. Luke continued,

'If an emergency arises, we'll be fine, I think I've solved the problem.' I looked up, only to see Luke make a dive for a large tree root stretching partly across the entrance, and there he was, my hero trapeze artist, pulling himself out and calling down to me.

'You were right, Freya; it is a beautiful sunny meadow overlooking the bay.' *Well, that's fine,* I thought, *but what about me?*

'Try to climb around those crags as I did; they are quite safe. I can then lean down and take your hand to pull you up.' So, I did and could not even nearly reach his welcoming hand, a hand that looked so reassuring and strong but was unable to bring us together again. I returned to the cavern floor and sat cross-legged with tears in my eyes, feeling lost and alone, trapped in a heavenly place surrounded by such beauty, but all I could think of was me, alone... separated from my friend, to die, alone, cold and hungry ... with my picnic sandwiches going stale!

Suddenly there was an almighty splash as Luke landed in the lagoon. He was smiling as he headed for the side where I sat, and although a bit wet, to say the least, he was back, and fear left me. It had become all boy's things, and I felt hopeless as a girl in circumstances outside of my control; no survival training, lost for ideas, and solutions, what to do?

I had to accept that chasm in certain areas between boy's and girl's things and desperately searched my mind for anything to equal up this divide. Then, from my little mental pink box tied up in pretty ribbon, I took out a solution, something delicate, with finesse and light years from this madness. I discreetly undid two top buttons of my floral dress, and then, to help him out, leant forward as far as I could without falling in.

All my wonders had been reinstated; his manly hand was once more wrapped around my small delicate white hand, that kind of thing. And I felt safe, the entire act garnished by his discreet glance at a maiden's delicacies by way of form, [actually two 'forms'] partly hidden in pretty fabric, far removed from old crags, muddy tree roots, and slippery slopes more suited to commando training. Luke had taken the bait and made the acknowledging comment,

'Well, that made my return worthwhile, which, actually, I did notice to a lesser degree, whilst looking down from up there, causing me to lean further and further forward, which was the very reason I fell in.' I simply smiled, as would have those 'cool', more experienced girls back at school, with not a word said as I glanced across at the small entrance we had arrived through, almost signalling our next move. I granted him a small trophy by way of a quiet, somewhat phony, '*whoops*' as I put chin to chest to do up my top buttons.

All felt equal once more, and I had found something to dwell on, in my tiny, ever busy mind, relating to the power of the sun, which could make hidden flowers look in certain directions, and the power I attributed to myself, bringing my Luke crashing down with noise and cascades of clear water rising, which in turn invited in a spectacular guest by way of a mini rainbow. In a quick attempt to drive out my silly mind games and rising ego, I asked,

'What to do Luke... you will know?'

He made a quick decision, adding some comfort by pointing out,

'Let's not get alarmed, Freya, we are not pushed for time and have several hours of daylight left. We must re-trace our movements, so follow me, back along the tunnel, which, don't forget, we have already managed once.'

We eventually reached the point on our first climb where we could see once more that higher sunlit entrance, but to my horror glancing down, the sea was there in greater strength, eating up the cave entrance, surely inviting us in, and we were not dressed for such bathing amongst rocks, sharks, and restless waves! Luke began once more to climb, offering up such encouragement for me with,

'Up we go, it's not far now, Freya; we'll soon be out!'

Just as I was beginning to think *I simply want to be a girl again ... to lie on that sunny meadow grass with Luke's arms around me,* he called back.

'Wait till you see this,' having spotted yet another sunny enticement off to the left, 'it's as though we have been led to a royal box for the command performance of a play called 'Heaven lies before us'.' *Not a bad 'end game'* I thought, until I entered that 'royal box' and stood in a small area with a low rock up-stand creating that balcony appearance Luke had conjured up in his mind.

My fear levels as I looked down this time reached a point, where I needed to lie down below the small rock up-stand or, I am quite sure, I would have fainted and fallen over it! You see, we had obviously climbed a great distance, and this particular 'royal box', was far up on a sheer rock face overlooking the bay. All around were nesting birds on 'crooks' and 'crannies', all seemingly looking at us, probably trying to work out what large wingless species we were.

There below, sat our beautiful little friend in blue, appearing in scale no bigger than a matchbox, with, I might add, what just had to be a high tide about to reach that very thing that could carry us safely home to a table with gingham cloth [in matching blue] and cakes thereon.

My exciting, grown-up, girly dreaming back in the last cavern was short lived as I laid low in fear, like a child wondering what on Earth was to become of us ... and to highlight my emotional falling apart, I cried out to Luke,

'But I thought everything here in 'Reality' was harmonious, and safe!'

By this time, our bonding became obvious, as he knelt down beside me, raising me into his arms, wiping my tears away with his by now grubby shirt sleeve, at which point I somehow knew all was okay, with a feeling of once again being safe, albeit with a grubby shirt sleeve as reassurance! You see ... he quickly brought everything back into focus for me with,

'Don't ever lose faith in 'Reality', lovely Freya, you are safe, and everything *is* harmonious. You simply allowed your mind to get the better of you with Earthly fears, which do not apply here.' I quickly added.

'Well do tell, my lovely friend, what is the solution this time, one that will bring us once again to a safe place ... and by the way, did you know, sea levels in the cave below have been following us up and, rising fast, which I didn't want to scare you with?'

'Keeping that to yourself, Freya, was pretty brave and thoughtful ... how on Earth did you manage that? Anyway, how shall we get you down ... any ideas?' He paused to allow my heart rate time to drop a little below 150 bpm, then, once more putting the entire situation back into my hands posed the question, 'what do you think would be helpful to get us down from up here?' Having dared to once more peer over the parapet with our nesting neighbours continuing to stare, I suggested, with just a hint of light-hearted sarcasm,

'I suppose a pair of wings might help.'

'And?' He responded, obviously implying I was missing something. Suddenly the penny dropped, and I looked up at him, while still lying down in total fear and declared…

'You're surely not thinking of 'Dippers' are you, and from this height? Might be easier to try climbing back down those slippery rocks at the end of the tunnel, prior, that is, to possibly falling down onto rocks and deep seawater below, to drown or at best be eaten by those sharks!' He eased my somewhat over-dramatized fear with.

'I do love you more when you do your amateur dramatics bit, said with smile one might expect from a film director having spotted a somewhat bad 'take'. 'We have tried our best and have had lessons on overcoming fear without applying our given gift to save ourselves. Try to see this adventure as extremes in *Reality* which will always have happy endings. Life is not always composed of walking by quiet streams and pretty wildflower meadows ... we will be fortified from now on, knowing there is always an answer!'

A good time, I thought, *for a very welcome tutorial*, as I quickly reflected back on how I had handled it all; *not bad*, I thought, with a couple of teary moments and extreme fears, but I had regained my prowess as a woman in the cavern, and I felt good about that! In the meantime, coming back to fear and possible 'death' following a 200 foot 'free fall' jump, possibly with that God source having taken a tea break. Luke's answer came,

'Birds are birds, Freya, and they fly, so if from the top of our Oak tree then why not from here?'

Well, of course, he was right, but this time it almost felt as if we were up in the clouds or the top of a certain building back there near Bridge St., Central London 'The Shard'.

Peering over once more, my eyes quickly scanned the surrounding rock faces at a sea of bird faces looking at me, all, I'm sure, smiling, as they eagerly awaited a spectacle about to take place. My eyes then moved from nearby smiling birds to a downward glance at such a pretty blue boat, so tiny as if in a scene from 'Gulliver's Travels'. My heart once more missed a beat as I said in an appealing kind of way,

'Can we really do this, Luke?' And, as always, his reassurance came; he lifted me up close to him saying, 'you did say the sea levels had risen greatly, so it's not as far down now.' *Oh great!* I thought ... *what a time for 'funnies'*.

'Please remember, Freya, you are safe. Now promise me you will keep your eyes on me, until with eyes closed, I say 'Jump' and do not look down, I repeat, do not look down! Try to imagine our launching as if it were from our Oak tree, ruling out any differences in the height.'

Not asking much then ... my mind reminded me of the difference between a 20 and 200 foot fall, not forgetting the time it might take. We stood together so close, and in total trust I followed his lead and carefully stepped up onto the parapet, with a little swaying as a gust of wind came off the sea, as the countless surrounding birds strained their necks to improve their view. I really do believe my heart stopped at this point as fear came back in good measure as we both closed our eyes. I wobbled a little with imbalance, knowing that to my left there was something firm, and to my right, there was absolutely nothing but space and the wind blowing. As that romantic saying 'the fresh smell of the sea air' left me, Luke called out,

'We are 'Dippers', have faith in your safety, Freya, now... 'jump!' So, we did, and feelings of weightlessness and the rush of air over my face really did take my breath away. As I continued falling, I knew I had failed; it's surprising what rushes through your mind when, at such a young age, you think you are about to die. I thought of my Ma, our safe little tree house with the table covered in gingham cloth [blue], and Luke and my togetherness, all about to be lost. Suddenly Luke, slightly below me, called out.

'Have no fear, He is ever near; close your eyes' (I'd already done that!) 'now spread your wings and fly ... now!'

Probably as a direct result of being shouted at, I did, and sure enough, those arms were now Dipper wings outstretched, and we were gliding safely down together.

Relentless in his attempts to keep me safe and instil confidence in this wonderful new world, he called across.

'You have to believe, Freya -- you have been given total control, you must believe this at all times... I'll show you, follow me.' We swept around in a large circle over the bay, apparently in order to be facing our friendly little blue boat sitting there totally unaware of the crazy happenings since the three of us were last together, appearing quite unconcerned at being gathered up by that 'High tide' soon to be bobbing about on the sea. Continuing to make his point on 'complete control', Luke suggested.

'We'll get to about three feet above the waves, slow down, and close our eyes,' which we did ... he then asked me to say out loud 'This is silly, humans can't fly,' so I did, and with an almighty... 'Splash', I was in the sea, not too far from the boat, once more as Freya. As always, there was Luke, heading my way in Olympic swimming style, calling out.

'Head for the boat sitting there in the sunshine, she's not far.'

Strange, how we see things. From so high up, with someone as fearful as me, and death beckoning, a little blue wooden boat felt like a dearest friend I so yearned to be with again. Now she was there, almost touchable, to save us and take us home. How can something without life have the power to exude safe and friendly feelings simply sitting there doing nothing?

With our lifesaving Dipper guise now gone, we climbed aboard, Luke first, after which he pulled me up into our dear little boat, which was by now beginning to sit in an upright attitude and just beginning to fully float on the rising tide.

We sat for a while to dry off, which seemed to take forever in the pose I had adopted, hands between my legs and a little hunched up, having noticed, being so wet, my cotton dress had suddenly become completely transparent and was clinging to my body like 'clear film'! Luke, always so discreet, looked to be struggling to find something to say, then, the only subject matter, which at that moment seemed at the forefront of both our minds, prompted him, having made an honest unrehearsed observation, to say,

'You better not stand up, Freya ... Are you wearing anything under that dress?' He had obviously made his first spotting of *secret things* and did seem a little lost for words on the boy/girl differences!

I smiled in an honest, coy kind of way, and replied,

'Next time we must bring a couple of towels. If we could sit here for a while, Luke, all will be quite respectable in no time as my clothes dry off ... don't worry.'

I began to ponder on the fact that I, at least, had had to endure those 'human biology' lessons, spelling out the differing body parts, whereas Luke had been created by my dreamy 'consciousness' imaginings of a lovely guy, and I think he was obviously pleasantly unschooled in such basic things ... so unlike my brief mobile phone tutorials forced under my nose back there! It all took Luke to such a high level of, shall we say, an untarnished, honourable, somehow beyond reproach type of a character.

Although unaware why, he must have sensed my shame and embarrassment, and he was having none of it.

'Nobody in sight, Freya, please don't huddle up in shame like that, stand up and be proud of yourself, as will I be, gazing at the wonders of you!' Seems we had much to learn in so many areas, but I loved it, the whole affair was magnificent, secret, for his eyes only, a million miles from smutty things and the degradation of budding youthfulness; this was me, standing all but naked, and the sun shone, and my dress was revealing every secret I had always to believe to be so.

How this guy could be so above it all in the things he saw, did, and said, I really did wonder. So, I stood, and he looked, and to avoid me having to linger on in my almost statuesque nakedness, he took me in his arms and declared.

'Thank you for sharing what appears as such uncomplicated perfect profile girls obviously have; these things really do have an effect on one's emotions, don't they?'

As if knowing exactly what was required, he dived into the cold sea once more, only to surface alongside the boat with arms and chin resting on her side, declaring.

'Now I feel normal again!' Not sure what that meant, so I coyly sat down, no longer hunched, and left the topic.

That feeling of being special had resurfaced as I again became aware, girls without realising it when growing up possessed secret things boys dreamed of learning about.

Poor Luke, I thought, *he takes it all in his stride, but he, as with me, must surely also be stirring inside with yearnings so new to us both!*

The constant dwelling on the fringe of boy/girl emotional wonders was always going to continue to develop I suppose ... slowly moving away from that 'fringe', inward toward a wondrous centre point to be enjoyed in full where two seekers become one. Strange how 'guilt' hovers ever near, but why? What is the rule my mind wrestles with, as I question the sense pleasures that all, apparently, are given, only to find shame creeps in during the journey of discovery and investigation? Almost like a child being given a 'lollypop' then getting a clip for licking it!

Were such things put there simply for us to learn to override the 'temptation'... if so, wouldn't it have been easier to leave it out of the divine plan in the first place, at least avoiding all those 'clips' around the ear? Or, should we all avoid the matter completely and seek only an inner journey of discovery like monks, nuns, yogis, etc? *I bet they think of such things, too,* I pondered. ... The answer must relate to age, where good behaviour is reasonable, I suppose.

I was becoming aware that no grey mists were forming as yet with Luke and me, as we teetered on that 'fringe', so, we would move on in our journey of discovery without guilt, I suppose. Luke, gazing so peacefully said,

'Sitting there with your chin resting in your hands looking seaward looks quite dreamy, Freya. Are you having happy thoughts?' I did love the caring way he said such things, almost appearing unaware of my inner searching and emotional stirrings; or was he?

This entire journey was, I had to recognise, a wonderful one to be gifted with. How many in my age group back there, I wondered, would be taking part in such a scene as this, Luke in the sea, leaning with chin and arms resting on the boat side, me sitting, elbows on my knees, chin in hands, both working it all out? Back home it would be all fun and games going on. Albeit so young, I was happy knowing somehow we were easing toward the right place.

With Luke by now back on board, I repositioned myself onto the front small seat facing forward to take in the view, also, if I'm really honest … to hide the little remaining embarrassment until I had dried off a little more.

HOMEWARD BOUND

With our little outboard motor turned up to 'Open-Water Mode', we made our way along the coastline, gazing down into crystal clear water, no more than 1.5M deep. Small fish darting here and there with such purpose, we hoped not in fear of us. We sat quietly, cruising along without talking for a while, I guess just reminiscing on the events of a day, which after all, had been full of adventure and somewhat contrasting excitements to say the least.

Luke steered us into the peaceful river estuary, changed the motor setting to the 'Quiet Running' mode, with the return of that rather pleasant 'putt-putt' sound ... taking us home.

We surely needed to keep clear heads regarding 'Reality', as so many facets were unfolding, by way of my visits home, Dippers, Squirrels, a beautiful butterfly, Luke and I as people and more, or we might well lose our way in such a contrasting lifestyle.

I thought to talk it through with Luke in such quiet contemplative surroundings, and, apart from feeling quite good about that new word 'contemplative' I had learned, I broached the subject with him as we journeyed home, by asking,

'Should we begin to formulate a lifestyle plan Luke?' This was my opening comment on a matter he had clearly been considering himself, as he came back so quickly with his response.

'Good, you are looking ahead from a harmony point of view, I quite agree, and thought best we formulate a plan that works for all; after all, our little riverside friends will by now be wondering what became of us; we became such trusting friends and everybody needs friends sometimes. Not forgetting the very pleasant Red Squirrel who watches over our little 'settle' ... any ideas?' he asked.

As we travelling quietly along in our little boat, I began thinking and made the not very well-thought-out, somewhat naive suggestion.

'Could we perhaps allocate a certain period for each situation?' Luke put his head in his hands and peered at me through his partly opened fingers then looked up at me, raising his arms in the air and, with such a smile on his face, declared something that made me realise, dear Luke was also learning certain wonders, and I really did have to stop so unfairly thinking he knew it all!

He had a way of teaching me by posing a question, then asking me to state the obvious answer, which, based on the nature of the question did usually seem, as I say, obvious. So, with a continuing smile, having put his hand quickly back on the boat's small 'tiller', which steered the boat, as we did appear to have been wandering a bit, he declared.

'When you return to your home back there, what becomes obvious immediately when your Ma calls out to you?' As expected, the penny dropped as, with such joy, I realised what we had both overlooked, which was the most important feature of 'Reality' in that time stands still for us between what can only be described as various manifestations in our dreamy world.

'I know!' I declared, as it became obvious that there really wasn't in fact any problem to be solved, and felt so proud to be able to say to him.

'Whenever, like whenever, we become, say, Dippers again, our friends will have no awareness of time passing, so, it will be as if we just popped away for a while, as would be the case with our Red Squirrel friend.'

'You got it!' Came Luke's response ... such a major point missed; I feel quite silly!

'I guess we simply need to formulate a plan between ourselves, like some kind of that allocation of our lives you mentioned to each part to play out, as it were. Or we can simply act as the mood takes us on any action we are both happy with.'

We arrived back at our welcoming Oak tree, tied up 'Mini Blue Bird' (that's what we decided to call her), and headed up to our tree home. Then, as do all grownups back there, we put the kettle on and sat to chat over a mug of tea, running through some ideas on that plan.

There wasn't really much to say, as Luke in his quiet contemplative manner did what he does so easily, bringing back an easiness that felt so right for 'Reality' as he pondered and finally came up with.

'I think we have agreed; we don't really need a plan, Freya. This would be introducing a restrictive routine of those lovely events; better we let things unfold in an easy kind of way, just letting our feelings guide us. After all, nobody else knows our secret world, so why not, within reason, do, and become, whatever we choose, whenever we choose?

'What's wrong with being a Dipper bird that flies up from the edge of the stream, then across flowery meadows, slows to that *stall* speed I mentioned, a quick morphing then, as a Butterfly, settle on the most beautiful flower in that meadow... It will all take practice, but what joy, to drift from one lovely apparition to another, isn't this what 'Reality' should be?

'Most people back there have dreamed, in troubled moments, of being free as a bird on the wing, unruffled by human affairs; maybe gazed at a trout in fast-running, crystal-clear shallow waters, hovering there seemingly untroubled, totally unaware of the unsettling agenda in the onlooker's world.'

'Well, that sums that up then!' was all I could add, as I became once more aware of the wonder of what I had found, plus the realisation that I was, although blessed, still a beginner, and Luke, I needed to remind myself, had a certain 'Dougie' with a degree of past spiritual awareness to turn to within for guidance when unsure. I felt led to say.

'Thank you, Luke, if nothing else, you brought back the realisation that I have been so blessed whilst so young to find 'Reality'. I have read of fairies only seen by children, based on their untainted innocence, but I was almost a teen when I managed to find such wonders. Why, Luke?' I thought to ask.

'There are many like you back there, Freya, who somehow know there are wonders to be found somewhere. It begins to show in the person by way of a disliking for dishonesty, greed, selfishness and, of course, at your age at the time, being averse to the degrading and sullying of natural growing up matters.'

'What is 'averse'?' I thought to ask ... to add to my little book of new words with such meaning I was keen to remember; after all, I was racing away from youth, and much grown-up conversation was now entering my life – that was for sure.

''Unwillingness' would probably sum up the word,' was Luke's reply. 'Just be happy to know yours, like all other youth actions and thoughts were, and always will be, being watched over by a Higher Source; your friend Jeni proved to be another close to that Source. If only all youth could understand, all actions and thoughts are known! Most, if not all of them, should be enjoying without shame, without sullying all areas of puberty, as it all forms part of the growing-up process.'

It was nice to get back into focus on the wonder I had found, so easy to drift along, taking it all for granted; I felt uplifted to a point, I'm sure, that was totally in keeping with 'Reality', and in a moment, had, quite alone, become what my Heart desired!

Luke, assuming I had gone into the next room to change, called out,

'Freya, look at this!' No answer came from me, and he wondered.

I was sitting as a beautiful Butterfly once more on an open page of a book he had been reading. I opened my wings and spread them across the page as I gazed up at my hero, completely amazed, like … 'gob-smacked', he quietly said.

'You did that all on your own … is that really you, Freya?' I opened my wings and closed them before once again settling with them spread wide open, as if in total submission. Luke placed his open hand down beside me, and I stepped onto the palm; I then flew up and out of the open window. This was 'Reality', all so wonderful, I glanced back as I flew, and will never forget what can only be described as the wonder of Love.

The look on his face, were I Freya, would have had me shedding tears of joy and sadness. He had a look of possibly losing someone close as I flew. Feelings of loss are deep and hurting, and I could see those very emotions there in his eyes with tears welling up.

I continued up and away, as if selfishly needing to increase his hurting over me; each passing selfish moment felt necessary to prove to myself how much he cared! Then, that selfishly imposed hurt on someone caused the scene to begin to mist over, even the beautiful colours of my wings began to fade, and I knew I was abusing something or somebody, and could so easily be denied my Luke and all my dreamy gifts given. I flew through the mist and quickly back through my open bedroom window of our Loving home and, immediately re-morphed into Freya, quietly slipped on a pretty dress and peered into our homely little room, only to see Luke still gazing skyward from the window with tears running down his cheek.

'Hi Luke,' I called out, 'I did that all on my own, what about that?' He eagerly turned to look my way, saying,

'I guessed you had,' trying to hide his eyes, 'I'm so glad you didn't lose your focus and become lost to us all here, we would have really missed you!' That statement came crashing home, as I recalled my frailties when jumping from that cliff and realised how much I really did need my Luke with me and that we should grow and do things together, which was clearly the intended way since the moment I arrived at 'Reality'. He did what he did so well and covered my somewhat hurtful action with praise.

'I'm so proud of you, Freya; you managed with an uplifted Heart to act out our dream... and all alone.'

The very word 'alone' struck home, and I ran into his arms, a bit like a romantic movie, I suppose, but without the lifting of a shoe clad foot behind me, and declared for the first time in my young years.

'I love you, Luke, and I give myself to you completely and forever, body and soul.' Said quietly, it didn't sound too much like that *hammy* Hollywood drama student at work.

He fumbled around a bit, still trying to hide the earlier sadness I had inflicted on him, and he was demonstrating no anger whatsoever, only absolute humility, responding.

'I feel so lucky to hear you commit yourself to me in such a way.' Still wiping his eyes with his cuff, he took me in his arms and that slight tearful demonstration, which might have been seen by some as a weakness, disappeared as he took control of the emotional chemistry that now consumed us both. Everything was changing. I suddenly felt smaller in stature, with him taller and stronger embracing me so tightly and so very close, a closeness with evidence that left me feeling as if in forbidden territory, and I loved every moment.

I was about to speak, as if looking for answers of what was beginning to take control of me, by way of a glowing sensations low in my tummy and a surrendering weakness to give myself to him without knowing at that stage what to give.

Luke always had the answers, but this time he was demonstrating without words, and I somehow knew he too was feeling similar new things stirring. He placed one finger over my lips, and I knew my place. He moved his lips forward and kissed me, so soft and gently, no rush, no nervousness, just an easy way that almost made my legs buckle. We were obviously moving into a wonderland together albeit with emotional differences -- his, and mine -- we were physically different, but equal in power, each in turn overpowering the other, merging into mutual uncontrollable joy!

We fell back onto his bed, still embracing so tightly that I felt an absolute oneness with him, as we had never been so close. I think we were both lost for the first time in something wonderful, a little frightening, and increasing in sensual power, with me under him, legs far from close together, and for some strange reason I didn't care!

Then, a little of that very essential 'fear' crept into my senses and, for some reason, I thought of my Ma back home, and all the guidance given to me without her being too explicit, and I called out,

'I'm just sixteen, Luke, should we be doing this?' Luke responded immediately, telling me he too had realised we were being a bit naughty, and so soon after we had met to begin a new life. We stood up together, adjusted our clothes and embraced so tightly with such joy as if to demonstrate a mutual consent of our actions, although both probably feeling a bit embarrassingly denied, but happy for very good reason, which felt amazingly encouraging and condoning!

We both sat holding hands on his bed once more, discussing, apart from such joy made possible, the fact was that we both realised the room had not misted over. After all, we had been playing almost limited degrees of life's games. We both knew then, for sure, at some time, the right time, we would be fully 'at one', and I would be taken to that unknown place that seemed to be arising in my thoughts more and more as time passed. Amazing how greed will so often rear its ugly head when one has found enjoyment. I began to consider, what with no mist appearing during those so secret and consuming togetherness moments of boy and girl, how much further could we have taken that enjoyment prior to promoting a *grey mist* to form. *It went a little misty!*

Having allowed our emotions to settle, we climbed to our tree top platform and continued to play our game of life. We held hands, closed our eyes, thought 'Dippers', and dived outward. In seconds we were in cool fresh air flight, together, just drifting around the skies, then down along the Mill stream, eventually to stop, bathe naked with white breasts exposed ... no need for shame!

The hurried morphing into the 'Dipper' world did seem a good idea, as for sure we both needed to allow emotions to calm, even the thoughts arising from that encounter, which bordered on some unknown physical union, was exciting to ponder over, so, us taking flight had steered the mind well away from exciting imaginings.

'I'm so happy, Luke,' I blurted out, 'will this be forever?' His answer came so to the point.

'Why don't we make it so? After all, that will make it unchallengeable by any person, or situation; it couldn't be diminish by even one particle.' Apart from bordering on 'atomic', that seemed to imply some foreverness!

It seemed a good idea to visit our Dipper home under the bridge; it always seemed so welcoming there, and, as Luke had previously pointed out, Dippers will often frequent the same nesting site down through generations, recorded as sometimes being as long as 120 years!

We arrived, tidied around by patting some newly obtained and existing moss by way of soft furnishings, and settled back. We were surrounded once more by those beautiful, coloured reflections moving around on the bridge underside. No need for much conversation; we simply watched the swallows diving down to skim over the mill pond surface, leaving just a hint of the broken surface, evidence of their insect catching skills.

Luke leant forward to gaze across the summer day silent water and point out our little blue boat to make a quite special comment.

'Seeing the swallow skimming over the water, leaving that trail, reminds me of an English man I have learned of who broke the world speed record in a boat he had spent almost his entire adult life trying to perfect.'

'What's the point you are making, Luke?' I thought to ask for some clarity.

'I guess you probably don't know many boats, Freya; have a guess at that boat's name.' Looking at our little blue saviour friend, just sitting there bobbing up and down, which Luke had clearly been looking at a few minutes' prior, I made my guess, "Blue Bird' which inspired you to choose 'Mini Blue' for our boat.'

'Well done!' said Luke, with a smile, 'how on earth did you possibly guess that.'

'Oh, I just read it on the boat down there.' That made him laugh, as he explained.

'I chose the name out of respect for a very brave man who lost his life on the lake Coniston, pushing those speed limits ever upward.'

'That's tragic, and very sad, Luke,' was all I could think to say, as such things don't mean a lot to a teenage girl, but I had to admit, I had witnessed Luke himself pushing ever upward in that seaside cave, which I did wonder about. Do all boys do that, or was that just another side of the male, an inherent driving force to win?

I was just happy to be back looking at life going on around the Mill; it offered everything, including Luke's fascination with speed, as two swallows zoomed under the bridge, causing me to look down in wonderment at a flash of deep blue, punctuated with little red caps on their heads ... friends just passing by. In a moment, there was a transition from such speed to tranquillity as my eyes focussed on a small area of clear water which, having missed the main water flow through the bridge, circled around to the side of the bridge's stone buttress in a small swirling eddy, as if awaiting the 'rite of passage' to greater things, surely to include the tiny trout resting there in passive water!

'When did you paint our lovely blue boat's name on her side, Luke?' I asked as I continued to gaze downward, 'you gave her such dignity by naming her; she deserves that recognition.'

'It seemed like fun, Freya. I did it early, when you were sleeping. I thought to paint it on both sides, in order that all little creatures on both the riverbanks will get to know us. I made the words in dark blue to match, after all she does have lovely bodywork, a bit like you, Freya.'

Such a cheeky quip, which seemed to endorse, apart from my bodywork, our developing friendship. I smiled without comment, side stepping the almost mandatory girly giggle, surely expected of a sixteen-year-old girl when paid a hidden compliment. Was I growing up too quickly? Maybe I should have giggled … what's wrong with giggling? That easy, confident smile I had just demonstrated was probably a direct result of that amazing grown-up tryst we had shortly before experienced in our tree top home. As always, Freya was working it all out again. Was such a silly thing worth pondering over? I just wanted to grow up at the normal recognised rate. I tried again and albeit somewhat belated, 'giggled', adding.

'Lovely bodywork … that's nice of you, Luke.' That made him smile, as if his somewhat inexperienced humour had been appreciated by a girl. Clearly, we were those 'rookies' playing the game of life; most modern girls back there would have probably responded with something along the lines of 'what do you mean 'Bodywork'... I'm on two legs not four wheels." In this, my case, it wasn't anything 'old' ... it was new, and blue, and most beautiful!

A peaceful day passed, with us just looking, as birds do, with Luke occasionally leaving to fly upstream, low above the water surface until settling on a half-submerged rock... a place to settle, to *Dip* up and down, as Dippers do. On his last trip of the day, he returned as if from the market with needs for the home, this time his 'big shop' was by way of home comforts, by way of a beak full of more soft dried moss.

We both busied around to make all ready for the night, finally settling down in a feathery bundle to sleep and dream. Strange, how the sound of water rippling under our home seemed sacred to the nighttime life of the wild, a constantly changing sound, unknown to the composer's pen, broke the silence of the surrounding quiet woodland and meadows. Then, as if to highlight the moment, the divine 'composer' introduced the call of a night owl as an accompaniment to fading dancing water reflections on a ceiling as darkness crept in, telling of time to sleep!

TRAVERSING TIME

I woke to the sound of a knock on my bedroom door with my Ma calling to me, a strong reminder that I was just a teenage girl and 'Reality' was taking me beyond limitations not only in certain mannerisms, but a somewhat accelerated growing-up in all areas of understanding. The 'parallel universes' were slipping apart.

Unlike my previous visits home, which were planned with my Luke, this transition had taken place during Dipper sleep, and as I awoke, I desperately tried to understand and found myself grasping at answers to ease my panic, even to the point of almost rushing across my room to my landscape of '*Reality*' to re-engage! Then my little voice called to me to 'Stop and think', I needed to focus my Heart, knowing '*Reality*' was there for me forever, and would be sitting, waiting, with the exact feelings as when I had left her.

I had need to gather myself, as living in two worlds was always going to be a matter for me alone to deal with. I did notice on previous home runs, it all seemed to go very smoothly, as I suppose it would, after all, this was higher consciousness unfolding, so it follows it was sure to be harmonic! The call from Ma came again.

'Time for school, Freya, it's getting late. Have you completed your art homework by the way?' I had, completed my art homework that is, and recalled one area of it that had referred to 'parallel' and 'perspective' lines, which had me considering that two lines can be 'parallel' but they don't necessarily have to be growing in length at the same rate, or in fact, remain at the same distance apart.

I couldn't wait to re-group with my Luke, to tell of my theory; after all, it was a recognition that *'Reality'* was obviously going to grow progressively more in all directions, thus becoming more attractive to me as time went on, ever posing the question: at what point would I want to shed my Earthly ties and move on to dwell permanently in that, my world of 'Reality'? After all, what more could anyone wish for? The very word *'Reality'* sums it up, as the place where anyone would surely wish to be?

I dressed and ran down the stairs, with a reminder being called out,

'You're going to be late!'

I had my breakfast and walked to school, trying so hard to come to terms with a dilemma buzzing around in my mind. You see, apart from my home life, I had become so disenchanted with life as a young teenager, which was the very earlier reason for my quest to find greater things, and I had actually succeeded. Now, with such fresh wonders found, I was left making comparisons as I glanced down at my feet in school shoes, taking me to improve myself in a world, which, in all honesty, I no longer really wished to be part of.

It would seem I had been granted one tiny iota of divine understanding, along with the small delegated 'power' it would surely embrace ... my inner voice whispered to me.

'Let me give you clarity, Freya, your decision as to which route to take is safe in terms of discord and hurt to others. Each of your two destinies is unknown to the other, you leave one, and that situation immediately goes on 'hold', you leave the other and that also immediately goes on 'hold', both simply awaiting a re-birth. One which might take a thousand years or the blinking of an eye in Earth time; the duration is irrelevant and meaningless. It's as if two entire lives go into hibernation.' This came so sweetly to my ears, but there was no one there like my Luke to hold a conversation with. Would

he still be there in that astral universe, warm and comfortable sleeping, unhurt, and not knowing I had flown away? My darling Luke! I was in love and missed him so!

'Did you complete all that 'b....' homework?' I heard from a girl class friend running to join me, which brought me back with a jolt to, not my 'Reality', but the reality of the current Earth world I was once again a part of.

'Yep, all done,' I answered with such confidence, somehow knowing I had. She was obviously hoping for some help on the main science subject matter, as she quickly asked.

'Did you get all that stuff about 'parallel universes'? It left me wondering, how could there possibly be two places?' Was I being tested? I wondered. That question did seem to be teasing an outpouring from me, but my secret was safe.

Clearly, there was still some control by that special Being that watches over us all. Maybe I had tarried for so long in 'Reality', and that very controlling force had not wanted me to sever my Earthly ties too quickly, made clear by the fact that I had journeyed whilst sleeping, but I somehow knew there would come a time when that decision would be mine alone to make.

I pondered often over what could be the purpose of my returns to Earth, after all, I had dreamed a dream of one day leaving a way of life that seemed to lack mental discipline and harmony in so many areas.

Time passed, and I began to recognise signs indicating reasons for my returns; it would seem I had left the school teenage 'Colosseum', a striving to move up through the 'pecking order' to be a 'top gun' teen. It had all been so like that 'Flavian Amphitheatre' in Rome I had learnt of in a history lesson. Now, for some strange reason, I attracted many, without effort, who wished to befriend me. There was the playing field, the dining hall, the walking to and from school, just to give some idea of the enormity of such changes in my life. No longer would friends sidle up to show me *nasties* on their mobiles and the like.

Something was shining through from that ever present 'Inner Self' that others liked; I had no need to try apparently; people simply wanted to be with me, to make conversation free from debase subject matter, or running others down in order to appear greater teen beings.

I never acted 'above it all', but with just a quiet countenance that came easy to me now!

A walk to school one day brought further surprises. That tall handsome school 'dude' that had previously made me look a bit of a nerd came chasing after me with a note pad I had dropped. He seemed so pleased to be able to offer up what must have seemed to him an opportunity to befriend me... possibly imagining this was a modern interpretation of an enticingly dropped white handkerchief or glove as of a romantic scene of old, as he continued to walk by my side, making fast contrived conversation, eyes darting up and down my front ... for my part, it all seemed at half the mental pace. No giggling, swooning, fumbling over words, just a cool quietness that came easy, a 'no comment', as he ran somebody down, a non-pursuance of anything negative, just a smile as I said,

'Must go, take care.' Prompting him to call after me

'Might see you tomorrow; I always come this way.'

'You never know,' I said. Words without eye contact coming easy, especially with a certain Luke on my mind!

Apart from moving into womanhood in a trouble-free kind of way, I realised there was '*something*' for me to demonstrate such as there being a pleasant, decent way of living one's life.

The question arose in my heart, what was it about me, that others were now attracted to? This seemed so important to understand. There was no 'selling' what I believed in, such as talking or writing about correct standards that could bring such rewards forever, one simply had to quietly demonstrate a correct path with a pleasant demeanour.

Having decided this is why I had to dwell in this 'parallel universe' for the time being, I studied my schoolwork, made friends, and gave help to some where I could, all without appearing too far out of step with my contemporaries like some kind of Good Samaritan.

It would seem I had been blessed with an understanding of this dual life, in that there was never a feeling of 'loss' or being denied or deprived of anything, especially my relationship with Luke. Unlike the world on Earth, where everything must drift away forever one day, the likes of loss of a loved one, the joy of looking at successful exam results, peering into the eyes of a kitten given to love, or a loving parental embrace.

In 'Reality', it had been deeply imbedded in my consciousness that all would remain absolutely fine there, all as when I left. It was almost like having a wonderful experience that one would do anything to hold on to, but the normal concept was always that it must, as mentioned, pass us by, leaving empty hands.

These countless moments would, for most, take albums to document. With mine, they were always there, just waiting to be rekindled back to the real! I could at any time, think of my Luke lying, warm and cosy, surrounded by soft green moss, sleeping, by now unaware of harmonic stream ripple sounds and night owls wishing him goodnight as he lay, unbeknown to him, continuing to grow older, as was I. I could re-engage with that wonderful fragment of life whenever I so chose... to wake him and peer together out at that crystal-clear stream, then raise our gaze to witness the sun coming up to reflect morning light across the mill pond. Not just a mental picture, but real, and in motion, 'Mini Blue' bobbing up and down close to water reed swaying. You see... I could take such things into my arms to love and embrace whenever I so choose!

I enjoyed the coming together with my Ma and friends, which especially included Jeni on some occasions, when we would smile in such a knowing way, wondering, I'm sure if either of us had recruited other lovely trusting friends to journey on to 'Reality'. I had two of my dearest friends who I hoped one day to share our joys with, taking them on that journey with me, one was English, the other of Indian origin; along with Jeni, the four of us had always been so very close, to the point of being called 'The palette' as in artist, due to us being white, black, and brown.

Having by now just moved onto college days, they all came to my eighteenth birthday party, which included a 'Karaoke' session... such fun to see Jeni smiling as I sang *'Somewhere over the rainbow'* ... followed by a 'wink'. I felt happy that she was clearly handling the secret, and nothing had been lost in our situation, it somehow confirmed, I was not alone in my parallel dreaming!

Time passed, and it began to feel that a piece of my life's 'jigsaw-puzzle' had been cut ready to form part of my life's picture and, it was now time to return back to 'Reality', back to my Luke, and if I am really honest, back to where my Heart truly felt at ease.

A WELCOME DAWN

I sat once more in front of my landscape picture to dream, remaining quite still for a while... no thinking, just gazing until I once more lost all awareness of my home surroundings. Then, my focus rushed to one of the smaller arches under the little stone bridge, a re-living of that first awareness of my successful journey there.

My new, such refreshing life, came by way of the sound of rippling stream water, and a rustling of waterside reed. I had, once again, been granted the joy of flying to the shallow water of the stony mill pond bank, just below our homely oak standing there, a custodian of happy lives and peaceful surroundings. He exuded such power, slowly developed over two or three hundred years from a tiny acorn embryo, not dwelling in a worldly woodland of planet Earth destruction, left to the mercy of a tree feller's chain saw, to send him crashing to the ground with such force, such majesty humiliatingly downgraded to smaller woodland things as he lays to ground, made ready for the 'planking' machine, then to lie dead for years to earn the grand title of 'seasoned oak'. Now just planks, unaware of their magnificent origins and lineage where they once stood tall as one body… that's gone... now made into tables, chairs and things for man to sit thereon and complete the depletion of that magnificence with the passing of wind upon!

I 'dipped' and fluffed up my feathers in the cool morning stream, thinking *I'll be pretty and bright eyed to meet my Dude. I'll tell him, I rose early for my wash and exercise.* Up I flew, and through the entrance hole into our cosy nest home. He opened his eyes and smiling, commented.

'You're up early ... it looks a lovely day.'

'Lovely' I thought, *it's more than 'lovely', it's what dreams are made of safe and happy with a feeling of togetherness once more.* In no time, we were gazing with heads over the nest rim, commenting on the stream ripple sound and sun rays resting easy on the still mill pond surface as she rose up over it... then Luke's perfect timing kicked in as he declared.

'Time to head back to becoming Luke and Freya again; what do you think Dilly?' Of course, he was right.

As we flew out from under the bridge, I still had a fading awareness in my consciousness of being a teen girl from that last journey home. Strange, how when the change of consciousness takes on that metamorphosis, for just moments, feelings arise relating to both worlds, as one moves from the one parallel universe to another, in this case, from a teen girl to a tiny 'Dipper' bird.

We had left the little confined space of our mossy cocoon home for two. Now we were climbing high in endless open space, bright and fresh with cool air rushing by.

'Homeward bound then?' Dude called to me with a smile, after all we could see our tree top landing pad directly below where we were circling. Hard to imagine we actually had two abodes so close to one another... one directly below the other, with a change in scale a little frightening and almost impossible to identify with, as just a hint of human-hood lingered there ... after all, as Freya that tiny little home under the bridge would nearly fit into my pocket!

We landed and were immediately surrounded by a wonderful ethereal glow, confirmation of something beyond normal understandings as we stood for a while enjoying the moment. It was as if we were being told that the morphing back into human form would always be a main event, with all other dreamy changes being of a secondary nature.

'You look lovelier than ever, Freya,' Luke remarked. I guess by now, having just reached eighteen, I had finally made the grade in terms of my obsession with my 'bumps' ... how silly I had been when at school, always, as do most girls, making comparisons with classmates. I was quick to point out, that Luke looked pretty cool himself, with a little unshaven stubble on his face.

There was obviously some explaining required, as we had both matured on that extended trip home, so, as I ran my open hand over his face 'stubble' trophy, I asked a straightforward question.

'You have always been one step ahead of me from the very day we met; tell me Luke, do you know something I don't?' At least I think I now knew a little more about certain things, and wondered if he was up for sharing. I was fringing around the subject of my recent journey home and the physical changes that had clearly taken place, along with more adult conversations having been had; even Luke's voice sounded deeper and manlier. He smiled in that familiar kind of way and commented.

'That guiding *'Something'* here in '*Reality*' takes care of everything, Freya, there is only a balance. It was obviously considered time for you to take a long break and visit home once more, you were doing something quite natural by falling in love with life here, in the knowledge that nobody back there, being as the clock stops, is ever hurt when you are absent! You thought I was sleeping when you returned, but I was peering out of our nest watching you doing your morning ablutions, with water flying everywhere, looking so sweet, 'preening' yourself... I hoped for me.'

Another tutorial was not quite what I had been hinting at, as I stood waiting for his insider information with a smile, feeling good that there could be no hidden agenda in our lives together, and eager to find out more, I asked,

'Do tell, Luke.' Obviously hinting at boy/girl things.

He continued with such enthusiasm on subject matter so normal, almost highlighting the need to sidestep my obsession with such 'growing-up' things,

'I had a job given me to do, come and see.'

He held his hand out for me to take. As he led the way, I glanced down at our hands entwined and loved the feeling of the boy/girl union. It all added to my mental book of knowledge on a recurring theme; his arm was strong, quite hairy... and mine, softer looking smooth white skin, and so much smaller. My hand seemed lost in his, and I wondered, how could such a strong powerful hand be capable of a gentle touch?

'You look quite starry-eyed, Freya, are you okay?'

Well, of course, I was fine; I had simply been drifting off into secret places which were mine alone to drift into.

'I'm fine, Luke,' I replied, 'can't wait to see what you've been up to.' He was quick to suppress a couple of doubts buzzing around in my busy little mind as I wondered how much we should be expected to take advantage of, manifesting things we desired, and he spelled out such important ground rules, if one could call them 'rules'.

'Good to start with the simple things in life, Freya. It would be so easy for us to try to introduce the development of a modern world, with all its 'gismos'. We are in an embryo of happy 'Reality', best to allow this wonderful world to evolve, which it will, and in an easy progressive way. I'm a little unsure what would happen if we begin to request those modern so-called improvements you have talked of at this stage, such as computers, TVs, mobile phones, apps, and so many more I.T. concepts and associated equipment. Who knows, maybe, we are following the correct path at this stage in our journey, and if we begin to seek out such so-called 'improvements', we will be shown that 'grey mist' as a guiding sign, but I don't want to test that 'guidance', as we are happy, and we are, on occasions, getting small degrees of some 'grey mist' steerage.'

I could see Luke's point; after all, why not stay with a state of happiness, we weren't in any hurry, and the thought of interfering with our somewhat limited CV in what was obviously a Divine creation was a mind-boggling trespass. For example, we might create a bus, along with a 'stop' outside 'Mrs. Pope's' corner shop, to take people where? Plus, she would probably faint at the very sight of something arriving from outer space, with people sitting upstairs with the lights on, looking down at her!

Reading my thoughts, well, of course he would on such matters, after all he had just raised the point of us 'seeking so-called improvements', and he could see my mind wandering once more.

'Buses will come along, Freya; after all we already do have a train. As long as things form part of our unfolding journey, it will be a harmonious transition. Do you want to go home next time on a bus?' Apart from me wanting to get off the subject of a return journey home so soon after arriving back, I was not wanting to relinquish my plan of the 'windsurfing' board with pink sail and me in matching pink shorts, heading out to drop over that horizon! He continued,

'My *Inner voice* with words of guidance, is pointing out, in the kindest possible way *'I created a situation once, called 'life on Earth', and hoped the dwellers thereon would cherish and improve it, but they spoiled almost everything*! *Your 'Reality' is, and always will be, inhabited by kindly Loving souls. Follow your Hearts.'* Ever the 'rookie', I was quick to ask,

'How did you hear that guidance, Luke? It sounds like my aunt Rosie, who, when I was quite young, I heard my Ma discussing with a friend, as that aunt being a 'Medium' who could hear voices from 'the other side'; sounded 'spooky' to me, and I remember asking, 'when you say 'the other side' do you mean over the fence?' That raised quite a laugh, with them suggesting that I leave such things to the 'bogeyman'. I know you're not a 'bogeyman', Luke, but you're not one of those so called 'Mediums' are you?' This prompted another laugh, this time from Luke, but at my age and ethereal learning, this was no laughing matter, and I wanted answers... I was not too sure of the meaning of the word 'ethereal' I had just introduced into my thinking. My education by now had moved on dramatically, but this one had slipped through the net of my 'A' level English ... it just made me feel important. He smiled and, quick to offer clarity on such an important issue, after all, he was referring to that *Something* within from where *All* things are made, he did, I notice, slip in a word surely for my benefit in his following statement.

'I'll try to describe this quite rare happening, Freya, but do understand: I am not a Saint or Avatar, it's just to help you understand this 'un-Earthly' 'ethereal' matter. If you close your eyes and allow yourself to be about to, let's say, whilst young, steal a cake in a bakery shop when the shopkeeper is not looking, *Something* would have reminded you: 'that is wrong', leaving you to decide what to do.' I closed my eyes to embark on this dreadful idea of pinching a cake, but in no time had to admit I was finding it difficult.

'I'm struggling with that, Luke,' I replied, 'as I've never stolen anything in my life, but if I am really honest, I have to admit, when arriving at the bakery, I felt awful at the very thought!' He then added,

'You see, *Something* was telling you that to steal a cake was very wrong, it's just that you heard words without sound!' I think I knew what he meant, as my mind had, on many other occasions, given me a nudge.

'That's what I hear, Freya, but there is a soft kindly voice attached, a voice that could obviously come in any language, but is not there to exchange conversation with, it's just a 'one way' unquestionable guidance.'

'Anyway,' I said, just to get us back on the topic of the job Luke had been steered into undertaking, I asked,

'What super task is my Luke up to now?' A bit cheeky, having introduced the words 'my Luke', and I noticed he did not look up, comment, or even smile. I liked that: it made the slightly possessive comment all seem okay, and that, just maybe, he was happy to be 'my' Luke.

NEW AMENITIES

It would appear Luke had been really pulling things out of the hat for us during my last visit home, so much so, I would become almost ecstatic with joy at what he was about to show me. Firstly, he felt the need to give me a bit of an explanation, as boys do, but I simply wanted to see the 'goodies' without a lot of tech stuff he was about to elaborate on, after all, I am a girl with girly things on my mind, but I listened, a little impatiently, I will admit, as he was obviously still seeing me as that much younger girl pushing our little boat and running around to the front carting round logs for her hero, well, he was still my 'hero', but he now had stubble on his chin and me, well, having looked in the mirror at home after showering, I thought I was looking just a little like 'Venus de Milo' but with arms. He began to explain,

'Do you recall seeing a small degree of what appeared as steam coming from the ground at the foot of our Oak tree?' Well actually, I had and answered.

'Yes... I thought that was early morning mist, rising from the Mill Pond.'

'Nope...' was all I had managed to glean from my man, obviously determined to play to his audience as a bit of a tease, and as girls do, I tried so hard to appear interested, but he caught me looking away at a passing swallow and, having glanced my way, did seem a little hurt. My 'girly' nature was called for, and I smiled so sweetly and held out one hand as if demonstrating to him he was my hero awaiting my wreath of laurels to be placed on his head.

I was, at that stage in my life, without swapping stories with school and college friends, learning all the boy/girl ploys played out in the growing-up game, a game that would surely drop away as years went on and real maturity blossomed, in this case I recognised a sequence which went as follows: Luke's desire to impress with man talk – my only interest being the end result – Luke seemingly a little hurt – my need to re-engage – Luke reassured but reducing his story – my need to overplay my interest – Luke coming to the point ... mission accomplished.

First, there was the *'Luke's desire to impress with man talk'* bit to be played out:

'Well, Freya, here's the wonderful news; that was not, as you put it, 'morning mist', it was warm water rising up from deep down in the Earth where hot water is formed by a natural 'heat source'. It can all start with rainwater passing down through 'granite' or up from above the Earth's crust through 'lime & sandstone' popping up through 'Jurassic' and 'Triassic' surface layers, and there you have it: 'HOT WATER'.' At this point, I was almost heading for my towel dreaming of a hot shower, but did not dare spoil what was by now becoming an obvious end result.

'It is only small, Freya, but we have a 'hot thermal spring' right under our feet. I had to obtain some large clean hollow bamboo to form a pipe route quite a way down, but not too far. Then what happens is a process called 'thermo-siphon' where, due to various effects on the water, it rises up through my pipes!'

At this point, it was like being at the cinema, and one standing to leave before the end of the movie, even though I could see a bamboo pipe going up behind where Luke stood. I held on as his enthusiasm grew, after all this whole project must have taken so much hard work, but by now, apart from being tempted in fun to ask for a 'hard hat', I was bursting to see the top end of that pipe. He continued,

'My 'phase two' is to obtain some glass to make a place in the sun higher up, like a 'solar panel' to help the warm water to raise up even more ... what about that?'

'Sounds amazing, Luke, but please now show me the top end of that pipe rising up behind you.' He turned to look.

'Oh yes, that's the important bit,' *well, fancy that* I thought, as he asked me to follow him up to a small new room he had made, and there it was: a shower head he had made. I threw my arms around him with such joy to think we could take warm showers at last. 'A nice surprise?' he asked with a smile. Well, it really was, although I had guessed what was coming about ten minutes earlier.

I couldn't wait to enjoy such a new amenity, and the thought crossed my mind, *how back there we all take such things so much for granted?* I did wonder, as I always seemed to, what Mr. Miller opposite might think, hearing me whilst in my birthday suit singing the song 'Singing in the shower' drifting out over the Mill Pond, with steam coming out of the top of this wonderful oak tree.

I was so impressed with Luke's achievements, but ,you see, any girl, in my opinion that is, would have offered up the appreciation sought by her man at the grand finale in any event by standing there showering in warm water for the first time in such a place, singing out through the steam: 'I'm in heaven'... no need to seek appreciation with all that man talk about pipes, brackets, the earth's crust, hot springs, or whatever it was, after all I didn't understand any of that anyway.

I really did enjoy thinking just a little about my growing up boy/girl learning process, well, quite a lot actually; it would all eventually make our life together easy when that 'blossoming maturity' reached full status, beyond that first flush of youth.

There are many subtle lines of attack a girl can adopt to win her man, for example, innocently leaning forward as mentioned earlier, in an open blouse offering a 60% glimpse of the promised land on offer for seeking eyes, knowing full well, those eyes would always be 'seeking'. Having mentally pictured that 'leaning forward' bit, I thought to quickly amend my game plan and decided, best to do up one more button on the next occasion, to reduce that display from 60% to 40%, as 60% at my age would be well out of order, but 40% a possible dressing error, the innocence of which would be far more appealing.

My mental meandering was brought back to reality with Luke's quiet voice whispering in my ear as I sat drying my hair.

'What are you up to now, Freya? You have that faraway look again.' His searching comment made me jump, almost as if he might know what I had been chewing over, then I realised it was all my secret little world, and I was doing what all girls do.

'Just dreaming, Luke,' I replied. That seemed a nice way to draw a line under my perpetual script writing of the actions a girl must partake of in order to be one step ahead of other competition. Then I realised there simply wasn't any.

We had been drifting along between life in 'Reality', my visits home, and morphing into wondrous things, trying to balance this dream journey and enjoy all its facets. We decided, being as I hadn't long returned from an Earthly life, a life that I was surely easing away from forever, why not introduce another adventure?

'What about another creature adventure?' Luke suggested, with, I sensed, a hint of that wanderlust inherent in his makeup... time to reverse the game plan and give the 'baton' back to my man, so I asked,

'Anything come to mind?' I answered, in a manner that demonstrated the wonderful simpatico we always had. There never seemed to be any disagreements or clashing of points of view... it was as if our two characters, apart from the obvious need for some individuality, were two peas in a pod.

'The season seems to be somewhat changing, Freya; it's getting quite cold, what say we have some time as 'furry' things with warm coats, I'm sure you know my thoughts on that idea. What comes to mind?'

'What a lovely change that would make, Squire,' I replied, making it quite clear I had picked up on his thinking by using that very name. 'Be nice to have a break from all that plumbing and things rising up from 'middle-Earth' stuff.'

'Great minds think alike, Squat, let's take that break then … when can you be ready?'

I loved the way he had asked 'when can you be ready?' it had moved away from me being a slip of a kid to that of a woman forming an important role in our lives together. Actually, I was ready to act on our dream journey immediately but played out the importance on offer as I suggested,

'Oh, yes, I do want to tidy round the home first,' knowing full well all was already tidy. 'And I have a few personal things to sort out in my room…' I really liked that I was introducing secrets, not that I really had any, but I was introducing some.

In no time we had morphed and were on our way, tracking along the margin of a corn field, long since harvested and processed into golden loaves of bread. There remained only stubble awaiting the farmer's plough to begin the cycle once more in the creation of that 'staff of life'.

We looked for the first tree to enable us to climb to safety, although we were convinced we were always safe in '*Reality*', an overconfidence that was soon to prove to be a wrong assumption, and one that would rock our little world, which I will explain shortly!

Although now getting quite cold, we travelled on so happily through various woodlands trying out every new species of tree we could find, noting how certain branches bent quite easily, with some in fact readily snapping due to last winter having taken its toll.

So easy to become lost when indulging in fun. We jumped, dived, moving ever further away from base camp, completely consumed with each other's company and the fun being had.

We had, up until now, had short experiences with new-found friends, but with this adventure we had allowed time to pass and in no time, the day was nearing its end with evening approaching fast, with me beginning to wonder where we were with, as always, a little fear creeping into my mind.

'Do you know where we are, Squire?' I asked, seeking some reassurance. He looked at me in a way never seen before, a look that spelled *'lost'*, a fallibility never evident in him before, a sign of imperfection in his makeup that made me love him more, and sure enough he replied.

'I have to admit, Squat, I have no idea, and I've lost my bearings completely.' He was always so good at solving problems, firstly with common sense and a little applied intellect. This time he went quiet. I knew we were in trouble, and his next remark confirmed it!

'Normally one can get a sense of direction with the location of the sun, but today we have cloud all around.'

This was all so new to us, a feeling of being almost abandoned and a little wondering if and when a delicate 'grey mist' would begin to form to save the day, but none came and I panicked, asking Squire,

'Why don't we morph back into something to save the day? And by the way I have just spotted snow beginning to fall.'

In no time, the entire surrounding landscape was covered in rapidly deepening snow, and we were getting very cold.

'Let's try to become 'Dippers' again,' I called out, thinking we could fly up to improve our understanding as to where we were, 'we could follow the river when found all the way to the Mill house and be safe in our lovely home.' Squire quickly squashed my glimmer of hope with,

'In this snow, which is getting heavier, we will not see very far in any direction.' He began to go into survival mode. For my part, I felt cold and hopeless as I looked on at my man scurrying here and there looking for a place to shelter. At the base of a large tree, I saw leaves and twigs flying out from a space between large, exposed roots, and he called to me to hurry to this partly covered little alcove. We huddled together in great haste, as the snow continued to thicken, holding hands we tried to morph into anything that could lead us home, but nothing came.

'I am mystified why the protecting force, that I always felt sure was watching over us, is not giving us a sign.' This was Luke's comment, one that spelled disaster, as he always seemed to know that, whatever situation arose, as long as he did his very best all would be well.

'I am unsure what to do, Squat; if I trudge out to find help, I might never find my way back to you, as the snow will cover my tacks. I think we must stay close to keep warm and hope the snow begins to ease.'

It seemed like eternity passed, and I wondered how long we could survive, had all my dreams of 'Reality' and the perfection it represented been dashed? It all rushed through my mind my home and Ma back there, my friends, not forgetting the new world of Love and unfolding joys we were finding together... what to do? I looked at Squire but felt the consuming Love and recognition of my Luke, and what we had found, or should I say, 'been given'. How could perfection and such degrees of Love simply disappear? I looked at my Loving partner and declared, in a way that moved far from any youthful thinking, it was a woman in Love, as I declared,

'I think we are to die here together, but please understand, I would not wish to die with any other living thing but you let's embrace so close that we feel to be one as we wait for our Loving memories to fade.' He looked at me with such sad eyes, as if taking the entire blame unto himself for helping to create a woman from a young innocent girl; I squeezed his cold tiny hand as he said,

'So sorry.'

We lay down together and quietly declared a faith in that Divine source that had given us so much. I could feel my treasure getting cold, thinking *we must surely have done something very wrong to bring this all about, but why no mist to indicate any misgivings*, when my Loving friend declared.

'I won't give up, I just know it will all be okay; such Love does not simply come and go so easily, it is a blessing, without which everything must be doubted … and I refuse to believe that all that we have found can suddenly disappear.' To my amazement, he stood and looked skyward, calling out,

'I know *You* are there! And would not bring two Lovers to an end in your divine game in such a way as this, it's painful to see my little friend lying there,' pointing his little cold hand down toward me, 'she deserves more than this.'

At this very moment, as if to highlight the trouble we found ourselves in, a large fall of snow came crashing down from the very tree we had taken to shelter under, in fact, under which we were about to be laid to rest. I wiped the mass of snow from my head and away from my face, looked up, and burst into tears at what I found myself looking at!

'Look up there.' I called out to my treasure, pointing to something that looked rather familiar. Although no longer a tall handsome Luke, but now a tiny fluffy creature standing in defiance of the bad deal on offer, he looked to where I was pointing and with such joy called out.

'I knew *He* would step in at some point to help us, that's our *'settle'* Squat, nestling up there in amongst that evergreen ivy.' He bent down to help me up, saying with much relief, 'No time for delays, let's climb whilst we still have a little strength left.'

We had been taken to the edge for some reason, but I was so happy to arrive up at such a welcoming shelter. I shook to remove any snow and scurried in along the small entrance passage, then into an opening up into what had all the cosiness of an Arabian tent. Dry mossy walls and ceiling, tiny bundles of moss like cushions, and a bed of thick, soft dry moss and lichen!

Squire, having completed his 'shake down', pulled the little leaf and twig woven door closed, followed me into this warm safe sanctuary, holding a generous supply of hazelnuts for us to eat, saying,

'These were behind the leafy entrance door, can you guess which dear friend might have left them for us?' And of course, it just had to be our Red Squirrel friend from that meeting during summer days, leaving what seemed to us both like lifesaving sustenance for distant friends.

With bellies full, we cuddled up so warm, gave thanks, and lay at ease before falling asleep in warm surroundings, so safe under a thick snow-covered roof acting as good insulation as with Icelandic Igloos. In my sweet sleep, I imagined, as evening fell, being on the wing high above, looking down at a completely covered white snowy landscape, knowing somewhere hidden below, there was a tiny warm green womb where two Lovers lay sleeping ... so safe!

WELL-DISCIPLINED

Morning broke to the sound of early bird song, so sweet and refreshing as if to welcome back the wonders of our new journey. Squire had been up earlier than me and was sat at the entrance looking out over a beautiful white landscape, no longer cold and threatening but wonderful, with signs of untroubled nighttime activity by way of footprints in the snow of varying size, all appearing to be going somewhere with such purpose and in all directions, it would seem. Where were they all going? 'My little voice spoke quietly to me this morning, Squat.' This was my friends' voice coming in an easy manner, telling of the need for us to be taught a lesson not to play too many games with the ability granted to 'morph' into whatever we choose or we could find ourselves in all sorts of trouble.

'Such as,' I enquired, somehow knowing in my heart this made sense, as we could easily choose a new guise that could present those troubles, I guess I was simply wondering what that guise might be. His answer came as a somewhat of a release as he suggested.

'The snow has stopped now, let's go to the entrance and morph back into 'Dippers'. I'm sure that will go okay now. We can fly up and look for the stream to guide us home, where we can sit peacefully and talk it over together. The important thing is I know everything will fine now.'

I stood next to my guy so high up at the entrance to our little sanctuary, when, having closed the entrance door, dared to look down at where we had lain lost in cold deep snow, wondering if we were about to re-house ourselves there having dropped down like stones.

'Stop that,' was Luke's gentle reminder that we were going to be alright once more ... a confident voice I desperately needed to hear. It was like that first flight we had made so long ago, it seemed, teetering on the edge of our oak tree platform, it required trust in every sense of the word, but this time we had experienced a failed attempt to morph the evening before, and I am not the one who had received that 'inner calling' from you know Who.

'Have faith, Squat, it will be alright, trust me and take my hand.' So, I did and squeezed it so tightly. We stared ahead, and his call came.

'We are 'Dippers', now jump!'

That first moment of falling will inevitably come with a degree of fear, I guess, but as always 'Dude' took flight first, but I was falling, thinking of a soft landing in deep snow.

'Fly 'Dilly',' was his loud call, and with that loud calling of my name as a Dipper that I could relate to, I spread my tiny Red Squirrel arms out, and, just moments before hitting the snow, they turned to wings, and I skimmed over the surface, creating a mini snow storm so large that for moments I couldn't see a thing, then there I was, in clean fresh air and beginning to climb, and of course in just moments my Dude was beside me calling out.

'Never any doubt we would be safe, you just have to practice your launch bit,' said with a smile.

We circled round, glancing down to where, the night previous, we had laid cold and afraid at the base of the tree holding safe in its outstretch arms our lovely 'settle' to rest in, safe and sound. Not too high we flew and there it was, in the distance, with warm morning sun reflections, the friendly stream in a location not far from where we had found those wonderful friends on that sunny summer day picnic. My mind was grasping at the differing mental scenes still lingering, comparisons of white cold bleakness of yesterdays with fear, now warm sparkling sun reflections reaching up to us as if welcoming us home.

Distancing himself from the seriousness of yesterday, Dude decided to have a little light-hearted fun relating to his love of flying when Dougie with his 'Top Gun' dream, he called out such silly things a girl would never do.

'This is Captain Dude to 'wing man', sorry 'wing woman' sorry 'wing person'... are you receiving me?' Not sure what response I was supposed to make to let him know I could hear, after all he was only a metre away, I called out what I had seen on films.

'Affirmative,' which I knew meant 'yes'.

'There it is... at *'eleven o'clock low ... that's ahead and down to your left'*,' called Dude, 'the Mill house and our wonderful Oak tree home.'

A feeling of absolute joy embraced us both, knowing what lay ahead, and for me a realisation that one must appreciate every happy moment in life as it can so easily be taken.

We landed on the snow-covered Oak platform, which engulfed us in that welcoming mist, but this time it had a coloured hue, as if in reassurance we were being watched over, and there we were, Luke and Freya in each other's arms looking out over snow-capped trees, with Luke pointing in the direction we had arrived from, commenting,

'Hard to imagine, Freya, such a short time ago, somewhere out there, we were lying cold, afraid, lost, and abandoned, and here we are, safe and warm in each other's arms gazing out over 'Reality'.'

Of course, he was right, and I stood wondering what to get more excited about, that fading coloured mist, or his comment on 'body warmth', you see, I always locked onto any personal reference to us and the glow created with close contact, after all we were just hugging with pure joy but, as always, my mind rushed to the 'body warmth' bit ... oh dear!

'Guess what I am about to suggest we do?' Luke said with such a cheeky smile ... a suggestion that had me in a tizzy, as my mind scurried around guessing, because that is exactly what it had been asked to do! The glow increased as my mind settled on the possibility that we were about to extend the togetherness we were so enjoying, then the words came drifting through this beautiful, elevated place of fading coloured mist where we stood.

'Let's go down to our cosy home, change into something more comfortable, then make a cup of tea and talk through the serious matter that we have just encountered.'

Umm! He was obviously thinking beyond the 'body warmth' bit, quite rightly so, of course. We did need to understand the misgivings of our morphing behaviour, something we must both understand fully. I always seemed to be grasping at any hint of certain togetherness and wondered why. Was I more in love with him than he was with me? Or was he controlling his emotions far better than me, after all, I always imagined boys do all the chasing and girls play hard to get … but did I really want to be 'got'. Oh well, all in good time, I knew he yearned for such things as do I, he just seems to know more about time and place.

'What are you musing over now, Freya?' said with just a hint that he knew full well what mischief my mind was dwelling on.

'Oh, nothing special,' I replied, 'just us and togetherness.'

'Well, that's far from 'nothing special', I think about such things just about every fifteen minutes.'

Now I felt embarrassed and gave away my naughty yearnings with a deep blush, feeling somehow happy that my man was controlling those yearnings better that me, and in such a mature way, after all, somebody had to keep things under control, we had been rather close to heading off to those 'Niagara Falls' moments, which I had been thinking about ever since that Human Biology class, aged about twelve.

We changed and sat quietly in our cosy tree top home, thinking how lucky we both were, leaning on our elbows, with a warm mug of sweet tea between both hands, ready to run through what Luke had to share regarding the words heard from that divine source. As he began to talk, I realised he was, as always, close to that guiding force and had been since the day we first met. His words came easy and with such confidence.

'It was guidance on the correct route to happiness, really, pointing out the need to manage our gift of being able to venture through 'Reality' in differing forms of life. When, in future, we choose to make that metamorphosis, we must be sure of the purpose for doing it, it doesn't need to be too restrictive, but not decided upon at just a whim for a change, as did we with our friends the Red Squirrels. That was motivated by you and me, thinking about fur coats. It has to have purpose. By the way, I was told the previous grey mist guidance forming will continue now for when we are a little out of line on various actions we might inadvertently take, so we will again have fair warning to stay within the joys granted to us.'

'Lesson learned, eh, Luke?' I felt to say this, if only to demonstrate that I had seen the occasional flippant error of our ways. He went on to say.

'Yesterday evening's winter wonderland in the snow event was intended to take us to the edge, to demonstrate how anybody in life who takes for granted wonderful things that come their way, if not careful, can end up with nothing!' This brought back memories of my gran telling me, when things were bad at school 'Never go down to a problem,' she would then add 'You can stoop and pick up nothing,' for many years, I struggled with the understanding of this, the second part had me thinking, perhaps 'stooping' to pick up a 50p coin, only to find it was something foreign. The underlying truth.

Reflecting back on us both gazing out over that vast snowy landscape, I did have a thought at the time and thought to raise the point with Luke.

'You know, Luke, when we arrived back to our tree top base after that snowy event, I looked out into space that seemed to go on forever, all the way to the far-off horizon, and it did cross my mind, where does my 'Reality' end? I saw myself as a tiny dot on the landscape, and couldn't put the two together, I mean that tiny insignificant, humble dot 'me' and such infinite space, which did at the time embrace somewhat of a bonus by way of millions of tons of snow. Knowing others have created their dreams in similar ways, what do they see, and what is theirs in terms of a divine 'Land Registry' idea?'

His response, as always, went straight to the point, which gave me clarity, but did seem to distance him from me, like off to another league, which I felt sure was his 'Dougie' inner knowledge. Being such a 'thinker', as Luke had put it, I needed answers which, when learned, would be done with and form part of my ongoing awareness. So selfish, I wanted knowledge, but I also wanted to linger on the simplicity of a boy/girl romance forming. I suppose academics consumed with knowledge can, be deeply romantic, too.

'The answer, Freya, might shock you, but you do need to be aware, or such wonders are being wasted. In fact, your 'Reality' goes on forever! Could you imagine being a bird you have morphed into and flying that way, pointing toward the horizon, then suddenly reaching the limits you have in your mind at this moment? What do think that limit might be – a wall, a screen or whatever? No, you simply fly on until you arrive here with me on our tree-top spot.'

'What? You would see me disappear over the horizon there, and maybe never see me again.'

'Well yes, to your first point, but no to the second, you would sneak up behind me, have you forgotten the Earth is round? I suggest you don't try it, not yet anyway.' Said with a smile and a wink, which made him appear 'cheeky' and close again, by stepping down from the tutorial role I had initiated by asking the question in the first place. But oh dear … it continued and went even deeper with,

'Try to understand, there is only 'where you are' at any given moment, remember the Mill House with nothing behind the doors or windows until you made it so? And the time you dreamed of 'wind surfing' over the horizon in a pink 'bikini' on some future trip home, with you thinking you might drop over the edge.'

'Yes, and you told me that was the 'Alness',' I replied, about which I knew nothing whatsoever.

'You're not meant to as yet, Freya, that is sacred space which goes on forever.' Then in a desperate attempt to reduce the intellectual gap, I made what I thought to be a smart comment.

'But that would be travelling around the curvature of the earth in a circle. So, what happened to your 'parallel universe' theory, Luke?' Well that didn't work, and he was quick in this, what had become a chess game on life itself , to take one of my 'Knights'.

'What happened to your Geometry lessons at school, Freya? Parallel lines can remain parallel around twists and turns, even around in circles.' Said, grinning ear to ear, running two fingers around the tablecloth. Sitting, gazing into each other's eyes on opposite sides of the table, I was determined to at least move a humble 'pawn' forward in a courageous move, with his 'King' glancing across at this audacious little 'squirt'! I thought to catch out my adorable boffin with a trick question that would bring about a possible 'stalemate', knowing full well 'checkmate' was far beyond my capabilities and, we could once more return to being *almost* 'lovers'. I made my move, pausing with one finger on the 'pawn's' head, as if planning a sneaky counterattack! I lifted my finger, sat back in my chair nodding my head slightly up and down, smiling, and offered up my gambit.

'You told me, Luke, that infinite numbers of 'seekers' achieve the wonders of leaving the Earth experience.' Knowing where I was going with this, he countered with.

'Yes… and?' said in a questioning manner with one hand on his 'Queen' whilst looking at me, him having spotted a corridor leading directly to my 'King', now completely boxed in. Ceasing a chance of defence, I moved forward in my chair and blocked that victory route to my 'King' by slipping a 'Bishop' diagonally across into that winning passage to scupper his plan by stating.

'Well, how could we all, and I include little me, see such wonders we are looking at out there? We would all see different views.' With such guile, having earlier discreetly positioned a 'Bishop' to my left, he moved a 'Knight' this way and that, reigning it in on a vacant piece of battle ground and called 'checkmate' with,

'It is each individual's consciousness that prevails; some will see golden sands, swaying palm trees and warm seas kissing a beach companion of old. What you do in private space in 'Reality' is yours alone, unseen by any other, as with all others who come to these places, which on Earth, only dreams are made of. Remember, Freya, this was, from the day we met, my home, with no Earthly ties, and you were sent to join me, now we are '*one*' so we see the same, isn't that wonderful?' I went a little quiet, reflecting on the way he could chase through intellectual matters and in a moment, bring it all back to what I love, that simplicity, almost childish way I love to hold tightly onto to. Guidance and required info can arrive in volumes of the spoken word but three words came my way … '*we are one*'.

I needed to end all this serious stuff, knowing it would now always be part of my knowledge 'database'. I got up and threw my arms around him standing so close, a closeness that to any other, would have been seen as embarrassing. For me, it was as near as I could get to achieving what would inevitably be mine to enjoy … 'oneness' with my Luke!

THE HOLLOW MOUNTAIN

Summer days were such fun, moving between the tree house and the white cottage where making a pretty garden at the cottage was a chance to create colourful flower beds to pick and place in vases all around.

Luke busied himself on things for the home, making it all seem quite domestic for people so young, including, apart from his, a pretty girly bedroom of my own. All created by his visionary consciousness, leaving me wondering, *how does he know such things befitting a female teen mind?* But he did, apart from asking my favourite colours and the general theme I might prefer, he put it all together so beautifully prior to asking.

'Anything you wish to change or add, Freya?'

There simply wasn't; he had done it all for me, and that made me feel great, and dare I say... quite important, without even a hint of 'ego' arising in me, which might have instigated that 'grey mist'.

I really quite liked the entire domestic idea as opposed to going to parties and the like back there, where everybody was getting jealous of everybody else about dresses worn, who was with whom, and who shouldn't be with whom. Was I being old fashioned? I didn't really care; I just knew I had entered a world where no such disagreements and restless mind wanderings existed, and I was happy.

One day, as I made tea, I heard Luke come down from the very dusty loft area of the cottage, calling to me to join him as he unravelled a roll of paperwork he had apparently found in a dark corner inside a box labelled with words printed, not written longhand, stating: 'I've been gone a while now but always knew you would find me one day.'

'Could these be?' Luke exclaimed in such a happy way, almost as if he had discovered treasure seeking documents, and of course he had! 'We have forgotten the lead Mr. Miller had given us about stories told. Could these be those Dougie drawings and maps revealing secret places to be found?'

We rolled them out on the kitchen table and placed two pots of flowers picked that morning on the top two corners to stop them curling down, one pot of white daisies, the other pink roses, creating, with us eagerly leaning over the document, a scene something akin to a cross between 'Treasure Island' and a Brontë novel.

'There's no cross marking the spot,' I said with a smile, and with a little wondering I might add, what we should be looking for? Luke replied with a sensible answer.

'As always with these things, Freya, it will be a mystery, with hints, clues and signs to read into in order to unravel treasures to be found,' said, clearly, with a boyish 'buried treasure' idea in mind. Then, without wishing to pop Luke's balloon, I pointed to a small note Dougie had obviously written which stated: 'No need to look for that cross I know you are seeking. You just have to follow the stream out to the sea, turn right along the coastline until you see a large open cave; watch the tides, it's easier to go in on a low one. You'll be in the 'Hollow Mountain', which offers fresh discoveries one after the other as you climb up toward the sunlight seen high above you at the top.'

We looked at each other in absolute shock, as we declared in unison 'but isn't that where we've been?' Luke looked at me in absolute amazement to say.

'To think, Freya, we have been to the beginning of one of his secret places without even knowing it.'

'I see,' he went on to say, 'The first plateau is my private 'box' to a theatre of new winged friends nesting everywhere, I knew many by name and could call them to come to me for company, as I was quite lonely in those passing years.'

We were feeling quite speechless at such fabulous news, to think Dougie had been right there where we sat in such fear, and we had no idea. Luke brought back to memory the moment when we had jumped, pointing out something that had not meant too much to him at the time, as we were consumed (at least I was) with thoughts of not landing on the rocks below... he began to explain something wonderful I had been too afraid to notice but did briefly reflect on later.

'Do you remember the small flock of birds circling around us as we fell? Could they have been his friends watching over us?'

Life seemed to be just one adventure after another, what with our river friends, life around the Mill, and so much more, I began to wonder, when such things would come together in one great story of life for us, so, I asked Luke what he thought of there being so much for us to associate with. His answer, as always, came in a way that gave me confidence that all was well in 'Reality'.

'There's an old saying, *'live in the moment'* which almost seems to imply not to leave one situation to seek out another, which will in any event inevitably come along, they are all meant for us to enjoy and partake of *'in the moment'*, and remember: we are, as discussed, together at the beginning... 'setting the stage' for our life here.'

I loved asking him for guidance; he always seemed to know what to say to make me feel fine, yet I knew sometimes he also felt a bit lost himself with nobody to turn to, and my Heart, as always, swelled with feelings toward him as we played this pleasant game of life. Back there, every participant would know all the answers, even if they didn't, leaving them open to ridicule by some who would refer to them as a 'know all'.

I pushed poor Luke, as I leaned on my new-found girly skills, by acting a little lost for direction, knowing full well in which direction I wanted to head!

'So, what's it to be?' I asked, putting him on the spot, 'an immediate return to 'Hollow Mountain' or repaint the kitchen wall?'

There was obviously no choice to make, really; destiny seemed to be calling out to us 'follow your Hearts to the mountain', so we did. Up early, and off we went in our little blue boat, heading for new special horizons, this time taking with us the maps and drawings in a small shoulder bag.

We finally arrived and sat in morning sunshine on quiet seas at the mouth of the large cave and thought to read some of the guidance in our newly discovered, priceless documents as we unfolded them on our laps.

'I can see the reference to the tunnel and our previously discovered balcony. Hard to imagine that spot was so precious to him sitting quietly with bird friends. He goes on to say 'When rested and refreshed by the small lagoon, track back along the passageway and begin to climb once more.' Well, of course, we have actually done this bit previously, so let's get started, Freya, up to the point where the second small passageway goes off to the left.'

Carefully, we again climbed, stopping to gaze along the first tunnel meant for 'rest and refreshing by the lagoon' as so nicely put by Dougie. It was, in fact, where Luke had done a little Tarzan and pool plunging. We gazed upward, somehow knowing there were wonders to be found up there, and to think we were treading in his very steps! We both had an inherent fear of having to go down again, which was far more difficult than the climb, but high above that ever-beckoning small piece of sky seemed to draw us onward and upward, a tiny piece of sky, not blue, but an effulgent, somehow soft pink tone.

As if to enhance the mystery, there were, according to the plans, some level plateaus, unseen until one had arrived at a certain level, then moved around a sort of corner stone I could see sketched.

It all seemed like a world within a world. We were consumed with wondering what could lie in store as we carefully moved over shiny, wet-with-dew, slippery granite, some covered in bright green lichen, soft and wet to the touch, some dry and safer to step on, and pleasant to sit on to rest a while … lost in countless questions with no answers.

We continued and finally reached a point where the only way up was around and finally arrived at a large granite corner post ... and sure enough, there it was, a second plateau made up of a magnificent crystal clear pool with, almost as if in friendly togetherness, a shaft of that light from high above pieced deep down into the pool, leaving us looking in awe, wondering as we gazed down, how far down it went, as it appeared bottomless.

We were totally entranced by what now spread out before us as we sat on one of those welcoming dry mossy areas leading right up to the water's edge.

We said very little for quite some time, 'blown away' by the beauty that surrounded us. Luke gazed across, I thought at me, but realised he was looking, actually gazing, beyond where I sat, as he asked,

'What is that, Freya?' Pointing to what appeared as a piece of paper in a small corner crag near to where I was sitting. I looked down and pulled it out from its resting place, feeling sorely tempted to take a peep but handed it to him. He opened it slowly, as if giving reverence to something which must surely be very important. It seemed like a lifetime of waiting as he pondered over words spelling out something about which I had no idea. I tried romantically to lean on his shoulder, gazing up at the side of my man's face, and then sneakily peered down to check out the action.

He was obviously digesting something amazing, made obvious by the look on his face. He turned toward me with the paper in his right hand held out for me to take, saying,

'You just won't believe what is written there; it will lift your Heart, it certainly did mine.' I opened it to lay on my lap with my eyes rushing to the first line, which read:

'So, you made it; I always wondered, when I discovered these heavenly places, who would be the ones to followed on, always knowing in my Heart it would be two Lovers together; it did all seem a bit of a waste on a man alone. I would sometimes look back to say 'just look at this' only to find there was no one there. There are composite wonders for both boy, and girl, such as strong granite faces to climb and delicate fine lichen strands of many colours from which to imagine pretty bonnets and gloves to be made'. He continued, almost as if talking to us directly as friends known. 'I found so many friends of a differing kind. If you are sitting where you found my note of long ago, lean forward and gaze deep down into the lagoon and try whispering ... where are you?'

It felt so wonderful to think we were following a journeyman of long ago into the unknown. But, as always, never to miss a trick, I grasped at the romantic, looking at Luke with my finger pointing to the words '*it would be two Lovers together*'. In such surroundings, I found my Heart beating so hard, I took Luke's hand and placed it on my Heart, well actually, my by now quite well developed breast, and spoke.

'In such a wondrous place, my Heart is about to burst out of my pretty dress. I had repeated thoughts as we climbed that I might fall, and if I did and failed to summoned up 'Dilly' dipper, I would not have actually told you 'I Love you, Luke.' It's not what you say, how you look, even the way you handle things and your general mannerisms, it's just you! We are, aren't we, Luke? I mean what Dougie stated '*two Lovers together*'.' Knowing full well we were, I just wanting to hear him say it, as I hovered around, as always, any line of reassurances hoped for.

There was a pause of about five seconds when I was alone in Love, separated, destined to live a life growing old, no one to hold my hand as the years slipped by ... and all that sad film stuff. It was, however, a real tear that fell into the lagoon, spreading out like radar waves as if calling for responses.

Luke's face said it all in such a simple way, as always, a smile as he struggled to find words from such a young, romantically inexperienced mind, with the clock ticking and my mental gymnastics by now in full swing, telling me I would have to accept enjoying a simple friendship with him -- and I didn't do too well in 'friendships'. My five seconds were up, and the door to my new life opened, welcoming me into a union of two, a Love affair, a giving and taking, caring and sharing, inside my blouse if so wished. His reply,

'I've Loved you, Freya, with all of my young, inexperienced Heart, from the moment I first saw you whilst riding my bike near to the Mill. I didn't know what those feelings were, after all, you were only thirteen. I Loved the things we did and said together, sometimes daring to look when you weren't aware ... seeing you as woman developing with female form, manifesting for me alone it seemed, based on the unfoldment that brought us together. I often wanted to touch, to learn of softness I somehow knew to be there, evident when you moved quickly or ran. I looked, and thought of it all almost daily without guilt, but had no idea as to what I should do or say.'

I interrupted him and threw my arms around him with a sudden awareness that we had, from the very start, been two happy individuals, both desperately wanting to be one.

Having been condemned to a five second period of a lonely life with no pets, family, or happy days of togetherness, I had been set free to step through that open door and suddenly became aware how much I really Loved him!

Was my timing bad, putting Luke on the spot with such an emotive question, when about ready to lean forward to call down deep into that crystal clear lagoon the words Dougie had proposed '*where are you*'? Well I didn't care, all the way up on the climb, with me imagining I might fall never having said 'I Love you', and now looking so deep, wondering if I might be about to drown. I looked at Luke and, having put everything in place, he had obviously dropped my 'girl in Love' stuff to the second division as he leaned forward asking me to join him, so I did, and there we were, looking at our reflections but seeing deep down beyond them as we whispered those words… '*where are you?*'

Young faces came rising up from deep down, then in a moment, they surfaced by the edge of the lagoon where we sat; up and out they jumped, turning through 180 degrees as they left the water, and there they were … six mermaids sitting on their hands in a row alongside us declaring,

'Don't be alarmed, we are your friends and knew one day someone like you would be calling to us; we were told by Dougie long ago!' Luke leaning forward to have all six in line and clearly in his view, declared,

'But you all look so young.' Prompting just one of them to answer, with a surprising response.

'There is no such thing as time where we live; how far up Hollow Mountain are you travelling?' We looked at each other, realising we actually had no idea, so we explained we had discovered Dougie's maps and drawings, and realised Hollow Mountain was the very place we had discovered on one of our trips out in our little blue boat, having ended up outside the large cave opening, a cave which almost felt to be inviting us in.

We pointed out we had found ourselves climbing up to the small passageway off to the left only to find another small lagoon and a balcony overlooking the bay.

They seemed quite excited to be able to explain: it was the place their old friend Dougie used to sit sketching and writing stories, with many of those sea birds sitting on the parapet top, sometimes for hours. We could see them from below; they were such a happy group of friends.

'Just like you and us now?' I dared to suggest, which caused quite a reaction as they adjusted their seating position so as all could be seen, calling out in unison.

'Yes, and there will many more for you to find.' We dared to mention the six large birds that surrounded us as we were falling from the balcony on that first visit, with me being a little late in making my change to a Dipper bird ... asking if they might confirm our thoughts on their presence.

'No doubt,' was the happy reply, 'we heard about that episode, and felt so excited that we had learned of someone being able to change into other forms of life. You see, we have friends living much higher up 'Hollow Mountain', in fact, near to the top, who told of people being gifted with the power to change. We knew immediately, when we heard about our six sea birds following you down as you fell, that you were two of those chosen gifted ones. Everyone in Hollow Mountain was talking about it, and here you are, our friends! Will you swim with us for a while in the lagoon?'

We sat in absolute shock that we were seen by dwellers of 'Hollow Mountain' as two 'gifted' people, especially as we were feeling totally in awe of these water angels, who had actually just asked us to swim with them. First thing that runs through the mind of people with more body parts than mermaids must surely be *'what about swimming gear?'*

Luke looked at me, probably thinking I had more to expose than him, and suggested

'Are we okay in our underclothes?' I looked down at my feet resting in the beautiful clear lagoon with my hands swashed between my legs, obviously looking unable to make such a dramatic decision, where modesty was about to leave my world, even more than the earlier episode by the boat at the cave entrance. Our new friends were, by now, 'giggling' like mad, leaving us wondering if they were aware of certain differences. The one of the six that had first said hello, leaned forward to ask,

'Does that mean you have more of those clothes underneath?'

'Well yes.' Was Luke's somewhat embarrassed attempt at modesty, obviously feeling a little outnumbered, as I was clearly nearer to them on the revealing side of things. Their giggling somehow reflected a complete innocence, more so an inquisitiveness, as would have been the case with so many sea creatures they would know of who were anatomically put together differently.

They all stared, giggling with smiles on faces, as we undressed and slid into the water. We were suddenly in their wonderful world, made clear by their eagerness to enter in, with water splashing everywhere, a harmony made up of laughter, clear water and feelings of joy erupted, and we were part of it all. Then it went eerily silent as Luke and I swam toward the lagoon centre, wondering where our new friends had disappeared to.

'Take a deep breath, Freya, and let's dive down to investigate; in such crystal-clear water, we must surely see them.'

So, we did ... dive deep that is, and they came from all directions diving in and around us with new sounds being made, like flute melodies, long flowing hair, fine and silky like sea grass, smooth soft bodies rubbing by, above, beside, over and under. I personally, probably with at least some 'female hormones' matching, felt completely at one with the entire sub-aqua sequence coming together, with a little wondering, how Luke was handling such beauty completely embracing us … and so up close and personal at that. I had lost all awareness of my humanness showing through my remaining underclothes ... as was the case, I'm sure with Luke.

It was like a large living ball of bodies, blending so close as if in a clear glass confining bubble as we moved and circled in an erotic like dance, at least I think that was what 'erotic' meant. A dance, with not one of us at any time losing contact with all in this sensuous ballet, and it was 'sensuous' but somehow completely innocent, never moving toward that human union that I had by now in my life with Luke been secretly yearning. This was Love in abundance; I was constantly being touched in passing by soft female breasts and arched backs and I loved it as the ballet went on and on!

Suddenly, as if each of them somehow knew the right moment, there was a rush of these angels to the surface, then leaped in complete unison, as at that first meeting, turning as they did, landing on the bank sitting side-by-side, and the 'giggling' recommenced once more. Luke and I, hardly appearing to be dressed in anything, with me certainly realising there really was such a thing as an 'after glow', swam to the mossy bank to join them as they sat slapping their tails on the water surface, calling out.

'We loved what we have created today and can't wait to tell our friends, we were six and became eight, in a dance of togetherness with Love feelings rushing from one to the other. We could tell you were feeling the same. We often play together, but that close intimacy is saved for very special moments with special people. Next time we may bring more friends to make the numbers greater, which will increase the sensations felt by us all. Did you notice the intense feeling of Love with each fresh individual contact being made? It's as if equal Love can be felt between Lovers of untold numbers, isn't that wonderful?' As if such a statement was being conferred, in unison without words, they were all leaning forward once more, nodding their pretty young heads and giggling, in a way that seemed to demonstrate 'innocence' and a complete, open, uninhibited honesty of sensual enjoyment.

It had been a demonstration of 'making Love' without those 'car mechanic bits' taught in my human biology class back there. This was a lesson given to two, though inexperienced, slowly becoming sexually aware, growing-up people, a lesson given by six innocent-looking, pretty, giggling girls, unaware of anything more being required by way of longing. A longing I had been developing from early teens. This had a 'completeness' to it, no talked of 'afterglow fading', with them, it felt to be almost permanent, a parcel tied in pink ribbon thrown into one consciousness. The very thought of there being more of these lovely creatures next time, with these six having declared 'will increase the sensations felt' was more than (and I speak for my innocent self) anyone could possibly be expected to absorb, be that mentally, emotionally or physically ... without popping like a balloon of ecstasy! Luke gazed at our by now most intimate six new friends to thank them, somehow knowing, with the obvious differences between us, it needed well-chosen words, which he narrated in *'spades'* with.

'I feel very honoured as a boy, to be taken by you all into a very delicate performance of Love; I was 'lost in Love' at every moment, not knowing who to Love the most, as each of you including, Freya, brushed me by. It seemed as though *'I found Love and lost Love'* in every passing moment, until I realised 'Love is Love', without jealousies and doubts, and I had, thanks to you all, been part of that, in an entwinement of bodies, as if in a full-size water-filled glass bubble of safe containment. I felt, and heard, 'humming' rising and lowering from one second to the next, as the touching of one, became another!'

The six, still giggling, having moved their heads forward, and their bottoms nearer to each other to make the line shorter, had a little team chat, and finally said between 'giggles'.

'What is a 'water filled glass bubble'? A 'Ballet Rambert' magnificence, reduced in thinking to a 'glass bubble?' An innocent simplicity that brought a smile to my face! I loved the massive, impromptu, innocent, sexual scoring of such a ballet, all without orchestration, we had fallen head over heels into. It made of nothing: the small, *everlasting,* implanted polluted memory facet, instilled by friends back there, talking of group things! Oh … how I knew, I had to leave, eventually forever! They continued,

'When you say 'feel honoured as a boy', we didn't know why you should *feel* different, although we think, we had all become aware, that as with Freya there were some differences, especially with you Luke.'

The 'giggling' increased as they all leant forward, I think, to glance at our 'nether regions', surely now made more obvious by the clinging white wet cotton underclothes. The maid, with more knowledge and understanding, was almost, apart from also being youthful in appearance, probably bringing the slightly younger ones along like students, made obvious by their intermittent silences and leaning forward to listen to her, expounding on delicate subject matter ... such as some of the references Luke had made in his 'inaugural bluster', she asked.

'You used the words 'lost Love', well that's impossible; in the mountain, it's ever present and grows and grows never diminishing, and you will find other types of Love to capture your Hearts, some, I believe you refer to as 'sensual', as a female I know Freya was feeling such things, but I know not of an end meaning, only that you will be consumed with those powerful 'humming' feelings times ten, Luke.' She smiled at him, as if she had focussed on his admission of being 'just a boy.' Having said his well-chosen words of thanks, much of which they probably didn't understand anyway, Luke was quick to move into more serious stuff outside of the being 'lost in Love' rhetoric we were all relating to.

'Where does this beautiful lagoon water come from? I noticed it tastes clean, fresh and drinkable, certainly not salty sea water.' The obviously more developed head of the group explained.

'It falls from high up on the 'Hollow Mountain' down a shaft, like an enormous internal waterfall, with rivulets feeding out to various lagoons; it eventually reaches deep down to join the ocean, that's where we swim down to in order to enter the sea, in secret pools we know of, usually on moonlit nights when strangers never come.'

Not sure if Luke was hedging his bets on the 'Making Love' bit, but he was quick to ask.

'Does this mean we might all meet again in those other lagoons here, or such 'secret pools' as you refer to them, in the sea below? We could meet you all there on clear moonlit nights, when the sea was quiet and tranquil'.

The 'giggling' began again, and I think he took this as a 'yes', in fact I know he did, because a smile came over his innocent face, like a boy in a sweet shop, prior to glancing at me when the raised corners of his smiling mouth dropped a little, as if seeking some approval. I had need to remind myself, Luke was actually completely innocent of 'taint' of any kind.

With by now a lack of interest in human biological novelties, made obvious by the absence of 'giggling', we stood and dressed, saying.

'We'd best be on our way now, to seek out other wonders higher up the mountain. Hopefully we will all meet again.' The senior maid was quick to endorse our hopes of such a reunion with,

'We will be around whenever you call, and, as promised, can take you into a more advanced aqua ballet, with more of our maid friends, and they are all experts at 'making Love,' the five younger ones, almost as if enjoying being included in such advanced 'stuff', were all nodding heads together smiling at each other … then all plunged into the lagoon, diving deeper and deeper until out of sight. Leaving me, with my limiting mind, deeply missing them, Luke probably knowing full well 'nothing here is ever lost', looked completely at ease.

For me, it had the same feelings of first loving infatuations at school, when seeing what I thought to be *'the one'* get on a different bus going home. If that makes sense, you know, not wanting someone to move into their own world, leaving yours, if only on a footpath, or a bus stop 'setting' for love.

Having by now dressed, Luke and I sat pondering over the wonderful new things that had come our way. The aqua bubble had taken us into true understandings of Love between, not just couples, but many together in innocent bonding, without jealousies and possessiveness.

Luke was luckier than me, as he had no knowledge whatsoever, of the way things were developing back there in that 'Wakey-Woke-World' I was rapidly nearing the point of leaving forever.

You see, as I have covered in great detail earlier in my story, I had been learning whilst so young the boy/girl 'goings on' in a tainted sort of way.

Without experience, I had tried to work it all out in my usual mind games kind of way. I just knew I didn't like the limited period in one's life where people seem to move through innocent adolescences, being told of certain criteria that would in all probability have come along anyway, but in that 'easy' kind of way I often seem to refer to.

Those so young, falsely assumed by authority to be all of a similar receptive mind-set [which they are not!] will have had 'words' thrown at them in classroom education relating to sexual behaviour and related bodily functions their bodies will need to encounter in those 'car mechanic' sex lessons at school – denying them the 'intrigue' and 'wondering' experienced since the beginning of time. No longer a step-by-step knowledge slowly drifting into their lives as days go by.

Myself, still young, I strangely found myself reminiscing on the words of that old man on the train telling of 'coming out the other side okay'. I was a modern-minded, new life young girl, and yet I think ... just think, I could make sense of his claim. Back to where life on Earth is heading like a fast train for a brick wall, with me, as referred to in my dad's 'Pink Floyd' album of long ago 'just another brick in the wall.'

I have always been a dreamer, and maybe I was again just dreaming. Dreaming of impossibilities as I compared two horizons light years apart One 'young life on Earth' and the 'thinning down' over adolescent years of the magic that has always been there for innocent discovery by teens in preparation for 'coming out the other side okay'.

It must have been 'okay' in earlier times: a 'natural progression' with simple formulae to solve 'temptation', all applied in varying degrees in the game of life – *I mustn't do that, shall I try that, I lost control and did that, I like doing that, I feel guilty doing that, shall I do that again, I'm rushing into things, that should really unfold in a lovely way, I'll leave the sweet shop now, for the time being anyway, as I somehow know I will wear my emotions thin too early!* I guess 'Jimini Cricket' was right all along!

The other 'horizon' free from those 'ears and tails' dear Pinocchio ended up with on the island was my 'Reality'... A place of many such islands, but free to journey to without fears of 'ears', where all could venture to, if they seek harmony in all aspects of life, including rewards such as the indescribable Love sensations I had just experienced. I'm so glad I waited in my Earth life and walked away with head held high.

HIGHER UP THE CHERRY TREE

We gathered our thoughts after such an event, which had completely consumed us with such Love and joy, both in and around the lagoon, as we considered what was going to be the next glorious phase. Luke, with feet firmly back on the ground, set the ball rolling for 'onward and upward'. For me personally, feeling high after the magic we had just experienced, I was left with feet far from firmly back on the ground, more so floating with romantic thinking 'up-up-and away in my beautiful balloon …' Luke's pragmatic approach popped my 'balloon' with.

'Why don't we look around for the next route to take us up? Knowing we are following someone special in such a lovely adventure, it will be far from obvious.'

We searched in every corner of the lagoon cave, only to find no possible way for the commencement of our next phase to that magic place 'Top-Town' so described in the precious notebook we had inherited. We sat quietly with feet in the clear water looking at Dougie's few notes and sketches, trying so hard to see if any clue appeared. Pointing to one little comment on life that appeared so general, Luke asked.

'Wonder why he decided to write this? It doesn't seem to relate in any way to such a special moment in time, knowing, as he would have, we are by now in the lagoon cave.'

As always, Luke could recognise reasons and discordant issues in life that must relate to something, often just simple little things, so I asked him to read to me that very piece he had pointed to... probably knowing nothing would jump out at my young emotional female mind. He read the following slowly, as if trying himself to fathom out any hidden meaning:

"In life, when problems arise, all is usually okay just beneath the surface, don't be troubled. A fresh approach is often required, one should wash away first thinking."

We sat quietly trying to think of the next somewhat essential step... well Luke was, I was trying to look intelligent, thinking where I could buy a new dress, to replace the somewhat shrunken one I was now wearing due to all that sub-aqua stuff, after all, I was now an eighteen-year-old girl, not a *'potholer'*. Suddenly, Luke stood, and once more began to remove his trousers, exclaiming,

'I think I know the answer,' which left me feeling totally emotionally unprepared for the male way of embarking on the wonders of boy/girl things, after all, I had heard of boys' acceptance of venues along the lines of even 'a plough up field behind a pub in the pouring rain' scenario. I looked up at my man, with eyes giving away my confusion and complete lack of desire. With me, there was Love there, but with no preambles having been offered up … not much was going on biologically below my heart level... all I could think to say was.

'What now Luke?' Only for him to reply.

'Yep.' as he dove into the lagoon.

I sat for a while, thinking *well that's a relief,* quickly followed by a sudden feeling of loneliness coming over me without him and a little wandering about what he had so suddenly discovered.

He resurfaced on the other side of the lagoon quite close to a rock face festooned in long draping green lichen and other such growth, smiling like a Cheshire cat as he called across.

'Get your togs off, bring the bag, and join me, Freya, all's well, make sure you do up the waterproof zip.'

This was the second time within a few hours; I was, in total trust, stripping down to my underwear and for adventure, not erotica. I arrived at the point where Luke was treading water, handed him the bag and asked,

'What on Earth did you read into those few words of wisdom?' To which he replied,

'Please trust me, Freya, I'll explain later,' so I did, and said, as I parted wet hair hanging down over my face like curtain drapes,

'You don't need to ask me that, Luke,' said pulling hair out of my mouth, 'anything you say is fine with me.' He smiled, and halfway through rising up to take a deep breath to dive down he called out.

'Follow me.' So, I did, and there we were submerged without our Loving Mermaid friends to guide us, with me wandering if from our Hearts, with my usual fear, we should call to them to come to save us, knowing their promise that they would.

Having just dived beneath the surface, we found ourselves swimming through a delicate veil of green swaying sea grass, moving here and there, with shafts of light accentuating its sway. The rays then driving deep down through the crystal-clear water. After just four or five strokes, Luke looked back at me, pointing upward, signalling time to surface which we did.

Wonder of wonders, there we were in another palatial chamber, this time with an opal blue lagoon. Those words in the little book which Luke had read into for his discovery suddenly made sense, with me thinking, *he is such a 'smarty pants'* as he explained what he had read between those lines:

'All is usually okay just beneath the surface ... wash away first thinking' that just had to mean beneath the lagoon *surface,* and the water statement was surely telling us to use that water to wash away all other thinking.'

Well, of course, I could see that, after all, I was not stupid... well, I didn't immediately, but I surely would have eventually. I do sometimes ponder over my makeup, which sees me drifting between an intelligent conversationalist like on the train, then when with Luke, I can sometimes feel to be a bit of a 'bimbo'. I guess everybody is different in so many ways. With our relationship, whatever it was, working with an end result of 'Love'. Not worth becoming a 'thinker' over that … although, just maybe, Luke would not feel comfortable being with a *'smarty-pants'* girl. Whatever, I like what I am … thinking about it I'll never be a 'Bimbo'! Mind you, thinking more about it, some guys like 'Bimbos' …Umm?

As if stage-managed, there, waiting, was another soft mossy bank offering somewhere to catch our breath, sit, and ponder holding hands and take in more magic. Having spotted something unusual, I pointed across to a small alcove in the bank just along from us and, smiling, said to Luke.

'I think I can guess what that is, how about you?' Well of course he could, it's not as if one expects to find little slips of folder white paper in such secret hidden places. I leaned over to take the message surely intended for the likes of us and again handed it to Luke for him to check out. He began to read what was obviously another Dougie message:

"Well, you made it. I wonder who you are, and how you first met in your 'Reality' so glad you can swim – be happy – there is so much more to discover as you journey up through 'Hollow Mountain'. I made this trip so long ago on my way to the stars after dwelling for some time up there in 'Top-Town' – you'll love it up there, when you make it that is ... and you will! - The people never leave their top plateau and live happily together. They remain in age appearance, in Earth years of no more than around twenty-five and know nothing of discord and inharmonious things. I won't tell you too much, but one thing nice for you to understand is that those lovely mermaid friends, you will both by now have met, are very much related to folk at 'Top-Town', and how they all get together will, as with me, be fun for you to learn. A secret I know they will have kept from you."

We had an immediate mental bond with Dougie and his welcoming words, I did wonder, how could he possibly have known when my journey first began when I had chosen the name 'Reality'. I asked Luke his thoughts.

'I think, fair to say, Freya as it was his world you stepped into on that magic day, he would know all about his new guest, and what she would call *her* dream within *his* dream.'

I needed to pause for a moment to reflect on that comment. It implied when I had made my first steps of discovery, I was actually being watched ... especially knowing I had often sat in my underwear gazing at his picture … apart from embarrassment, that felt a bit spooky.

Before doing any more 'reflecting' or, for that matter, anything else, I needed to dwell on the joy experienced during that sub-aqua aspect of our trip and thought to ask Luke.

'As we swam through that pretty curtain of swaying green drapes, did you see those beautiful, coloured fish swimming around us? At one point I veered to the left, and they went into a bit of a frenzy, before darting forward toward you as if to say: 'no, this way'.' He replied.

'I didn't see that, as I was ahead of you, seems our mermaid friends were right, when they had said 'you will make lots of different friends.' Looks like you already have. They were there to help us like 'pilot' fish around a shark, not that you look anything like a 'shark', Freya, more like a pretty mermaid.' I really liked his 'hammy' compliment to a girl, so far removed from life back there, especially, the distancing of me from a shark likeness to a 'mermaid' vision.

We spent time taking in the surroundings: white streaks of limestone, and different coloured minerals in the rock walling, highlighted by opal coloured water reflections dancing around us, possible resulting from that ever-present shaft of light from high above. The very thing that drew us on to find that unknown 'Top Town' place so sought. It was as though the light had power, more radiant than sun beams known to us all out there in the world outside 'Hollow Mountain'... What, I wondered, could be up there?

There was a constant peaceful sound of running water, probably from that inner 'waterfall' feeding its thirsty lagoons with fresh water on so many different levels, prompting me to ask Luke.

'Do you think we will find these beautiful lagoons at every level, which does seem hard to believe?' His response was as always to the point without figments of the imagination, simply honesty in everything he said, no daydreaming as with me, and I knew we really did need his 'sense and sensibility'.

'I couldn't really say, Freya; we won't know what wonders await until we reach each level in turn, that's what will drive us 'Onward and upward' like adventure stories written by imaginative authors. They might call this one 'Topping out on Top Town'.' Well, that did have a little of the 'imagination' I referred to, and I liked that; it's what a girl likes to hear, although sometimes, those 'adventure stories' promote degrees of fear of the unknown, which brings to the surface the fact that the girl has her man to work it all out. Girls can 'work it all out' [said to cover any 'Woke' damage] it depends on how the girl 'ticks', often preferring to hide behind the delicacies of life. I just know the arrangement Luke and I had worked for us. Picking up on his reference to 'onward and upward' prompted me to ask.

'This all seems such a magnificent, very different adventure, do you think we will ever return 'downward' back to 'Reality'?' After all, I really did think I had a good understanding and liking of all that was going on in our lives down there, I just sometimes needed Luke to reassure me, which he did immediately with,

'What makes you think this is separate from 'Reality'. It's all part of our story, it's just that in 'Hollow Mountain', we are almost moving through one of those 'parallel universes', safe, and still falling under the power of that great 'Source' we know to be there. I say this with confidence, Freya, because we are unable to 'morph' into other life forms whilst within the mountain, so we must give ourselves to that 'Source', knowing we are always safe!'

My mind was racing in circles as I pondered over all the wonders to date; it all seemed so advanced for people like us, and still quite young. As I reflected on earlier times of tea and cakes on the riverbank with animal friends, along with frolics around the Mill with them, and others. Then there was sleeping safe in a soft-lined 'settle', and under a bridge with cold mill stream water running beneath a moss lined 'dipper' nest. Not forgetting home life at the Oak and our pretty cottage downstream, then there was 'sky diving', 'flying', and on and on. - I needed to pause to take a mental breath but ended with walking hand in hand by that riverbank with my Luke, feeling so in Love as we moved through teen life, with all the exciting things it embraced. I decided to talk it all through with Luke prior to our next phase of 'onward and upward' to some wonderland called 'Top Town' that would surely settle the jumble of joys in my head before moving on to what was inevitably going to be a new door opening.

All this mental wrestling must surely be due to the fact that, back there in my other life, it is never a continuous roller-coaster of wondrous adventures. Maybe, if I reminisced for a while this would prepare me for more to come.

He always seemed able to focus my busy little mind on positives, never negatives, and in a few words he had me back on track, feeling full of joy and, so grateful to be on this somewhat strange, what-dreams-are-made-of lifestyle.

'Try to quietly go back over this journey in your mind.'

'I've just been doing that...' I said.

'I do agree, it's good for you to talk, Freya, if nothing else it shows your appreciation. I am aware that back there...' nodding his head to one side, as if pointing to life on Earth '... there is the saying 'taking things for granted'. Can't you see? You are simply not doing that ... and it will be noticed.'

'That's quite a reward, Luke, but not sure if I feel comfortable with all my actions being monitored' I said.

'They're not,' said Luke. He then continued, 'your mental wrestling was simply your consciousness rising nearer to the 'One' that has all the answers! Whenever we silently call for help, as in fact you have been doing, by not wishing to 'take things for granted' – that call is heard; how else, could things be made to go misty or, a warm squirrel 'Settle' suddenly appear out of the cold, if poignant moments in our lives were not being managed by Someone?'

'Thank you, Luke, I understand what you are saying,' I said, feeling quite reassured, and he continued in a pleasant way.

'You recognised the sad direction the world seemed to be going in, and although so young, wanted something 'Higher'; well, you found it! What could be higher than 'Top Town?' said with a smile, 'On your thoughts, regarding going down: well, how do we know, just maybe all that we have dreamed and created into 'Reality', might exist anywhere we so choose?' A final comment made, with one finger pointing upward, I presumed toward 'Top Town'.

My mind rushed back into its interim girly hideaway places, leaving outside much confusion, wrestling with somewhere between 'parallel universes', 'three and four dimensions', and 'a small new world perched on top of a mountain' sort of thing. I had given in, to leave such deep subject matter for another day, and was left simply staring upward at that 'light source' with a look of amazement, wondering what lovely scene it was shining down on up there. With a blank canvas, the mind will fill in empty space with imaginings; could it be a buttercup meadow, fairies dancing? Such wonderings now surely drawing me upward, not downward.

Was it inquisitiveness on such an unknown scene or was it the very thing Dougie had embarked upon so many years ago, staring at a massive blank white canvas, allowing his consciousness to drift through a pastoral dream ... then, simply applying coloured pigment to make it so?

It just had to be my consciousness doing just that, after all, I had already painted fairies dancing happily around on a 'buttercup meadow'. How blessed I was, staying in the light, as within the embrace of a rainbow arch, leaving those who so chose to remain outside of such a divine 'bow' where it always appears darker in tone … where many choose to remain. Were I to allow them into my dream, they would surely see their own scene above where I stood, a scene of dark things to contaminate my dream, to entice, to hover around at length, sufficient in time to grow 'ears' and 'tails', now looking foolish … to become 'misfits' anywhere … except in their 'consciousness' scene, so far removed from mine, of dark clubs, drugs to fool, drinks to ego raise, and other's loved one's to steal!

I knew, having created that beautiful, perfect embryo back then, which was to develop into my 'Reality' I had to grow with it, as a woman, to include all the wonderful things that go with being just that! Near to Miss Pope's little shop I'd create a pretty gown shop that also sold the accessories needed … yes … that's what I wanted to do, and I would.

Just thinking about it would take me away from immersing myself into this boyish adventure story that was clearly developing. I could see there were many interludes of real feminism, even naughty feminism, I was surrounding myself with, so, not suggesting Luke was having too much influence on our lives because, to date, all that he did and said had helped me grow from a developing thirteen-year-old girl, into what I was am, and I loved it all, not least my Luke. And … we were a million miles away from that 'Tarzan and Jane' stuff! However, I suddenly realised, I had not even changed my dress since arriving in my new world and my boobs were beginning to, to put it mildly, overflow, denying me that 'Venus De Milo' profile to be gazed secretly upon … mine was heading toward my 'Ma's dumplings'. So, the first thing I would do when arriving next at the cottage, or our own little 'Top Town' at the top of our tree; I'd hang many lovely dresses and t-shirts, then there would be drawers of pretty underwear, then there would be a line of modern shoes, then there would be

'You look so happy, with such a smile on your face, Freya … where are you are you? In the sweet shop?' I guess that's what lovers do: feel for each other, almost knowing what the other is thinking. Luke had spotted my interlude in our 'Top Town' campaign. I immediately knew, somehow, he had no idea of my wanderings around my 'boutique'. I hurried out of the shop and, with my own key, closed and locked the door.

THE FLOWER FINALLY OPENS

I was learning to love the game of life being played out wherever we were. This, of course, included 'back there' as well as my 'Reality'. You see, boys, I was learning, are usually so wonderfully obvious in their thinking and contemplated actions. Whereas girls are jamb packed with mysteries, secret thoughts, and complicated, quite innocent mental shenanigans. I did wonder do all girls do that, like, 'Woke' thinking? I did … but I nipped in, then nip out before anyone can catch me! I really must share my scheme with my old gentleman friend, when I next saw him on the train, or of course, if I visited 'Harmony Town'. I knew he would like my plan for sowing seeds 'back there', which, who knows, might keep people out of trouble, one of the very things that had driven my desire to find better! That life of treading on 'Woke' eggshells, made up of 'what you say' -- 'what actions you take' – 'what you support' … Oh dear.

We walked around this new beautiful lagoon toward that other light source seen from where we had sat on arrival, and sure enough, there was another route to the outside, made more obvious by the sound of sea birds calling.

With a degree of impatience surfacing to go upwards, not sideways, we did feel compelled to, at least, check it out, so we did and found another chance to view our lovely blue boat below, by now appearing the size of match head, no longer the box that it came in, as seen from the lower level. Above our heads was a massive cliff overhang as if denying us any idea of what may lie in wait above, prompting Luke to say, whilst leaning out far enough to scare the pants off me,

'The question is when I lean out, am I *in* the 'Hollow Mountain' or *outside* the 'Hollow Mountain'? That's rather important, because, as you know, we cannot morph inside.' His conundrum had obvious implications in that 'if' *'inside'* and we jumped, calling out 'we are dippers', that might be the end of our blessed journey. 'Not sure if we would be spared for breaking such a well-defined rule?' We were clearly being tested.

'Well, there we are, Freya,' said Luke, 'we are being offered a choice of either a risky 'morphing' at the outside of the mountain to return to the aspect of 'Reality' we know, and I know you hanker for... or, we climb that stone stairway,' pointing to a formation in the rock face ... a slippery, dangerous-looking, steep flight of possible stepping places leading upward. Back to decision time. Having by-passed the idea of a possible flight down, maybe simulating 'Newton's apple', possibly ending up on the rocks, or as shark bait – or, the temptation on offer of heading up there on the 'Top Town' adventure, I asked.

'What to do Luke?' There was the usual pause as he thought things through, by which time, I was on my way up that inviting climb. He looked up with such a smile and said,

'Glad to see your spirit of adventure shining through, Freya, no longer your constant wondering about going down, and, in fact, how we would do just that? We shouldn't have to choose between new adventures and going down to the existing, that's like having your feet between two worlds. If only to make you feel at ease about those wonders 'down there', there must be a safe way down if called for.' Keen to learn more about this implication of possible lifts, secret stairways, and the like, I continued with my usual questionnaire.

'How do you know, Luke? After all, we might have to reverse all we have achieved to date like tunnels to crawl through, lagoons to swim down into, and slippery slopes leading down to raging sea and rocks with sharks waiting.' I had added the bit of drama of 'raging sea, sharks, and rocks', just in case he might be getting tempted to postpone the magic climb already under way! He was quick to demonstrate his fast thinking by asking.

'Have you not stopped to consider where we found the very maps and paperwork that brought us back to the 'Hollow Mountain'?' Well of course I knew the answer to that and answered,

'Do you mean in the loft of the cottage Luke?' To which he replied, raising his head just a fraction, adding 'yes... and?' as if inviting me to continue. The penny dropped, with me standing in a tiny 'Bimbo' hat, as I suddenly realising what he was smiling so smugly about.

'Dougie must have returned from this adventure at some point, or all his paperwork about 'Hollow Mountain' would not have been in the loft.' Now I felt good, knowing 'Reality' was like an expanding universe I had heard referred to in physics lectures back there. 'In any event,' he continued by pointing up the climb, 'up there, we will be outside the Mountain, and we might find we can morph from the dream beyond a door leading out from the Mountain, and drift down to our little blue boat, patiently waiting in the bay, an experience Dougie, in his time, did not have the pleasure of enjoying.'

The very thought, in any event, of jumping from so far up, almost standing in cloud, had my knees knocking, and I needed some assurances on that, after all, we always had to stand on the edge, prior to closing our eyes to jump!

'I can see fear in your eyes again my lovely, Freya... what are you up to now?' So, I told him; he sat on the next available step and answered.

'Okay... prior to us jumping, I will take away all your fear by demonstrating something brilliantly clever, a solution I have just thought of for you, but not until we are up there.' Pointing his finger up the stairway. I felt better about that, but did think, *how could he solve such a mega situation in just two seconds, without being up there to check it all out? It can't be that good.*

Luke stood and began the ascent once more, with me following, still thinking nobody could come up with a solution to a brand new, so fearful thing, in just two seconds. He turned, smiled, and winked then continued upward calling out.

'Trust me, Miss 'mumble-jumble' mind.' I had been caught out once again.

By this time, we had climbed a considerable distance with both of us although unsure how, both realising return trips to Reality [phase 1] at ground level, sorry sea level, were on the table if this appealed to us. After all, at this stage in our journey we only had a mill, and one corner shop, with little else to form a community of some kind, and what about 'Top Town'? This prompted me to ask.

'Assuming we will be meeting new folk in 'Top Town', how will we introduce ourselves as they will soon learn that we live together... totally unaware of our innocence to date?'

He was about to put a blessing on our relationship, one that broke away from the term back there of 'living together' which, of itself, now seems quite the norm, but did so often embrace a freedom to move between relationships, the religious endorsement of marriage was weakening year-by-year, I presumed due to an implied unwelcome permanency in the marriage. 'Tell death us do part' was sadly fading in favour of a rubber stamp with a 'sell by date'.

His answer took our closeness beyond the emotional turmoil back there of boys losing girls and girls losing boys [having 'nipped' into 'Woking', I nipped out, and added 'Trans losing Trans, and Trans losing Trans'] with a constant wondering, how long any relationship might last, and who would be most hurt and out of pocket! With divorce Lawyers rubbing their hands, feeding off such sadness.

'We were blessed by a divine force from the moment we met Freya, remember, there is no such thing as discourse and lack of harmony here. You will never meet a Mr. and Mrs., nobody here will know of such titles.'

I was beginning to realise the enormity and boundless reward of acting as a decent person and spending quiet time back there, seeking *Something* higher that embraced only good.

'Don't dilute your blessings with 'Reality', Freya; it's yours, you created this magic, take it, and embrace it, it is something available to all; it's just it would be in another place and setting. Everybody's consciousness is different, unless, of course, you are planning to arrange coach loads of troubled souls to view that picture back there in your bedroom. I think your mother would have something to say about that.' Said with a smile and another wink.

I'd never seen him 'wink' before, and I'd had two in one day ... that was quite cheeky. Of course, the landscape picture in my room at home was my doorway to 'Reality', and here, we were about to pass through another doorway into another magical place ... a world within a world?

We had been chatting away with much wondering as we followed what felt like a never-ending stone stairway, somewhat resembling a spiralling access up through a church tower. Then, at last, there before us was the enormous oak door, with just a large handle and no locks visible, almost appearing as an open invitation to enter through ... but to what?

We definitely needed to prepare ourselves, with at least an extended pause, if only to give excited imaginings chance to come out to play, not forgetting other 'coming out' with my need to do a little 'tucking in' adjustment. Dougie's paperwork had hinted at wonders almost beyond belief, steering cleverly away from specifics, leaving us feeling just a little apprehensive. Compounded by the fact that there was a large door and there, high above, was sky but oh so different, as in that pink hue seen when looking up from well down in the Mountain.

During that 'pause', my mind, as do 'minds' so often, selfishly drifted back to that other life back there, with thoughts arising would others be led to the 'Hollow Mountain' and find their way through the lagoon sub-aqua secret access 'beyond the veil' in this case, a divine veil of green swaying drapes of giant sea kelp? Would they eventually come, spoiling this paradise with degrees of tourism? A slight grey mist came and went, and I was so glad it did but had quickly faded, leaving once more the colours and magic setting that surrounded us. I'd been given another short reminder not to adopt such selfish negative thoughts, in shame mentioned my misgivings to Luke, which always seemed to work, and sure enough, his words flowed easily and straight to the point of all this being ours, to cherish and to enjoy, as it was within our consciousness and no other.

Knowing we were soon to discover new adventures and discoveries beyond normal understandings, I thought I would call this elevated place 'Reality 2', as I could see we would be living between these two worlds, confirmed earlier in the knowing that Dougie had journeyed back to the cottage on an unknown number of occasions, and, of course, we, unlike him, maybe would be able to fly down ... who knows?

'I feel quite nervous, Luke.' An honest admission, perhaps with nervous excitement being nearer to the truth… whatever, I knew from reading the notes we were in for quite a shock when we learned of what he had wanted two lovers to share. We took each other's hand, as if in preparation to enter this magic place full of unknowns.

Nervousness left me as Luke threw open the door, and we stood wonderstruck at all that lay before us, tempting us to part and run separately across a sunny meadow of strangely beautiful flower species unknown to compliment a 'buttercup meadow'. *Well, there's a thing* I thought.

I found myself skipping, as if becoming a child again, dancing and stepping between each flower like a ballerina in my attempts to avoid harm to my new pretty, smiling friends. I stopped my pastoral ballet, which did begin to feel a little 'the hills are alive'-ish. Glancing across at Luke, by now some distance away, standing beneath a tree in full blossom, waving both arms from side to side, a demonstration of such joy! Then back into each other's arms we ran, to rest beneath that tree, to savour the beginnings of 'Reality 2' before venturing out into this newly discovered dream, so beautiful.

We lay… a setting worthy of romantic novels, as delicate blossom petals fell on two people, surely endorsing that union of Lovers I had repeatedly dreamed of. Luke leant my way to brush from my face one or two of those petals and kissed me, not on my cheek or forehead as if in a caring 'all is well' kind of way, but on my lips … and it was done! I was lost, in Love, in submission, in bliss and a knowing, it would be now. A dissolving of guessing and pondering on something that had to belonged to all, from the beginning of time, and that 'time' was now mine to take, to immerse and drown myself in ... feeling safe, and Loved … as two became one, in mutual joy, above and beyond my many imaginings since early teens. I can't say what my Luke was experiencing, that was for boys and unknown to girls only to recognise with someone so strong, his gentle manner in dealing with a girl's delicate expectations, was applied so well. Innocence taken, but innocence still there, as in that innocence we took of each other, nothing was any longer his, or mine, it was all ours, to share each to the other, two made one! We were now 'Lovers', sharing, uniting, maybe procreating, who knows, and whereabouts, who knows, and who cares!. I didn't care!

Many, over time, have written song lyrics, poetry, and verse on this moment, each trying to capture such ecstasy as they fringed around the edges with words, but they were their interpretations, not mine. Mine was that very private beautiful moment in *my* 'now', beyond words, lyrics, and verse on times belonging to 'others' which were theirs alone, lost to me, not to be reflected on by strangers, as with films back there, when the story line weakens and the Director saves his day and throws such false union into his camera lens to be projected into minds that really only seek a continuation of a great story line written by an author, dreaming his narrative will be well cast.

Minutes, hours, days and lifetimes passed, who knows of such limitations, lost from kiss to 'afterglow' ending. I had found another world within another world, within another world. *Where will this creation end?* I wondered. Finally, I was reinstated back into Reality with my sensually endorsed partner Luke, by now *"beside me singing in the wilderness"*

[--Omar Khayyam] still embracing me so tightly, as if not wanting to relinquish me, his first time prize, bless him, well, he couldn't … because it was '*our* first time prize', a contract of Love, not for dividing 'Amo'--'Amas' -- 'Amat' … that's it … it had to have been; 'Eros' love to 'Agape' Love … and back again!

Having drifted back toward normality, our 'union', 'unity', 'unite' moments were compounded, as in unison we gazed at each other and whispered 'I Love you' in a way that drifted away from romantic novels and movies of times gone by like 'Love Story' and aptly named 'From Here to Eternity' ... it just had to be unique; it was Freya and Luke and no others.

My mind was selfishly clawing at anything to make what had just happened the best thing that ever happened since the beginning of time, because it was, if only just *our* 'time'.

I was fully aware of how much I had moved away from life back there on Earth when I consider my age now. My life was obviously unfolding in a different way. So many girls back there, be that right or wrong, had long before reaching my age been doing 'togetherness' stuff , here, there, and everywhere.

By now, out of the private 'bubble of bliss', my busy wonderfully inquisitive, humorous mind sprung into life, as I turned and lay looking at those blossom petals still falling, *for us alone* I thought. Luke, with his quiet mind, lay with hands behind his head looking skyward, probably thinking nothing more than ... WOW, when next?

I began pondering over the analogies of life, like the child in the sweet shop, also wondering if guilt had any interfering place in my world, with the likes of Is there anybody nearby? Should we have done such things in this new wonderland? Should we have been in the cottage? Did Luke close the oak door? Then I thought of Miss Brown back there and her 'Niagara' analogy, thinking *what had the crafty old bat been up to during half-tern?* I was a grown woman now and could think of such grown-up things. I had drifted away from childhood imaginings... now, no longer a 'freshman', I was left wondering what precious thing of mine I had bestowed on my Luke. It was gone! Luke, looking across at me, smiling, said,

'Bet you're drifting through those blissful wonders shared?'

I immediately realised, of course, it had been Luke's precious moment too, and he had given of such things to me in equal measure! And yet, he had just referred to 'sharing', and I had dared to ponder, just a little second, on 'loss'. I felt shame and moved closer to rekindle another close embrace, to be once more oh so close to my Luke.

We had by now stood, hand-in-hand, just gazing about, as if lingering on a 'togetherness' we both seemed unwilling to relinquish. Luke moved away, bent down to pick a beautiful flower... we had now parted, and, if only for one moment in time, I recognised that 'parting'.

He put the flower in my hair, and I retained it for the rest of my life in a locket, always there as a reminder of precious moments granted to me ... strange, on into old age its colour never faded.

We could see out beyond this plateau's edge to that mysterious line, supposedly above some lower 'parallel universe' Luke had referred to. I began to wonder how one could descend to such a place, but immediately put the lid on my busy mind, as there was obviously so much here in this dreamy place to be discovered, not forgetting finding 'Top Town' presumably inhabited by people with whom to make friends in true Loving fellowship.

With feet back on the ground, we once more became two people, not one, with me wanting, prior to going on, that 'something brilliantly clever' solution I had been promised by Luke about jumping off a cliff! So, just in case of emergencies, I asked him.

'So, you haven't forgotten … okay,' said Luke, 'it might also be an idea to check out our 'morphing' concerns, and, I suggest, with 'flights down' in mind, we should become 'dippers'. Now give me your word... you will trust me totally?' So, I did.

'Close your eyes and take my hand, as always. Now walk with me for a few minutes.' By now, my mind had reverted back to becoming possible shark bate, but I had given Luke my word. An hour of fear later... actually just a few minutes but it felt like an hour to me... we stopped, and he asked me, still holding hands with eyes closed, to step up onto what felt like a wall. He continued with his instructions, by asking me to stand by his side and keep facing forward. By this time, with a strong warm wind in my face, I must have been shaking in fear, as I began swaying on legs still weak from a certain event under a blossom tree, now almost toppling forward into what was surely a massive void of nothingness *keep facing forward, Freya, and remember how much I Love you, and would never want to lose you*? This was turning into a drama of 'Weathering Heights' proportions, and so soon after such romance, but I had to demonstrate a full trust in my Luke.

'Now, knowing I have checked things out below, let's count to three, call out loud we are 'dippers' ... and jump.' The call came, and with clenched fists and white knuckles showing, we jumped and within seconds, I knew it was right to have trusted my Luke, you see we were now dippers, the only thing was... we were still on the ground in 'Top Town' country, having jumped off a small wall just two feet high. Having struggled between wing flapping and tiny leg adjustments, we finally stood, me getting over the shock, and Luke laughing uncontrollably at his own joke.

'Happy now, Freya?' was his first comment, by now accompanied with a cheeky smile. 'I think I am forgiven for testing the 'morph' scenario, especially as it was to assuage your terrible fear, and we now know, we can make that change up here, isn't that great?'

Not only had that fear of repeatedly throwing myself into space left me, which in this case would have been to the tune of around 500 ft up, but I had a fabulous realisation, one that I was absolutely sure Luke had not yet plugged into. He always seemed to spot a 'twinkle' in my eye when I made a fresh discovery, and sure enough he popped the question.

'I can see mischief in your eyes, Freya, what are you up to now?' Determined not to give away my discovery in word form, I thought to demonstrate it, which I just know he would be impressed with, so I said,

'Just watch this,' pausing for a moment, thinking to myself, only moments ago as Freya and Luke I had been fully participating in the most wonderful equal emotional bonding one could ever dream of, 'oneness' ... now I was about to take to the air quite alone, as a dipper bird. Knowing Luke would be wondering about my movements, and therefore not the obvious, I walked slowly [as dippers do] back around and onto that small wall where Luke had augmented our very first space launch ... like from twenty-four inches off the ground.

With such confidence gained from earlier flight training by my man, I took off and flew at low level around the beautiful meadow, then, suddenly, turned and headed out over that once fearful edge where nothing but open 'space' surrounded me. There, far below, my eyes focussed on a tiny little blue boat the size of a pin head. Luke, realising we were once again dippers, immediately flew up onto a large rock on the very edge of the cliff and stayed there, watching, as if offering his approval of my very first 'solo' flight.

I returned to my by now loving partner, flapping his wings in what appeared as applause, with something really important to report,

'You must do the same Luke, as there is something I want you to explain to me.'

'Which is?' he responded.

'Well, at one point, I tried to go down just a little, as if being called by our little blue friend down there as I say 'just a little', if only to prove to myself it was within our grasp.'

'And… what happened Freya?'

'Absolutely nothing in terms of flying matters.' Was the best flight expertise I could offer.' I tried to fly lower, but it was impossible, I remained at the same height apart from being able to fly upward.'

So unlike Luke... he didn't seem keen to fly off to investigate the situation, and I wondered why. He suggested we 'morph' back to Luke and Freya then gave his considered explanations, the first two of which made good sense but did, however, promote a little wondering if in fact we might be trapped.

'There are three reasons I can think of, Freya: one, is that as with all cliff faces, especially when flat-fronted, there is often an upward wind force called 'wind shear' ... you will often see hovering birds above high cliff faces effortlessly enjoying the ride. Likewise, if I am wrong with that, then similarly, when winds are light and the air quite warm on a nice summer day, remember warm air rises, this would present the same effect of keeping one up, making it more difficult to descend. Had it been either of those two options, you might have found it difficult to break free to return back to being over our meadow here.'

I wasn't sure if he was giving me sound aeronautical guidance or a slight hint of me misbehaving by slipping a little fear back into the equation, leaving me considering... I might still be out there fixed in space. It couldn't have been that, as we were now 'lovers' and he wouldn't want me to have fear... because true lovers don't dish out such things. I'd fallen into the mental embrace of a girl's expectation of what she should feel, once that complete togetherness had been enjoyed as it had with us!

Having completed my usual 'thinking' process, working out what life should, or might not be, I quickly moved on from a girl's thinking on such an emotional commitment made. Then I began thinking, once more, the word 'commitment' was awful, and I re-thought it along the lines of us having drifted into 'oneness' ... That felt better. Getting back on track with this journey, I asked Luke.

'Please tell me then the third 'reason', Luke, now we have put aside the weather influences on flying.'

What he shared made me Love him more, knowing I could rely on him to offer more common sense than my way of just drifting around in a kind of daydream. The last reason he was about to expound on had a mysterious happy future for us both, and on thinking about it, it was obvious really.

'We are here for good reason, if you think of my origins long ago relating to Dougie. Here he shares his dream with us, by way of the guidance found in the cottage, just waiting to take us on his dream journey. I refer to the scroll at the cottage, the slips of folded paper, all seemingly addressed to us. Consider the last lagoon space note, which read, and I quote:

"Well, you made it. I wonder who you are, and how you first met in your 'Reality'," he goes on to say regarding 'Top Town': . you'll love it up there, when you make it that is, and you will. When you become 'high flyers' you'll find so much to learn high up there, please remember this ... nothing is worse than taking oneself to the edge!"

'Do you not realise it was you, Freya that brought him back as a young guy by being drawn to his picture many, many years on! And that's where I came in'.

I thought to stand and throw my arms in the air, gazing around at such wonder, daring to call out 'This is all due to me.' No grey mist appeared, which dissolved my fear of being caught 'ego surfing', especially having made such a profound albeit *very true* gesture. Better to show my gratitude in a humble way... I fell to my knees on the grass, bent forward with face in cupped hands, trying to be a tiny as a ladybird, and said 'thank you!'

Luke had obvious been taking note of my attempts to hold onto the past with constant reference to things such as how to get down, our little blue boat friend waiting, can we fly down, can we find our way back through deep subterranean lagoons once travelled, as we journeyed up through the 'hollow mountain'. He finally lent forward with both hands outstretched to raise me up, and with such a lovely smile said,

'As I have already mentioned, Freya, this all forms part of 'Reality'; it's simply a continuation of it. We are here on a road once travelled by your past hero, Dougie. He paints a wonderful picture of joys to be found that way,' pointing to far distant hills bathed in sunshine. Do you need a road sign to convince you that it leads to 'Top Town'? Nothing created to date is lost ... or ever could be ... Shall we go?'

We held hands and, smiling at each other, we were off to find that place ... probably both thinking along the lines of a certain 'Yellow Brick Road'. As we strolled toward somewhere unknown, I gazed up at Luke, realising he had had a past life as Dougie, which left me reflecting on the occasional *'inner guidance'* he had received along the way as we had travelled together through my world of 'Reality', along with some unseen power on high that could cast 'grey corrective mist' to help us on our way! *Who, or what, was that force?* I wondered. *And where is that other 'place' beyond any understanding?* I was thinking like a grown up, and I guess, now nineteen, I really was -- a grown woman that is. I decided to ask my Luke if he knew more that he could share with me, so, I asked the most important question in my story,

'Tell me about Dougie, Luke, and where he went.' He responded,

'I have only been with you in my thoughts and deeds, in this place 'Reality' you created, a place where you gave me fresh horizons to be enjoyed with you ... if, however, I ever choose to be really still in my mind, I think you might know that as 'meditation', then, I somehow know I could tell you more!'

He squeezed my hand, and went 'still' in his mind as we walked ... still smiling, he appeared distant, but that 'squeeze' remained, almost as if he knew I would feel somewhat detached, and I did a simple 'squeeze' of my hand drove away a sudden inrush of loneliness, hours, minutes, or was it seconds passed by, and he spoke so quietly,

'He's gone on a journey, a bit like you, Freya ... a seeking journey to a place beyond normal understandings. Looking into those deep, oh so deep, crystal-clear bottomless lagoons, the moonlit skies above us where we slept in our little home above the mill pond waters, peering over the edge of that second 'parallel universe' you fell down to, on your pink 'wind surfer' when going home … Let me take you to the limits of your now bright 'Uni' understandings: Imagine your mother rolling pastry dough into a ball, made up of all the planets in our solar system, including the sun … the sun would account for 99,8 % of that total mass! Having got over the shock of such magnitude, now drift on in your imaginings to the following if the largest star now found in space were to exist as near to us as our sun, it's curvature would appear to us as an almost straight line apart from 'scary', and you, in your modern term 'freaking out', how am I doing? Well Freya … he is beyond all of those parameters, discovering things we could never understand until we go there.'

'Could we?' I asked, interrupting his 'stillness', 'go there, I mean?' He was back with me, smiling, offering, as always, sound advice, surely gleaned from his 'inner' guide.

'Yes, we can, but all in good time.'

'Sounds frightening!' I replied, 'but take me there, Luke,' I asked, and, if only in understandings, he did, and in such a simple way, with words my tiny, now adult mind could gather up as if crumbs from that astral table he had laid before me.

'You see, Freya, all of that mentioned, is in the 'three dimensional' parameters of thinking known to [man/woman/person!]… However, ***'I Know a Place'*** is beyond all of that… it's in a 'fourth dimension', found within, and you've already been there, Freya, and as a thirteen-year-old girl at that, can you believe that? It was always there as in every person … It's called 'Consciousness' one simply has to find ***IT!*** Somebody once said, "seek and ye shall find"! All a little deep for a now nineteen-year-old Freya, but rest assured, a seed has been sown, one which you will ponder over throughout your precious life, and if watered it will grow so beautifully. I'll always be there to comfort and guide you!'

He had said it! We had found 'foreverness', together!

Lost for words, I gazed at my man, lips tightly closed together, and smiled!

THE END

www.ingramcontent.com/pod-product-compliance
Ingram Content Group UK Ltd.
Pitfield, Milton Keynes, MK11 3LW, UK
UKHW040900040525
458182UK00001B/25

9 781805 417156